"A heartfelt delight from start to finish."
—F. C. YEE, bestselling author of the
Chronicles of the Avatar series

"Melissa Yue's *Misadventures in Ghosthunting* is one of the most original ghost stories I've read in a long time. Creepy, magical, and full of heart, it heralds the arrival of a talent to watch!"
—JOEL A. SUTHERLAND,
bestselling author of the Haunted Canada series

"A funny and action-packed adventure that cleverly explores how stories and traditions connect the children of immigrants to their culture."
—JULIE C. DAO,
author of *Team Chu and the Battle of Blackwood Arena*

"I thoroughly enjoyed *Misadventures in Ghosthunting*, an original, action-packed debut that balances high stakes with humour. A fantastic fresh take on ghosts!"
—CATHERINE EGAN, author of *Sneaks* and *Julia Vanishes*

"What a ride! Funny, heartfelt, and action-packed.... This is an adventure you don't want to miss!"

—SARAH SUK, author of
The Space Between Here & Now and *Made in Korea*

"Breathlessly adventurous and imaginative, *Misadventures in Ghosthunting* provides chills, twists, and sly humour galore.... Melissa Yue's debut entranced me from the first page and never let go."

—MARY AVERLING, author of *The Curse of Eelgrass Bog*

"Witty, hilarious, and with a cast of characters that readers will grow attached to from the first page, Yue's *Misadventures in Ghosthunting* will remind you of the people we leave behind, and the importance of lifting our own spirits to see the life still ahead of us."

—M.T. KHAN, author of *Nura and the Immortal Palace*

MISADVENTURES IN GHOSTHUNTING

MISADVENTURES IN GHOST-HUNTING

MELISSA YUE

HarperCollins*Publishers*Ltd

Misadventures in Ghosthunting
Copyright © 2024 by Melissa Yue.
All rights reserved.

Published by HarperCollins Publishers Ltd

First edition

HarperCollins books may be purchased for educational, business,
or sales promotional use through our Special Markets Department.

HarperCollins Publishers Ltd
Bay Adelaide Centre, East Tower
22 Adelaide Street West, 41st Floor
Toronto, Ontario, Canada
M5H 4E3

www.harpercollins.ca

Cover and interior art © 2024 by August Zhang.

Library and Archives Canada Cataloguing in Publication

Title: Misadventures in ghosthunting / Melissa Yue.
Names: Yue, Melissa, author.
Identifiers: Canadiana (print) 20240386094 | Canadiana (ebook) 20240386701 |
ISBN 9781443470919 (softcover) | ISBN 9781443470926 (ebook)
Subjects: LCGFT: Paranormal fiction. | LCGFT: Novels.
Classification: LCC PS8647.U32 M57 2024 | DDC jC813/.6—dc23

Printed and bound in the United States of America
24 25 26 27 28 LBC 5 4 3 2 1

If you've ever felt like you were a ghost,
that you were invisible
and didn't matter—
this is for you. And you matter.
Take up your space and live.

CHAPTER 1

The first rule of dealing with ghosts is you don't.

Which is why, when I crept down the stairs, I didn't look in the mirror hanging above the table on the landing, and I definitely didn't catch a glimpse of an eerie figure darting out of view. I also didn't look over my shoulder into the dark, empty hallway behind me, head pounding, before I eased my way down the stairs. And when I snuck another peek at the mirror, I didn't see two eyes peering down at me. The pounding in my head intensified.

When I sighed, the house seemed to sigh with me.

Some people think you have to believe in ghosts to see them. Well, if it worked one way, it worked in reverse. I didn't believe in ghosts, and neither did my family. A vivid imagination, Dad called it. Too many computer games, Mom said. My grandma, Mah Mah, staunchly refused to talk about ghosts at all. One mention of the G-word and she was spooning medicinal soup into your mouth in less than five seconds flat to chase away whatever delusions you had.

So, ghosts didn't exist. Period.

I had real problems to worry about, like how I was going to hide my final exam in math, and the big red D at the top of the paper. Thankfully, Mom was vacuuming the kitchen for the third time that week, so I managed to sneak past her and into the living room.

As soon as I did, my headache vanished. Relieved, I slunk over to the ancestral altar. The altar stood in the corner of the living room. It was three layers tall with intricate curls carved into the dark cherrywood, and it bore its plate of four stacked oranges in solemn solitude. I tried to ignore how it seemed to glare down at me, silently carrying the judgment of all my ancestors like *they* never got a D on an exam before.

Carefully, I slid out the bottom drawer of the altar, the one that no one in my family touched, not even my grandma, and I slipped my folded test paper inside.

Then I shut the drawer.

I peered over my shoulder, heart racing. Thankfully, the vacuum was still running.

Look, it's not like I wanted to hide my test. It's just that Mom would have gone nuts if she saw it, and then I'd have to call the ambulance to save her poor heart. I was doing her and Dad a favour. It was only until I could buy a red marker that matched what the teacher had used, and then I'd turn that D into a B and everyone would be happy. I'd head over to the corner store after school and pick one up.

"Emma," Mom said from behind me, and I shot up.

She had her arms crossed, and she was looking at me

with her Disappointed Mom™ frown. I plastered a serene smile on my face.

"Morning, Mom."

"What are you doing?"

I looked up at the altar behind me and cleared my throat. "Paying my respects to the ancestors?"

Mom's frown deepened. "You know you're not supposed to touch the altar. Mah Mah says—"

"—I'll invite bad luck into the house if I mess with the altar," I finished with a sigh.

Even though Mah Mah didn't believe in ghosts, she was a firm believer in superstitions. From making sure our beds weren't pointed towards the bedroom doors (it looked like we were dead) to making sure we never stuck our chopsticks upright in a bowl of rice (because the gods were going to mistake our fresh rice bowls for offerings for the dead), a lot of it had to do with making sure we didn't associate with death, and all the unlucky things that trailed behind it. She even made me carry around a stash of protective talismans in my backpack—little rectangular papers with great, sweeping characters written in black ink.

The altar was especially off limits. No one explicitly said why, but an unspoken agreement had been planted around it: touch the altar and Mah Mah ends you. I shivered. Luckily, Mah Mah was nowhere in sight. She was probably out in the backyard, watering the garden before the summer sun grew too hot.

"Hurry up, then, otherwise you'll be late for school.

It's the last week before summer vacation." Mom dusted off a speck of nothing from my shoulder. "And make sure you come straight home after. Your cousin Dylan's red egg and ginger party is tonight, and we still have to get you an outfit."

I barely stifled a groan. My cousin Dylan was a hundred days old now, so that meant we had to celebrate with a red egg and ginger party, and *that* meant a family gathering where I was going to be pinched and prodded within an inch of my life. But today was the day I'd promised to go over to my best friend Michelle's house to help her with the last tweaks on her DiverBot project. I didn't think I'd be needed back at my house until dinnertime. "But—"

Mom marched back into the kitchen and took out my packed lunch from the fridge. She shook it at me. Glumly, I took it.

"Mah Mah will take you to the mall since your dad and I will be working," she said, scrutinizing the hastily closed top of my lunch bag. She un-velcroed it, then velcroed it back with precise movements and a satisfied smile. "Pick something nice up, okay?"

I was torn. Michelle had said the project was a matter of life or death. "I can pick something up on my own."

"Mah Mah will go with you," she repeated firmly. "Are you taking your bike to school?"

I bit my bottom lip. Mah Mah had coughed up a storm last night, and I didn't want to bother her in case she was getting sick. "Mom—"

"Ride carefully," she said. "And make sure your helmet straps are tightened properly."

Before I could say anything else, she turned the vacuum back on. A loud whirring filled the space, and I swallowed my brewing frustration. She never listened to what I wanted to say.

I lugged on my backpack and left the house to grab my bike. I kept it in the tin-roof shed in the side yard. Outside, the breeze nipped at my ears, and I shivered. Something felt different in the wind today. It left a creeping chill on my skin, which was weird, because even on the coldest days of winter, being in the garden around the house had only ever made me feel warm.

I'd helped Mah Mah plant many of the flowers and shrubs. Being in our garden smelled like instant noodles sneakily eaten after school before Mom and Dad got home. It sounded like Mah Mah's calm voice instructing me how deep to dig into the cool, damp soil. It was warmth and sunshine, even on cloudy days. We'd built the garden up so that the hydrangea bushes clustered around the house like a protective fortress, and the plum trees reached towards the sky like spires. Even the neighbourhood deer seemed to steer clear out of respect—or, you know, because Mah Mah had ambushed them with her gardening rake enough times that they finally got the hint.

I shivered again, trying to shake off the feeling of ice in my veins. I wheeled my bike out of the shed, and promptly stopped.

Under the shadows of my house, a boy was standing in the middle of Mah Mah's hydrangea bushes. His face was cast in darkness. It almost looked like he was standing *in* the bushes, which would've been really hard to do, since I discovered how dense they were when I fell into them last month while I was helping Mah Mah re-mulch the bushes to protect them from drying out in the summer heat.

"Can I help you?" I asked suspiciously.

"Yes," he said, and he stepped out of the hydrangea bushes. They didn't rustle when he moved through them. Something about the way he moved made me feel nervous, as if he was a panther waiting to pounce. He was clad in a black jacket with a hood, and it opened to show a charcoal shirt. Even his pants were black as night. They were tucked into the tops of calf-high black boots with thick white soles. If he was trying to make a fashion statement, it wasn't working.

He held up a familiar piece of paper.

"What the—" I squinted, but there was no mistaking the big red D at the top of the paper, and I flushed. "That's my final math exam! How did you get that?"

He scowled like I'd said something brainless. "The game's over, Lin Wai."

Whatever he'd called me sounded rude. I took a really good look at him in case I needed to file a police report. Despite it being a sunny morning, the light didn't shine off his black hair. His skin was sickly pale. He looked around my age, but there was a menacing air about him. Fear crawled around in the pit of my stomach like it wanted to come out. It made me feel slightly nauseous. It almost felt like he was a ghost.

Which, again, was impossible, since ghosts didn't exist.

I heaved in a deep breath. It was way too early in the morning for this. Ghost or not, if the boy had been in my house, that was breaking and entering. That was a crime. I was dealing with a *criminal*.

"If you want this back, come with me." He extended his opposite hand out. Like the rest of him, his fingers were extraordinarily pale. They were lined with even whiter scars, criss-crossing along the length of his hand.

My hands tightened around my handlebars. "Where?"

His face twisted into a sneer. "An adventure. A vacation. Hawaii. Wherever you want. Come on."

"No."

The sneer dropped. "What?"

"I'm going to be late for school, and I've got math first thing." I pointed at the test, trying to keep my hand steady. My heart was loud in my ears, and I swallowed. "So if you could just give that back . . ."

His nose wrinkled. "Sure. If you come with me."

I thought about it. The longer I took to answer, the more agitated the boy became, and the more suspicious I got. He was nearly bouncing on his toes by the time I replied.

"No, thanks," I said.

I dropped my bike and sprinted back inside the house.

"Hey!" I yelled.

7

Mom popped out from the living room. Her eyes were glued to the suit jacket she was running over with the lint roller, but she still managed to look chagrined. "Why haven't you left yet? You're going to be late!"

I was about to tell her about the trespasser outside, but I froze.

Because over her shoulder, I spotted the boy.

He was in the living room, standing beside the altar. He pulled out a calligraphy brush from a black drawstring pouch hanging off the side of his belt. I recognized its teardrop head and polished handle from my miserable afternoon lessons at Chinese school. But while the brushes at school were made of white-haired tops and yellow plastic, his was entirely ink-black, just like the clothes he wore.

"Uh, Mom?" I whispered. I didn't have a good feeling about this.

"—maybe you should start taking the bus," she continued, giving her jacket a few more whacks with the lint roller. "It's safer, anyway, and it's so hot out in the afternoons—"

The boy pointed the calligraphy brush at the altar and wrote something out—and for a brief moment I could see what he'd written. It was a Chinese character, but one I couldn't read. The lines hung in the air, shimmering and silver, and beautiful in the way that a frosted leaf is in the dead of winter.

My mouth dropped open. I'd never seen a ghost do *that*. I mean, I never saw ghosts. But if I did, I wouldn't imagine them being able to write out calligraphy that hung in mid-air.

The strokes of the character hovered for a second more before vanishing into wisps of silver. As soon as they did, a tendril of smoke curled off the altar in the living room.

I warned you, the boy mouthed at me.

And he disappeared just as I caught sight of the first flickers of fire at the top of the altar.

"—riding your bike to school is perfectly fine in good weather," Mom rambled on. "But what about winter?"

Transfixed, I watched as the line of fire hungrily ate its way up the side of the ornate carvings. The flames spit bright orange. Plumes of smoke puffed off the wood shelving, and dread filled my stomach.

Fire—that's all I needed to say. But the word wouldn't leave my mouth. The first wafts of smoke, heavy and acrid, drifted over to where I stood in the entryway.

"Uh," I said. The flames were licking higher with each second that passed. "Mom—"

"—you don't have nearly enough reflectors for the rain, and—"

"Fire!" I screeched. I heard her gasp right before I ran into the kitchen. In an instant, she was beside me, grabbing pots out of the cupboard and filling them with water. We rushed back out into the hallway, and I nearly careened into Dad and Mah Mah, hurrying down the stairs. They took one look at the dark smoke billowing out of the living room and joined us in grabbing water. Mah Mah threw open the windows, coughing as she did so. My heart squeezed tight.

The smoke burned the inside of my nose and made my eyes water. It was probably bothering Mah Mah even more.

Finally, the fire was out and we were left staring at the blackened remains of the family altar. It wasn't until I reached up to wipe my face that I noticed my hands were shaking.

"Are you okay?" Mom asked, frantically patting me all over like I was the one who'd been set on fire. For once, her perfectly coiffed hair was a mess.

"I saw who did it," I wheezed. "It was a boy, but he disappeared, like a ghost . . ."

My voice trailed off, and my stomach squeezed tight. Uh-oh.

Mom's mouth flattened into a disapproving line. "This again? I thought you'd grown out of these stories. You can tell us if you had something to do with the fire."

"I didn't!" I protested.

"We've been over this, Emma." Dad ran a weary hand over his soot-covered brow. "If you don't want to tell us what's going on, that's fine. But don't lie."

"But he threatened to take me to Hawaii—"

Mah Mah laid a gentle hand on my shoulder and it felt as heavy as a bag of soil. Today she was dressed in a paisley buttoned shirt, and her soft grey hair was wound in little curls. The subtle shake of the head she fixed me with somehow felt more dangerous than the fire we'd just put out.

"Don't bother your parents," she said quietly in Cantonese. "Go to school and don't worry, okay? Mm sai geng."

"Okay," I said, equal parts miffed and relieved that she wasn't spooning her bitter tonic soup into my mouth.

Except the unease didn't leave me, and when I hesitantly made my way back out of the house, Mah Mah followed. She closed the door behind us, and her mouth dipped in concern. "Do you still have talismans?"

"Yeah," I said around the tightness in my throat.

"How many?"

"I don't know. Two, maybe? Three?"

She glanced back at the house. I followed her gaze, and even though nothing was there, a chill crawled through me. She turned her head to the side and coughed.

"Are you okay?" I asked. "You've been coughing a lot more lately."

"No, no. Here." Ignoring my question, she reached into her pants pocket and withdrew a small stack of protective talismans. She peeled off several from the top and placed them in my palm. Like with the altar, she never fully explained what they were used for. All I knew was that if I felt that something wasn't right—which was exactly how my entire house felt at the moment—I was supposed to stick one on the closest entryway. It wouldn't work if my parents did it, she said. Only me.

I swallowed, looking down at those several protective talismans. "Did you see anything . . . strange inside the house?"

She gave me a careful look, like she was scrutinizing me more than my words. "No. Did you?"

"No," I said, just as carefully.

"Good, good," she said affectionately, patting me on the arm. "Now go to school, okay ah?"

"Okay," I said, still unsure.

I expected her to go back inside, but she didn't. She simply watched as I got onto my bike and pedalled down the street, and the weight of her stare followed me until she and my house disappeared from sight.

CHAPTER 2

Life had done nothing to prepare me for what to do if a ghost was trying to burn your house down. Even worse, I'd got no advice on what to do if your entire family didn't believe you could see ghosts but Grandma snuck you protective talismans like it was a black market dealing.

So I did what any reasonable person would do: I pretended it hadn't happened and furiously pedalled away.

I pumped my legs until they felt like they were on fire. I sped past parked cars and red maple trees. Finally, because I didn't know where else to go, I skidded to a halt in front of the doors to Saanich High School.

Carefully, I got off my bike. Students streamed past me towards the front doors of the school, giving me odd looks. I ignored them. I was only looking for one person. Ghost Boy was nowhere in sight. I wheeled my bike over to the bike rack to lock it up. Jitters ran up and down my arms and legs from the terror of the fire.

"Emma!"

I flinched. Luckily, it was only Michelle Zhang, my best

friend. She jogged up to me and looped her arm through mine. Immediately, I relaxed. She'd tied up her hair today, and the short strands poked up from her head like the top of a pineapple. TRY ME was written across the front of her hoodie. Anxiously, I shifted in front of her in case someone tried to pick a fight like the last time she wore it.

"Hey," I said, relieved to be with a normal human being. I finished locking up my bike and we walked over to the front doors of the school.

She grinned, showing the electric-blue elastics on her braces. They matched the blue streaks in her hair. "You've gone granny, Emma Wong."

"What?" Panicked, I looked at my hands, flipping them over. Had the ghost done something to me? They looked normal.

"Not your hands. Your *hair*. It's covered in white powder." Her nose wrinkled as she dusted off my hair. "What happened?"

"Nothing," I coughed. The entry was packed with students streaming down the hallways.

"Doesn't smell like nothing." She leaned over and sniffed at my hair as we walked through the doors and into the crowd. "You should've invited me if you've been lighting fires."

I tried to keep my expression neutral. "Right. Lighting fires."

Her face softened. "Is everything okay?"

Michelle and I had been best friends since first grade. If there was anyone I could trust, it was her. I threw open my locker and stuffed my backpack inside. "What do you think you need to do to set a fire in somebody's house?"

"Well, first you need something for tinder— Wait, you stressed out or something? Because trust me, arson isn't the answer."

I slammed my locker shut in panic. "It wasn't me!"

Oops. *That* caught her interest. She slid over closer until her elbow was digging into my arm. "Confess."

I winced. "The family altar caught on fire."

"What?" she screeched. The conversations around us stopped, and all eyes in the hallway swivelled towards us. I dropped my head into my hands just as Michelle continued, "Oh my gosh, I can't believe I just won a lifetime supply of Cheerios!"

Because no one ever willingly eats Cheerios, everyone turned back to what they were doing.

"You're kidding," she hissed. "Isn't that super unlucky? Your grandma's going to freak."

The morning bell rang. I tucked my math textbook and binder under my arm and hurried down the hall to class. "She didn't. Because it *wasn't a ghost.*"

"Oooh, so it *was* a ghost? Extra unlucky," she said sympathetically. "Hire an exorcist."

"I'm not going to do that." I shivered as I entered the classroom. Math gave me bad vibes most of the time, but had the room always been so nippy?

"Why not? Are they too expensive? We could fundraise, like what they did in *Turning Red.* We might not have a giant red panda suit, but with a little tweaking I could make DiverBot 9000 just as cute." Her face twisted unhappily. "Or at least make it actually swim. One of us has to, and it's not going to be me."

DiverBot 9000 was the current project of the Robotics Club, which Michelle was co-leader of. The other co-leader was Nathan Kim. They were trying to place in the National Robotics Competition with it, but it kept sinking when it was supposed to swim, and it made strange zapping noises when no one was touching it. I still wasn't sure why Michelle had agreed to making a swimming robot when she was just as scared of water as I was of pigeons. They had bobbing heads and evil, beady eyes and stole my corn chips when I wasn't looking.

"No fundraising," I said quickly, and glanced around at our classmates. Thankfully, they seemed oblivious to our conversation. But it was odd—it felt like someone was watching us. "And you promised not to bring up the G-word anymore."

"You're right." She tried to snap her fingers, but it didn't work. "We could be the exorcists."

"No!" I shout-whispered. "Absolutely not!"

She gave me a withering look. "You can't pretend you don't see ghosts for the rest of your life."

I lugged out my textbook and slammed it on my desk. "I can, and I will."

"Why? Because it's easier to pretend they don't exist?"

I opened my textbook and nervously flipped the pages.

"Yes, okay? My grandma gets really upset whenever I bring them up. I'd rather just ignore them if they're going to cause that much trouble."

"Even if they're setting fires in your house?" she coaxed.

"Especially if they're setting fires in my house," I said adamantly.

A crafty grin spread across her face. "Why don't we go over to your place after school instead of mine? DiverBot doesn't care where it goes, as long as it's near its battery charger."

"And water," Nathan Kim piped up as he plopped into the seat next to us. I stiffened, wondering how much he'd heard. Thankfully, he only pulled his textbook out of his bag like nothing was amiss. He had dark hair that curled around his ears, and freckles on his face from being on one of the local soccer teams. Usually he sat on the other side of the classroom, but Nathan had supersonic hearing when it came to anything to do with one of the Robotics Club projects, and selective hearing when it came to anything else. "It's DiverBot, not HydrophobiaBot. Today's the day we'll test the new edition of the user manual and make it swim."

Michelle shuddered, but nodded. "Or die trying."

"That's kind of extreme," I said. "And don't come over to my house."

"It's not too extreme," Nathan said gravely. "This is the future of humanity we're talking about. With DiverBot's small size and home-friendly charging, we could deploy thousands of these into the ocean and rivers to establish new salmon breeding grounds. Maybe we could even fix the coral reefs."

Once Nathan flipped open his notebook, I leaned in close to Michelle and hissed, "Let's pretend that ghosts really do exist. The ghost burned down the family altar, Michelle. It's too dangerous to have you over."

She pursed her lips. "So what? You're just going to go to the bathroom in the middle of the night knowing there's a ghost walking around?"

I shuddered. "Don't."

"I promise I won't try anything. I'm worried too." Her smile dropped a fraction. "No one in your family ever helps you with this stuff, aside from your grandma's flimsy talismans."

For someone who couldn't see ghosts, Michelle was surprisingly nonchalant about the whole paranormal world. She was both supportive and overly interested, which made for a bad combo with my possible newest creepy house guest. Still . . .

"All right," I grumbled, finally finding the right page in my textbook. "But you two will have to stick with me. Don't let Nathan go wandering off down empty hallways or open random closet doors. And if you see anything, run. Leave the house."

"Deal." She grinned again, then waved over at Nathan. "Hey, Nathan! Change of plans. Emma's house tonight."

"Cool, I'll bring an extension cord and extra copies of

the manual." He gave us a thumbs-up before diving back into his notebook.

Math passed uneventfully, but I couldn't shake the feeling that someone was watching me. The sensation brushed across the back of my neck like a cold breath of air. Whenever I glanced behind me, though, nothing was there.

Deep down, I knew that ghosts really did exist. It was hard to explain away seeing things that other people couldn't. But Michelle was right—it was easier to pretend they didn't than deal with the consequences. Keeping the family peace was more important than proving I was right.

Unfortunately, ghosts liked existing—around me, specifically. I'd been near enough ghosts to know that me being paranoid wasn't enough to determine if one was around. Most ghosts liked to play it up. They'd make lights flicker, or drench me in a freezing chill. I usually felt sick, too, like I had a mild case of food poisoning from the hot dogs at the mall. Some ghosts gave me headaches—pounding ones that made me want to cover my eyes and bury my head into my pillow. Those were also the ones that usually made me feel a looming sense of dread. I tried to stay away from them as much as possible.

By the time I got to Social Studies class at the end of the day, I'd had enough. The feeling of being watched wasn't going away. Twenty minutes to the end of class, I raised my hand.

"Can I go to the washroom?" I asked.

"Sure," Ms. Singh said without turning around from the whiteboard.

Michelle watched me with a raised eyebrow as I left the room with my backpack. I never left in the middle of class. If I had to rub the back of my neck one more time to shake off the feeling of being watched, I wasn't going to have any skin left there.

Casually, I walked down the empty corridor to the washroom at the end. When I reached the end, I looked over my shoulder.

Perfect. No one was around.

Instead of heading into the washroom, I hurried over to the closest entryway. It was a side door leading to the sports field outside. Once I did another sweep of the hall, I unzipped my backpack and dug around for a paper talisman.

The talisman was the length of my hand and a bit wrinkled, but the black ink characters looked the same as they always did. Probably. I couldn't actually read what they said. Hiding math tests was one thing—hiding tests from after-school Chinese class was a whole other realm of chaos. Luckily, I sucked enough that my parents had let me drop out last year.

I flattened the talisman as best I could and stuck it on the wall beside the door. The characters briefly glowed red right before the whole paper vanished. Mah Mah said that was normal. Her definition of normal was a bit off, but I wasn't going to complain.

I went around to the next-closest entryway, the one by the gym. When I slapped the talisman against the wall, some of the unease I'd been feeling all day lifted. Ugh. So there *was* a ghost. Being haunted at school was the worst. Everyone looked at you when you screamed.

I managed to cover all the doors on the first floor except one. The final door was by the art room. I raced over. School would be finished soon, and there was no way I'd be able to smack a talisman on the wall by an exit without anyone noticing the strange red glow.

As I passed the art room, I slowed. My head started pounding. It felt like someone was knocking on the inside of my skull. The hallway was still empty. I looked around and caught sight of the monthly exhibit of student work across the hall. Someone had made a sun out of mirror shards, and the whole thing was bright enough beneath the school lights for me to need sunglasses.

I did a double take. In the reflection of the sun was a man. He was wearing a bowler hat, so I couldn't see his eyes.

No one was across the hall.

Slowly, I backed up—and as soon as I did, he opened his mouth. Inside was a swirling red-and-orange ball of fire. Heart pounding, I whipped around, only to smack into someone. Michelle stood in front of me, her backpack hanging off one shoulder. The last bell of the day rang, and students swarmed out of classrooms.

The giddiness on her face faded to concern. "Yikes. You look terrible. Bathroom was that bad, huh?"

"What are you doing here?" I hissed.

"I went looking for you when you didn't come back after ten minutes."

I snuck another look at the sun mirror in the art display. The man was gone. I opened my mouth to tell her about the ghost, then stopped. She was already too excited about coming over to my house. I didn't want her to start a Paranormal Investigations Club at school.

"Yep," I agreed. "Huge line at the washroom."

Nathan squeezed through the crowd of students. He looked slightly frazzled, as if he'd run around the whole school.

"There you are," he said. "Ready for tonight?"

Michelle grinned and shot a fist into the air. "We're going to ace this. Nationals, here we come!"

"Yeah," I said. "But let's stop by the corner store on the way to my place. I need to grab a red marker." Ghost Boy was eventually going to show up again to convince me to go with him. My math test was his bargaining chip. Once he did, I'd grab my test back and fix my grade before my parents called the school to ask about the missing exam.

"And snacks?" Nathan asked hopefully. "My tuna sandwich was ages ago."

Michelle rubbed her hands together gleefully. "All-dressed chips! Mom's banned them from the house because she always binge-eats the whole bag in one go."

"As long as I can get that red marker, you two can buy whatever you want."

As we filed out the door to grab my bike, I couldn't resist taking one last look at the sun mirror. I thought I caught a flicker of darkness at the edges. But I blinked, and it was gone.

CHAPTER 3

"Soonshine?" Nathan read incredulously. "Shouldn't it be 'Sunshine'?"

He was staring at the name of the corner store. It hovered above the awning in huge neon-green letters.

"Don't look at it for too long," I said. "You'll get eye damage."

Michelle smiled dreamily. "I like it. It's poetic."

Soonshine Market had a stucco exterior and brass door handles, the kind that Dad liked to admire when he thought no one was looking. Outside the door was a wooden sandwich board advertising a sale on bouquets of peonies and blue poppies. The windows were covered in an assortment of ice cream flyers, from orange Creamsicles to chocolate drumsticks to strawberry-shortcake bars.

I wheeled my bike outside the store and popped up my kickstand. Usually I'd lock it up, but this area was safe. We'd be in and out. Once we were at my house, I could help test DiverBot's user manual.

"You can't stay too long," I said. "I've got my cousin's ginger and red egg party to go to tonight."

Michelle's eyes lit up. "Is there going to be niàng xiè qián?"

"No Mandarin, remember?" I said. Michelle's family spoke Mandarin, and mine spoke Cantonese. As hard as we tried, we couldn't understand each other. The languages weren't mutually intelligible. Not that I was fluent, anyway. Far from it. It was a little embarrassing—okay, a lot embarrassing, especially at family functions.

"Oh, right. You know, those shrimp crab claws. The deep-fried ones with the claw sticking out."

I squinted as I racked my brain for the Cantonese translation. "Yeung hai kim?"

She shrugged. "You tell me. If they serve them, take pictures. I'm going to live vicariously through you."

The shop owner gave us a nod as we entered. He had a tablet propped up against the box of Coffee Crisps in front of him. "Hello, Emma and friends."

"Hi, Mr. Levesque," I said politely. I caught the telltale blue and white of the Victoria Royals on his screen, the local hockey team. Mr. Levesque gave another nod before returning to the highlights of a previous game on his tablet. A swish, a thwack, and a cheer crackled through. If he wasn't watching hockey, then it was lacrosse. I'd only ever caught him once without a game playing, and that was because his granddaughter was visiting from Ontario.

I grabbed a shopping basket and headed towards the stationery section. It was small, but I spotted the red marker I needed. Bingo. I dropped one in my basket and made my way over to the produce aisle.

I couldn't go home empty-handed—not after my whole family suspected I had a budding career as an arsonist. I needed something. An offering for the family, both alive and dead. We didn't have an altar anymore, but I suspected that Mah Mah would find a way to keep making spiritual offerings until we got a replacement.

I got within two metres of the oranges when my head started pounding again.

Uh-oh.

Nervously, I scanned the stacks of lettuce and tomatoes down the narrow aisle. Michelle and Nathan were chattering loudly away somewhere in the store. I started to make my way to them, but turned down the canned goods aisle and froze.

A person with a bowler hat stood in the middle of the aisle with their back to me. They did a quarter turn—and a wave of dread soaked me from head to toe.

It was the ghost I'd seen in the sun mirror at school. This time, I could see his eyes. They were rheumy and hazy, like a fish that's been out too long at the market.

He opened his mouth. Inside his throat was a ball of fire.

I dropped my shopping basket and ran towards the back exit of the store with the ghost following. Hurriedly, I wrenched off my backpack and groped around inside for a talisman. As soon as I felt the edges of one, I slammed it onto the wall beside the door. The ghost flickered, but it kept coming towards me. I shoved open the door.

Outside, I whirled around. The door shut with a soft click, and I backed up between the dumpsters on either side of the door. My heart was beating loudly in my ears, and my head pounded along to its tempo. A sick feeling swirled in my stomach.

Usually ghosts looked like normal people. They walked on the ground, even if they could keep on walking right through walls. They smiled and kept to the right side of the sidewalk and generally wore clothes. But every once in a while I'd come across an anomaly—a ghost that had its head on backwards, or a pinpoint for a mouth, or long, slender needles for hair.

I had no idea what to do with a ghost that carried fire in its mouth.

Just as I expected, the ghost came through the door, moving through the solid barrier as if it didn't exist.

"Come on," I goaded it, backing up. I had to hope it would continue following me. I could lead it away, and then . . .

Then what?

The talisman hadn't worked. Michelle and Nathan were still inside the store. Same with Mr. Levesque. If it went back inside, I'd have to pretend it wasn't there while it was breathing fire down my back.

I swallowed and walked away from the store, keeping an eye on the ghost as it advanced towards me. Its jaw had unhinged to the point where the ball of fire was larger than half its face.

I walked around the side of the store and looked back again. Panic shot through me. It wasn't following me anymore. Instead, it had its attention focused on a dark-haired boy standing near the bus stop.

Despite the warm weather, the boy was dressed in a dove-grey peacoat that went down to the tops of his legs, and he was looking down at something in his hand. The brown messenger bag at his side wavered slightly in the wind. He stood there, oblivious to the ghost coming closer.

Without thinking, I sprinted over—and just as I got close enough to warn the boy to jump out of the way, the ghost turned towards me. Instantly, a wave of heat crashed over me, hot enough to throw me off balance. I squeezed my eyes shut as the terrible heat licked over my skin.

When I opened my eyes again, the ghost had vanished. The boy was staring at me. I wanted to sink into the earth and never resurface.

"Sorry," I said awkwardly. "There was a . . . a bug on you."

His eyes widened in alarm. "A bug?"

"A huge one. Massive." I smiled, but maybe I was too enthusiastic, because he seemed to shrink back a little. "Anyway, bye." I started walking back to the store.

"Wait," the boy said from behind me. "Are you okay? You almost fell."

My skin prickled from the memory of the heat. "Never better."

Unfortunately, that only seemed to encourage the boy. He jogged up beside me and flashed me a worried look.

"You saw it?" he asked, but it was more of a statement than a question.

I skidded to a halt.

Wait a second.

Was he asking about the ghost?

"*You* saw it?" I asked, completely failing to keep the disbelief out of my voice.

Something in his expression shifted. "You did."

"Nope. Didn't see anything." I shook my head adamantly. "Nothing at all."

The worried look intensified. Strangely, it suited him, the way pugs looked extra cute because of their mopey wrinkles. The corners of the boy's mouth dipped. "You are pretending you did not see the ghost. Why?"

My stomach gave another unpleasant lurch, but this time it didn't have anything to do with what I'd witnessed.

He could see ghosts.

Even worse, he didn't get why I wanted to pretend I couldn't. How did he not understand that seeing things other people couldn't was a curse? It was going to take a lot more for me to admit to my embarrassing ability than one person swooping in and admitting they could see ghosts too.

He shifted the strap of his messenger bag. It was made out of a soft-looking brown leather, with brass buckles and thick threading. He looked like he was in grade nine, like I was, but no one carried around a bag like that anymore.

"You need to return home," he said, looking around in concern. "You are not safe here. Judging from its spiritual energy, it was most certainly a ghost. A malicious one. I'm sorry. I should have done a better job, but I was not expecting you to have the Sight. You never gave any indication you had it before."

My head spun as all my internal red warning alarms started beeping simultaneously. "Uh. Right." I jabbed my thumb in a random direction. "I'm going to go now. Friends are waiting for me inside and all that." Before he could get another word in, I ran around the store to the back exit.

I'd almost made it to the door when a bird darted in front of me. I shrieked. It was a pigeon. A *pigeon*, all fluttering grey wings and ominous beak, ready for pecking. I ducked my head and tried to swat it away. The pigeon soared around me—

I jerked back, away from the door handle. The bird was gone. In its place was the boy. Who was supposed to be far, far behind me.

"Wait, I need to talk to you," he said between gasps of air. A stray feather, grey and soft, floated down by his ear. He extended a hand to me in a bizarrely formal fashion. "My name is Leon. I am sorry to meet you this way."

I looked at the earnest smile on Leon's face, looked down at his outstretched hand, and my brain fizzed out.

"Oh, no, no, no," I said. "Nice try, but I'm pretty sure you're not supposed to use actual animals in casting roles if it can be helped. Animal rights and all that, even if they're pigeons."

He looked extremely perplexed. "I'm sorry, but I do not understand—"

"You're a special effects artist."

He paused for a long, long moment. Then he said, "Excuse me?"

"You're a special effects artist," I repeated. The words spilled out too fast, but I didn't care. "That's why you've got a creepy little pigeon and a stunt actor. That's neat. Fun job. I didn't know they were filming a movie out here. Is it a scary movie? I mean, I guess they often film movies on the island, it's just I didn't expect a crew to be out here, because I never heard anything was going on."

"I'm not a . . . special effects artist," he said patiently. He clasped his hands behind him like he was preparing to settle in for a comfortable chat. "And that was not a stunt actor. It was a ghost. A geoi hau gwai."

I pretended to consider this detail while I scoured the area for the best route around him. "Oh, wow. That's fascinating. Now if you don't mind, I'm heading back inside, *where my friends are.*"

To my dismay, the boy didn't budge when I tried to reach behind him for the door handle. "I'm afraid we have gotten off on the wrong leg—"

Foot, I shouted in my head, tugging on the handle. It didn't budge.

"—but that pigeon really was me." He paused, as if he

had just revealed the secret of the century. "I am sorry that you had to find out this way, Emma."

I let go of the handle. The guy knew my name. Slowly, with one eye on him, I withdrew my phone from my hoodie pocket. I'd never had a stalker before, but this guy fit the bill.

"Listen, Leon. I'm going to count to three," I said carefully, trying to keep the tremble out of my voice. I held up my phone and gave it a little shake. "And if you're not out of here, I'm calling the police."

"Ah." With a sigh, he ran a hand through his hair, brushing it out of his eyes. "Okay."

"One . . ."

Instead of booking it, he gave a small nod.

"Two . . ."

Frantically, I looked from him to my phone and back again. His face was the embodiment of serenity. Even his eyebrows looked relaxed.

"Three?" I said tentatively.

He cleared his throat. "I help maintain stability in the world by monitoring ghosts in the Mortal Realm. I'm afraid I must apologize. I have not been doing a good job."

Speechless, I watched as he got down onto all fours, right between the dumpsters on either side of the door, and touched his forehead to the ground.

"What are you doing?" I hissed.

"I apologize," came his muffled reply, "for being unable to prevent the fire in your home this morning. But I assure

31

you I will catch the ghost responsible and bring them to face the justice of the Underworld."

And that was when I turned on my heel and hightailed it around to the front entrance. I slammed the doors open. Michelle, Nathan, and Mr. Levesque all stared at me with shocked expressions. Michelle had a taro Melona bar in her mouth.

Mr. Levesque searched the windows behind me. "Everything okay?"

"Wasp swarm chased me," I panted, then gestured to my friends. "Come on. Let's go."

"Oh." Michelle's eyes popped. "*Oh*. Is it a . . . ?"

She wiggled her fingers creepily, and I coughed. I *wished* it was a ghost. At least I had semi-logical explanations for those. Nathan looked between the two of us. He shrugged and pulled a ten-dollar bill out of his wallet for his stack of chips.

"I'll put out some wasp traps," Mr. Levesque called out after us as we left the store.

"What about your stuff?" Nathan asked.

"I'll come back tomorrow," I replied, which was a lie because I was never coming back to Soonshine Market.

This time, when I looked back at the windows, I didn't see any ghostly apparitions. The headache had almost completely vanished. But something tugged on the periphery of my attention. My gaze went to the treetops, and my stomach dropped as a pigeon flew off into the distance.

CHAPTER 4

I had to force myself to cycle back to my house at a normal pace with Michelle and Nathan. The house was uncannily dark. Once we were inside, I flipped on the lights and called out, "Mah Mah?"

No one answered. Maybe she was out.

I locked all the doors and windows in the house and drew the curtains. We headed upstairs to my room.

"Wow," Nathan said as he entered. "This is very . . . green."

"It's *fresh*," Michelle admonished.

Nathan wasn't wrong. Posters of garden herbs and native plants and their uses hung above my bed. In the centre of the ceiling, a spinning mobile of air plants inside open glass baubles hung down, twirling slowly so that the glass shimmered with light. And against the window was my desk.

My computer sat on it, as well as a stack of some old textbooks and a pile of mechanical pencils—but on every other inch of available space were pots and vases of plants. Succulents and cacti crowded the edge closest to the window. Spiky aloe reached towards the ceiling. A monstera with giant split leaves hid my secret stash of fruity Sugus candies. And right beside my computer, positioned where I could always see it, was the perfectly preserved lotus flower Mah Maḥ had given me. It was suspended in a clear gel inside a glass vase. Its pink petals almost glimmered gold if you looked at it from the right angle.

I triple-checked that the latch on my bedroom window was closed, then sat on the floor with Michelle and Nathan. He pulled DiverBot out from its special case, which was really just an old cooler bag from the Saanich Strawberry Festival.

"I think we need to recalibrate the sensor," Michelle said, typing away furiously on her laptop. "It's not reacting the way we want."

"We've already tried that nine times," Nathan said dubiously. He flipped DiverBot over. It was a stumpy block of metal, more cube than robot. Someone had drawn a face on it. It had two dots for eyes and a sideways 3 for a mouth.

Michelle heaved herself into my computer chair and swivelled around with a groan. "Snacks, please."

While Nathan rummaged around in his backpack, I peered out the window again. I couldn't ignore the fact that I'd seen a pigeon transform into a person. I'd tried explaining it away through countless excuses. Maybe it was a hyper-realistic bird drone that could disappear in the blink of an eye. Secret military technology. Or maybe my eyesight just sucked.

In the end, though, all I knew was that a bird had gone poof and in its place was a real live person.

Nathan held up two bags of chips. "All-dressed or ketchup?"

"Emma?" Michelle prompted.

I blinked. "Yeah, let's go with all-dressed."

"I knew it," she crowed triumphantly. She held her hand out, and Nathan tossed her the bag.

Something slammed down the hallway, and I shot up.

"Do you hear that?" I asked.

Michelle frowned. "Hear what?"

My mouth went dry. "There was a noise, like a door slamming."

"Maybe your family's back early," Nathan suggested. "Should we head out now?"

"Not yet," I said. "Wait here."

I left my room and closed the door quietly behind me. The long, dark tunnel of the hall stretched out before me. I resisted the urge to look in the mirror above the display table. Instead, I crept in the opposite direction, listening for anything out of place. Maybe Mah Mah really was home. But when I pushed open her bedroom door, no one was inside. In fact, all the rooms were completely empty. Strange. The slamming door had sounded close.

With a sinking feeling in my stomach, I turned around and walked over to the top of the stairs. I stopped in front of the table. Nothing looked out of place. Slowly, I lifted my eyes. Nothing was in the mirror.

Relieved, I flicked on the light. The length of the stairs was lit, but I kept imagining shadows moving where there were none. My hands felt clammy. The last thing I wanted to do was venture off into my empty house, looking for exactly what I didn't want to see.

I descended the stairs anyway and looked around the house, pretending I wasn't on the verge of shrieking every time I brushed against a wall. The living room was tidy. Nothing of the fire remained, but a little shard of guilt slid into me even though I'd had nothing to do with it. I was about to head back upstairs when a door slammed again. This time it sounded faint, like it was coming from outside.

I was almost finished checking the house. The yard was the last place to look. If there were any poltergeists hanging around, I needed to know.

Outside, the big maple tree in the backyard hung over the shed with clambering branches. As quietly as I could, I unlocked the shed, turned on my phone flashlight, and shone it inside.

The shed was just large enough to fit in Dad's small workshop, the old push lawn mower, and a few random gardening tools. We used to have a working light hooked up on the corrugated metal ceiling, but Dad removed it after every light bulb he installed kept burning out after a few days. Faulty wiring, he'd said.

Now I was wondering if it was something else. If it was some*one* else. I glanced back over my shoulder, then stepped all the way inside the shed.

In the corner where my bike usually sat, wedged between the lawn mower and a pile of dirty plant pots, was the broken family altar. Dad probably thought he could fix it, but it looked like it was toast. A shelf was missing and one whole side had been burned off. The objects that usually decorated the shelves were in a pile beside the altar. I bent down and dusted off a porcelain statue of the Goddess of Mercy, Kwun Yam.

Mah Mah was going to take the loss of the altar hard, especially with it being so close to the Ghost Festival. The Ghost Festival took place soon, and was a time to honour our deceased ancestors—*not* ghosts, as Mah Mah liked to remind me. For as long as I could remember, she'd always started her mornings off by lighting the joss sticks in the incense tin. The smoky fragrance would fill the living room and greet me as I came down the stairs in the morning.

Okay, so maybe I didn't believe that the altar was the physical connection between the world of the dead and the land of the living, but it was still an important memorial. A way to remember family.

I sifted through the remains. Pushed aside charred spirit tablets with embossed gold characters. Moved around broken offering plates. The whole time, I was tense. I kept expecting a ghost to pop out from the wreckage. The wind was picking up outside. When the shed door slammed shut behind me, I jumped. I tried to open the door.

The handle didn't budge.

Confused, I jerked the handle forwards and backwards. The door jostled, but didn't open. A tiny spark of terror shot through me. I'd never been afraid of the dark—not even when I was a kid—but this was different. My phone flashlight only did so much. Even in this small space, the light didn't reach into the cobwebbed corners.

Something rustled outside the door. Like leaves, or paper.

"Mah Mah?" I called out tentatively.

No response.

"A little stuck in here," I tried again more loudly.

The smell of burning wood reached my nose.

I whirled around.

One of the spirit tablets was on fire. Just the corner, but as I watched, the flame grew bigger, racing down the edge, melting the last of the embossed golden characters.

"What the heck?" I squeaked out. Frantically, I brought my foot down on the tablet. Stomped on it again and again, yet the fire didn't go out. It was like it was eating up a line of fuel. I stumbled back, heart racing, as the fire consumed the tablet—and spread up the side of the altar.

With all the force I could muster, I aimed one last, hard shove at the door—and tumbled through.

Sweet, cold air greeted me. I crawled away, coughing, towards the maple tree. I pulled myself up using the tree trunk for support—and spotted Leon, pacing the row of chrysanthemums outside my home. When he caught sight of me, his face brightened. I groaned.

"Thank goodness," he said. "You are okay."

And then he hurried over to me, like he was actually concerned. He stopped in mid-stride when I held my phone up in the air.

"This looks like a great scene for the police to walk in on," I gritted out. "You part of some arson gang or something?"

The corner of his mouth dipped, as if he was offended but trying not to show it. "I have not set any fires."

"And I've never drunk water."

His brow creased quizzically. "You haven't? But that is impossible. All mortals require water, air, and food to survive."

He pulled a brush out of his messenger bag. I sucked in a sharp breath. It was the same type of calligraphy brush Ghost Boy had wielded. He wrote something on the side of the shed, and for one unbelievable moment I could see the character he'd written. Gold and glowing, it shimmered against the wall before it sank into the dark canvas of the shed. A distinctive dripping pattered inside the shed. Rhythmic, with a clear ping.

It almost sounded like . . .

"Wait a second," I said incredulously. "Is that *rain*?"

A hesitant smile crossed Leon's face. "Indeed. A particularly heavy one, too. It will extinguish the fire very quickly. The one I did not set," he finished resolutely.

I took a step back, watching as the smoke from the shed began to lighten. My head felt cluttered, like there were too many boxes to move around inside. I looked at the brush in Leon's hand. Took in the shed with its cloud of steamy smoke. And then slowly, as if I was considering a new botanical find, I examined Leon from head to toe. He looked normal. Too normal, actually. All polite smiles and respectful distance-keeping. It was almost more creepy than the sudden fire in the shed.

"All right," I said, shoulders slumped in resignation. "What are you?"

He proudly drew himself up like he was about to do an important presentation. "I see. I should have given you my full name before. My name is Cheung Li Gwan, but my English name is—"

"No," I interrupted. "Like, *what* are you? Why are you able to do"—I waved my hand uselessly at the shed—"*that*?"

"Ah." His whole body seemed to deflate with the word. "You can consider me a guardian."

My stomach churned. "Like a guardian pigeon?"

He tilted his head in consideration. "Yes? I am not a ghost."

"I know."

"How?"

I bit my lip. I didn't want to tell him too much—not when he was a suspect in criminal activity. Instead, I interrogated, "Did you set the fire in my home this morning?"

"No," he said.

"What about this one?" I pointed at the shed. "Was that you?"

"No," he repeated, and maybe it was the mopey puppy expression he was wearing, or the fact that he'd rescued my family shed from a fiery ending, but I believed him.

I inhaled to steady myself. "I can look at you from all angles and you stay in my field of vision. You don't flicker in and out like static."

"Pardon?"

"You asked me how I knew you weren't a ghost. That's how. You also don't feel . . ."

"Nauseating?"

I glared at him. Was he trying to be funny? No, he was back to hands clasped behind his back, all innocent head tilts and sympathetic nods.

"I wouldn't say nauseating, but yeah, being around a ghost makes me feel under the weather. Like there's an atmospheric pressure drop, and I'm reaping all the consequences, and—"

My throat hitched. Michelle was alarmingly enthusiastic about my ability to see ghosts, but she couldn't see them herself. It was a lot to be talking about something I'd buried so deep. Now here it was, out in the open. I kept expecting him to brush me off the way all the kids on the playground had when I invited that lonely girl ghost over to play on the swings. The way my teachers had. The way my family had.

All he did was sagely incline his head. "An unfortunate side effect of the Sight."

"The *what*?"

"The Sight—the ability to see ghosts," he explained, taking a step forward. "It often comes with physical sensations such as headaches, nausea, or other digestive issues. You may also experience seizures or overwhelming feelings of dread if the ghost is particularly strong. Luckily, the geoi hau gwai who started this fire is not at that level yet." He looked at me expectantly. I flushed as memories of flunking tests in Chinese school came rushing back with painful clarity.

"Oh, uh . . . sorry, I don't know what that is," I said lamely, fully expecting a lecture.

Leon raised his finger up, exactly like he was about to give a lecture. "Geoi hau gwai are a type of hungry ghost. They are the fate of rather . . . ungenerous mortals. Their afterlife is filled with endless hunger because everything they try to eat is burned to ashes before it reaches their stomach."

"Hold up—hungry ghosts? Like the ghosts that my grandmother is always worried about attracting whenever we break one of her superstitions?" I snapped my mouth shut. Mah Mah had only mentioned it once, and when she had, she'd looked embarrassed, like she'd slipped up. After that, she only referred to breaking superstitions as unlucky.

He brought his hand to his chin in thought. "Yes. Hungry ghosts are not pleasant spirits. They are born from mortals who were immoral during life. They are cursed to wander the Mortal Realm in search of offerings to sustain themselves."

Hungry ghosts. Offerings. I rubbed my temple a little more vigorously than I needed to.

"I will search for the geoi hau gwai responsible for burning your family's altar and storage facility. For now, you should be cautious when you enter your house. Do not step on the doorsill. It will break the barrier of your home, and ghosts will be able to enter."

"A little late for that," I grumbled, remembering Ghost Boy lighting the family altar on fire.

"And be careful who you talk to. Some ghosts can change appearance, and they may steal faces to trick you into talking to them—"

"Emma?" Michelle called.

She and Nathan were coming around the side of the house. Desperately, I gestured for Leon to go, only to discover he'd already vanished in the second it took for me to spot Michelle and Nathan. For someone who wasn't a ghost, he sure had the whole disappearing act figured out.

"We were wondering why you were taking so long." Nathan sniffed the air. "Is that smoke?"

Quickly, I swung the shed door shut. "The neighbours must be using their wood stoves."

I caught the last few puffs of smoke rising from the altar like apparitions. And above the shed, perched on a long, spindly branch of the maple tree, was a pigeon. Its beady stare glued me to the spot.

Michelle followed my gaze into the tree branches above. "What are you looking at?"

Nervously, I looked back up. The pigeon was gone. Phew. I didn't like keeping things from Michelle, but I also didn't want Nathan to know about my sixth sense. I'd tell Michelle later, when it was just the two of us.

"The leaves are really green," I said, then pasted a bright smile on my face.

She looked skeptical, but before she could say anything,

I continued, "Did you figure out the issue with DiverBot?"

"No," Nathan groaned. "Sorry for wasting your time. We can't get you to test the manual if DiverBot doesn't work at all."

I was about to tell him that I wasn't in any rush to test the manual again, but the mechanical whirring of the garage door started up, and my parents' car pulled into the driveway.

Panic shot through me. I'd completely forgotten about dinner. I still didn't have my outfit picked out.

"You two should get going," I said. "I need to get ready for dinner."

"Jealous," Nathan said. "Have fun at the celebration. Thanks for having us over."

"Yeah. Thanks," Michelle echoed. As soon as Nathan headed towards my parents' car to say hello, she pointed two fingers from her eyes to me, drawing an invisible line of sight. "You and me. We've got lots to talk about. Later."

"Later," I promised, but it did nothing to ease the queasiness roiling in my stomach.

CHAPTER 5

Back inside the house, Mom's face went through a rainbow of colours before settling on horrified white. "You haven't gone to the mall with Mah Mah yet?"

"I completely forgot," I said, hoping that I didn't smell like smoke. "I've been working on a project with Michelle and Nathan. Mah Mah's not home, anyway."

Her brow uncreased a smidge. "Well, if it was for school..."

"It was," I quickly said.

The mention of school work seemed to pacify her. She hung up her jacket and her handbag on the hooks beside the front door. "What do you mean Mah Mah's not home? Where is she?"

"I don't know. She wasn't home when we got here."

Mom looked me over with a resigned sigh. "You're just going to have to wear something from your closet. There's that nice blue dress you wore for the Zhangs' Christmas party. You'll fit right in with your cousins. How about that one?"

The dress did look nice. It was also incredibly itchy, like a million barbed plants decided to unleash their revenge

45

through one specific piece of clothing. But Mom looked halfway to a fainting spell at the prospect of me being underdressed at a family dinner, so I headed upstairs.

Once I was inside my room, I closed the door quietly behind me and breathed in the silence. Being in my room alone reminded me of the strange noises I'd heard earlier. A chill ran up the back of my neck. I swatted it away before digging the blue dress out of my closet with a grimace.

The dress was midnight blue with a shimmery skirt that came to my knees. I tugged it on and the itch started immediately. They'd used a cheap netted liner to fill out the skirt, and it poked out along the inner seams of the waistline. As long as I didn't shuffle around too much in it, I'd survive.

I looked at myself in the mirror on the back of my bedroom door. Pleased, I gave a little twirl. I *did* look good in the dress. My aunts would have one less thing to fill their gossip cannon with tonight. The dress even had pockets, and I slipped a few paper talismans inside. You could never be too prepared when you were suddenly the VIP for all the ghosts in town.

I hopped over to the washroom across from Mah Mah's room and shut the door. I was almost ready, but there was one more thing I needed to do.

I peered at my reflection and tucked a strand of long black hair behind my ear. People told me I had my mom's eyes and my dad's nose. But most of all, I was me, and that was enough. I didn't have much makeup, but I had some eye-liner, eyeshadow, lip gloss, and a facial moisturizer Michelle gave me for my birthday back in September. I dug out my makeup kit and put the final touches on my look.

When I was finished, I opened the door.

Nathan was standing outside. I let out a tiny shriek.

"You're still here?" I placed a hand on my chest to try to calm my ricocheting heart. "Didn't you go home already?"

He rubbed the back of his neck. "I did, but then I came back. I forgot my notebook. Have you seen it?"

I paused. He looked really uncomfortable. I couldn't quite put my finger on it, but he didn't seem . . . right. I stuck a smile on my face. "It's probably in my room. One sec."

I had to walk past him to get to my room. But as soon as I got near, tension seared through my head. I crumpled, hands to my head—but just as quickly as it came, the headache disappeared.

Stunned, I straightened. What was *that*?

Too many seconds later, I realized I was just standing in the middle of the hallway, not doing anything. Even weirder, Nathan wasn't either. Normally, he'd be asking what was going on—and that's when I knew something was really wrong.

Rigidly, I turned around. "You're not Nathan."

His eyes narrowed. "Ah Wai, you've gotten slow."

Before I knew what was happening, Nathan transformed into Ghost Boy. Short hair, black as midnight. Dark eyes, intense and focused, and as sharp as his cheekbones. Like last time, aside from the charcoal shirt beneath his open jacket, everything he wore was black. The colour made the paleness of his skin all the more stark. It was an instant transformation, and just as quick, he pulled his calligraphy brush from the pouch hanging off his belt.

I ran into my bedroom and slammed the door shut before remembering that ghosts could go through doors. Right on cue, Ghost Boy stepped through the solid door as if it wasn't there.

"What did you do with Nathan?" I demanded, hating that my voice quivered with fear.

"Nothing," he said. He tossed something up in the air and caught it, his eyes never leaving my face. It felt like he was watching every breath I took.

Then I took a closer look at what he had in his hand.

"What the— Is that my test?" I shouted. It was folded into an oddly lumpy shape, but even with all the creases, I could see the big red D right on the side.

"No," he said sarcastically. "It's my test, which I'm hiding from my parents because I'm too ashamed to let them see how terrible I am at arithmetic."

"Why'd you fold it into a hat?"

"It's a boat," he said, gritting his teeth.

I took a deep breath. "Give me my test. If you leave now, I won't call the exorcist on you."

"The exorcist?" Ghost Boy's eyebrows pinched in confusion, and then his whole face relaxed and he laughed, a full sound that came from deep within his chest. It sounded like the laugh a final boss would do right before he whipped out a devastating attack to end the battle. "Real funny, Lin Wai. You can stop pretending now. If you wanted to hide, you should've reincarnated into a different family."

"Stop calling me that." I edged my way closer to the door. "It's rude."

He snorted. "How can your own name be rude?"

That was it. I spun around and snapped, "My name's not Lin Wai. It's Emma."

His face twisted in disgust, but then his gaze focused past me, as if he was searching for something not visible. "Hm. You're right. You're not Lin Wai. That makes Plan B a lot easier to carry out."

My stomach dropped. "What's Plan B?"

"You take a short trip to the Underworld."

He took another step closer, and I hunched over, dizzy. The sickening feeling travelled through my body. With a lot of effort, I threw open my bedroom door and dashed into the hallway. I looked over my shoulder into my room.

He was gone.

And then I crashed into something solid.

I teetered back, rubbing my nose.

The ghost stood in front of me, a massively unimpressed expression slant to his eyes. He brandished his black calligraphy brush in front of me. Desperately, I dove back into my room and grabbed the first thing I could—and flung it at him. It flew through his head and hit the wall behind him with an audible crack.

"Emma! What are you doing?"

I whipped around. Mom stood behind me at the top of the stairs, mouth open in dismay. She had a plate of sliced apples in her hand.

"I . . . uh . . ." I stuttered. "There was . . ."

Ghost Boy leaned against the wall, smirking. He flipped his calligraphy brush into the air and caught it again—and then he took one purposeful, short step to the side.

A splash of wetness. Glossy rivulets, running down the painting on the wall. A cup on the ground, rolling to a stop at Mom's feet.

Oh, *crap*.

I'd thrown a cup of water. And it wasn't just any old painting I'd thrown it at. It was one that Mom had done years ago, before she stopped picking up her watercolours and began replacing them with calculators instead. A billow of clouds and herons in flight, evenly spaced amongst the strokes of white.

At least, that's what it used to depict before I ruined it.

Mom bent down and picked up the cup. "It's okay. I should have taken it down a long time ago." Her fingers tightened around the plate in her hand. "It's not very good."

"Mom," I said, my throat tight. "I swear it was an accident. I love your work."

She finally came up to me and pushed the plate of apples into my hands. "It's fine. I'll go get some paper towels to clean up. What is this? Water?"

"Yes," I whispered.

Mom's shoulders sank down. She looked tired. "Hurry

and get the towels from the washroom. We have to leave for dinner after." She headed back downstairs.

"It was an accident!" I called weakly down after her, but she didn't reply.

"Your poor parents, stuck with you for a daughter," Ghost Boy said with a sneer. "Maybe I should just take all four of you. It'd be a family trip."

I turned back to him and said, "Get out."

"Or what?" His lips curved. "You're going to call the exorcist? A Western exorcist won't know how to get rid of a ngo gwai unless he fancies a trip to the Underworld too."

The heat drained from me. A ngo gwai was a hungry ghost, and I had no offerings to appease him. But if it was me he was after, maybe I could at least lure him away from my family.

I dashed over to my bedroom window. Shoved up the glass. A cool gust of air pushed into my face. The ground below was far away. But not too far.

Okay, I could do this. Think Girl Guides. Survival skills. Tuck and roll. Or was it roll and tuck?

I jumped just as I felt him come up behind me. The air flew out of me when I hit the grass. For a second, I couldn't breathe. A burning pain tore through my shoulder. I wiggled my fingers. They worked, at least.

I groaned and wobbled to my feet. The boy was already outside on the lawn with me. He sat on his haunches, examining his fingernails.

"Time's up," he said coldly. He rose to his feet with the

ease of an uncoiling snake and pulled a bronze disc out of his inner jacket pocket. It looked like a mirror and was a bit bigger than the palm of his hand, and I knew, just by looking at it, that I did not want to go near it.

"What's your name?" I blurted out.

He thought for a moment with the bronze mirror in his hand. "You can call me Henry."

"Who's Lin Wai?"

He froze, caught off guard. "Someone I knew."

"You said you needed her to help you."

"It doesn't matter now." He stood up and tossed the disc into the air. Briefly, it glowed silver before he caught it in his hand. The light vanished. "She's dead."

I cringed. He'd mistaken me for a dead person. That seemed offensive, somehow.

I slipped my hand inside my dress pocket for a paper talisman. He moved towards me, but I moved faster. I sprinted right for him. He must not have been expecting me to come towards him, because his eyes widened. But just as I was about to slap the talisman onto him, he clamped his fingers around my wrist in a crushing grip.

"What do you think you're doing?"

His tone was icy, and his glare even colder. I gave a hard tug, but it was like fighting a concrete block. The talisman fluttered to the ground.

My face flushed with anger and fear. "Let go, jerk."

He yanked me forward so fast I tripped. "Try it," he hissed. "Go ahead. I dare you."

"Okay."

And then I kicked him. Hard.

He released my wrist and stumbled back a couple of inches, surprise splashed across his pale face—and a pigeon swooped down in front of us.

I let out a huge exhale of relief as Leon transformed into his human form. His rounded eyes darted between us, as if he wasn't sure who he needed to approach. He shot Henry a distasteful grimace, like he'd eaten something rotten. "Do I know you?"

"Unlikely." There was more than a touch of annoyance in Henry's voice.

Leon stepped towards him, hand slipping inside his coat pocket. "Return to the Underworld before I exercise my duty to uphold the balance between the Three Realms."

"Immortals are always such troublemakers." Henry slid the bronze disc back into his pouch. "You of all people should know better than to interfere with Underworld business."

"Me of all people?" Leon looked even more confused than I felt. "I think you should leave."

"Wait," I said. "He's got my math test."

"Give her the test, ngo gwai."

"Of course," Henry said smugly. He held my folded test paper out to the side. "It's all yours, Emma."

I didn't even have to trust my gut feeling to know that it was a bad idea.

Leon slammed into Henry's side, throwing him off

53

balance. I sprinted over. I didn't know what to do. I only knew I wanted him to go away. To disappear. A warm energy swept up in waves inside me. I reached out. Smacked his arm with a talisman.

Disappear, I thought.

And just like that, Henry vanished.

CHAPTER 6

"Emma!" Mom shrieked from inside the garage. "We're going to be late!"

"Coming!" I called back. I turned to Leon. "Holy crap, did you see that? I didn't just imagine him disappearing, did I?"

"That talisman was a ghost hunting tool," he said slowly. "Where did you get that?"

Suddenly, I felt nervous. I thought I'd done something good, but Leon's face was telling me otherwise. "My grandma has a whole stack of them."

His expression went flat. "A stack? Did she mention anything about using them?"

"I'm supposed to stick them near entryways if I feel something's off." I wiped my sweaty hands on the skirt of my dress. "Not necessarily anything paranormal. She's never talked about ghosts. No one in my family believes they're real."

I said the lie like I believed it. But as soon as I said it, I realized that Mah Mah hadn't exactly said she didn't believe ghosts were real. She'd just avoided the topic like it was made out of bad luck.

"This is very odd," Leon muttered under his breath. He paced back and forth, gaze focused on the ground like I wasn't there. "Why would she . . ."

When he didn't continue, I prompted, "Why would she what?"

He shook his head and smiled warmly, but I could tell it was hiding his worry. "It is of no importance. What matters is that you are safe. You are, right? Are you hurt anywhere?"

"I'm fine." My shoulder throbbed a little from where I'd landed on it, but right now the most discomfort I felt was inside my stomach. Did Mah Mah know the talismans she'd given me were ghost hunting tools? Why *did* she have a huge stack of them? This whole thing was starting to give me a headache. "So . . . is he gone? For good?"

"He would have returned to the Underworld, but as he has already travelled to the Mortal Realm, he may return." He gave me a funny look. "I have never seen someone send a ghost to the Underworld with a protective talisman. As your grandmother informed you, they are only meant to ward off evil at entrances to buildings."

I shivered and wrapped my arms around myself. "I need to go, but thanks for helping."

"Stay safe. I will try to identify the ghost."

He gave me an awkward pat on the shoulder. I thought about awkwardly patting him back, but decided that was even more weird than getting chased out of my bedroom window by a ghost. Leon was a bit of an oddball, but he was nice. I bet he would help Michelle and the real Nathan test-drive DiverBot as much as they needed.

He transformed into a pigeon and flew away, slipping between the treetops into the cloudless night. With a determined huff, I swatted off the grass and dirt on my dress and marched over to the garage. I slipped my hand into my dress pocket. Two more talismans.

If Henry showed up again, I'd send him right back to the Underworld.

• • •

Jade Garden Restaurant was bustling, noisy with families and clanking dishes. The restaurant looked the way the world did when I was on a roller coaster: half was a blur of a kaleidoscope of colours, and the other half . . . well, let's just say I wasn't the biggest fan of feeling tossed around by my surroundings. Servers whizzed around at a dizzying speed, their arms laden with fragrant, steaming dishes. One server whipped the yellow tablecloth off a table and quickly replaced it with a fresh one before four people plopped into the seats.

We wound our way through the busy diners, slipping between packed tables and dodging twirling servers. Just when I thought I wouldn't be able to squeeze through another set of chairs, we stumbled out into the banquet room at the back of the restaurant.

"We're late," Mom panted, her eyes roving over the full tables.

"Just be glad we made it," Dad wheezed, straightening his tie. "One of the servers nearly spilled boiling soup on me."

"Come," Mah Mah said, completely unfazed by the tornado we'd just travelled through. I was dying to ask her about the talismans, but before I could, she beelined straight towards a table with empty seats, and I tried to rub away the headache that was starting. My head felt a little funny with all the noise.

The banquet room was separated from the rest of the restaurant with sliding partitions. Everything was red for the occasion: the chairs, napkins, and tablecloths. Even the plates of eggs in the middle of the big round tables, with their dishes of pickled ginger, were dyed a vibrant red. The side wall was covered in scarlet satin. Gold figures of a dragon and a phoenix hung on it, watching over the table in front where my cousin Josephine, Uncle Eric, and their baby, Dylan, were seated with their parents. I wanted to go up and say hi, but as soon as we reached our table, my aunts swarmed me.

"Oh, Emma!" Auntie Lynn shouted close to my ear with her big crimson lips. "Your hair's gotten so much longer! Has it really been six months since I last saw you?"

I glued my Good Niece smile onto my face and resigned myself to sitting down. "Yes, Auntie Lynn."

Auntie Vivian swept up to me in her sparkling rings and necklaces, bumping me in the process and jostling the cup of tea I was sipping from. "Goodness, it's been that long? I just saw Emma over spring break! She and Beth had such a lovely chat about their school work. Beth only got 92 percent on her last math test, and I was hoping Emma could give her some advice since she's a year ahead."

I slouched in my seat. Oh no. It was coming.

Auntie Lynn's eyes narrowed a smidge. "Oh? Beth is in grade eight, isn't she? I remember Jonathan was having *such* a difficult time. He passed, of course, but now he's in pre-calculus. I'm wondering if I should pull him from hockey so he can focus on his studies, but you know, his team is headed for Seattle next month . . ."

"Well, universities look for extracurriculars. Emma's been putting in so many volunteer hours at the community garden," Mom said, casually raising a glass of water to her mouth. "Aren't you, Emma?"

"Yes, Mom."

I slouched down lower and washed down the groan rising in my throat with another swig of tea. I wasn't volunteering at the community garden to impress some university I might not even go to. I was volunteering because I liked feeling the earth beneath my fingers and helping things grow. But even Mom was getting sucked up into the vortex of one-upmanship. At this point I might as well just disappear under the table and be done with it.

My aunts exchanged a glance with each other.

"The community garden?" Auntie Vivian echoed. "The one down by the landfill?"

"It's the Fairview Community Garden," I corrected. Something about her tone rubbed me the wrong way.

Auntie Vivian tapped a finger against her temple. Her large diamond ring caught the light above, momentarily blinding me and letting me imagine, for a split second, I was still at home, swiping off talismans at ghosts like a deck of cards. Fighting off another ghost was sounding really good right about now.

"But why a garden? There are plenty of better volunteer opportunities—"

"Emma's been doing a wonderful job of helping the community garden prepare for the summer," Mah Mah interjected in Cantonese. She placed a plump fried shrimp crab claw—yeung hai kim—onto my plate. "Half the food from that garden goes to the food bank. You could have an expensive education, a fancy car, or a large house, but if you have no food, it means nothing."

Red splotches appeared on Auntie Vivian's cheeks. "Of course, Nai Nai," she muttered, using the family term for mother-in-law. "How's your health? Are you still—"

"Fine, fine," Mah Mah said dismissively, even though she seemed to be fine less and less these days. Dad chalked it up to getting older. Mah Mah said it was because she always had to remind him to lock the shed door.

As soon as Auntie Vivian looked away, Mah Mah nodded at me. I flashed her a grateful smile. We ate the rest of our dinner in comfortable silence. Dish after dish arrived at our table: sesame oil jellyfish, succulent roasted squab, steamed fish with hot soy sauce drizzled on top, and cream sauce lobster. Finally, when the last course had arrived and no one could eat any more, a tinkling sound rang out. Uncle Eric was tapping his knife against the wineglass in front of him. Josephine beamed and held Dylan up in one arm. With her opposite hand, she raised a glass.

"Thank you all for joining us today," she said. "We're so lucky to celebrate Dylan's first hundred days with the family."

Uncle Eric pecked Dylan on the forehead. "Very lucky."

"We're also excited to share Dylan's Chinese name with you all." Josephine gestured towards her parents, and they stood with their own glasses in hand.

"Welcome to the family, Leung Kit Hong!" They raised their glasses. "Yum bui!"

Everyone around the banquet tables raised their glasses and clinked them together. "Yum bui!"

I tipped my glass of ginger ale towards my mouth, and then I made the mistake of looking outside.

Uh-oh.

There was a pigeon outside the window closest to me, beating its wings furiously so that it hovered in place. When it saw me looking, it dropped to the windowsill and pointed its wing to the side. My jaw dropped. That was *not* normal pigeon behaviour, which meant . . .

Leon.

Quickly, I looked around, but no one else seemed to have noticed the pigeon. Yet. With the way it was jabbing with its wing, someone else would notice soon.

"Go away," I mouthed frantically as it started doing circles with its wings over its head like it was leading an impromptu yoga class. I made a shooing gesture, but it only sped up its circles.

"Everything okay, Emma?" Mom asked suspiciously.

"Just practising my presentation for tomorrow," I lied.

Grandma's gaze followed mine to the window—and then her eyes widened. There was no way I could lie to her about something she'd already seen. Face burning, I shot to my feet. Family dinners were already enough of a trial without a magical pigeon pooping the party.

"On second thought, I'm going to the washroom," I announced, loudly enough for half the banquet room to hear—and, hopefully, Leon.

I dashed off towards the washrooms at the back of the restaurant. As soon as I rounded the corner, I veered towards the exit. The back door had an Employees Only sign. I shoved the door open.

Sure enough, the pigeon was waiting for me outside. It hopped down from its perch on the lid of the dumpster beside the door and vanished. In its place stood Leon, the biological anomaly, adjusting the collar of his neatly buttoned shirt beneath his unseasonal wool coat. I stumbled backwards with a small yelp.

"How are you doing?" he asked. He wore a benevolent smile on his face, as if he'd been invited over for tea and was delighted to accept the offer.

"You can't be here." I slammed the restaurant door shut behind me. "Dinner's still going on. I need to get back before my family wonders where I am."

"I know." He winced apologetically. "I would not bother you unless there was imminent danger to your mortal life."

I stared at him. Hard. He stared back, horror dawning on his face as he realized what he'd said.

"That is . . . I mean . . ." he stuttered. "I have discovered the identity of the ghost who attacked you."

"He didn't attack me. He pretended to be my friend and chased me out of my bedroom window. On the second floor." I paused. "So, am I going to die?"

He winced. "No, you are not. My apologies for scaring you. I was not expecting the head ghost hunter of the Underworld to come after you."

The heat drained out of me. "The head ghost hunter of the Underworld? That's who Henry is?"

He shifted uncomfortably. "His actual name is Lam Kai Ming. He was born into the prestigious Lam family of the Three Great Hunter Clans." His face darkened. "But he has changed. Now he works for Tin Hong, one of the Ten Ghost Lords of the Underworld."

Tin Hong. A chill cut through me at the mention of his name. I shivered.

Leon rubbed his chin, confused. "Henry is usually responsible for reining in unruly ghosts who cause trouble."

"But I'm not a ghost."

"No," he said miserably. "I am at just as much of a loss as you are."

We stood there in silence. I plucked at a loose thread on my skirt. "How are you able to transform into a pigeon?" It was far from the right question, but it fell out of my mouth before I could stop it.

"Years and years of study, I'm afraid." Leon smiled tentatively. "You had best start studying now."

I refused to laugh. "Why a pigeon?"

"It's inconspicuous. I could choose a different bird, but no one ever questions the sudden appearance of a pigeon."

"Right," I said faintly. He chuckled, which was funny because I didn't find any of this amusing at all. "Why do you think Henry is trying to bring me to the Underworld?"

"I do not know," Leon admitted. "You seem to be a completely average mortal girl with no special abilities. None at all."

"Thanks," I huffed.

"But until we find out, keep your shield up—"

"Guard."

"Keep your guard up around Henry. As you saw with your friend, he is skilled at taking on other appearances. He's infamous throughout the Three Realms for his ruthless dedication to his job." He gave me a meaningful look. "I don't think he has ever failed to complete a task."

"All right." I hesitated, then asked, "So what can *I* do? There must be a way to drive them off."

He raised his pointer finger and said earnestly, "The best way to protect yourself against ghosts is prevention. Make sure you close all windows and doors before sundown. And don't step on the threshold of the front door. Ghosts can follow in behind you once that boundary is broken—"

I crossed my arms, trying to settle the queasiness in my stomach.

"—and try not to talk to people who are acting oddly," he continued. "Ghosts can be very deceptive, and it's not always easy to tell them apart from real people, so—"

"Got it. I'll never leave my house again," I said, before I remembered that he didn't understand sarcasm.

He nodded gravely. "I know you need to go to school, but stay inside the house when you can. I will keep watch as much as possible for Henry and other ghosts—"

I drowned out the rest of his words with a very loud groan. Regular ghosts were bad enough. Finding out that my personal poltergeist was the head ghost hunter of the Underworld was like being told I only had math courses for the entirety of the next school year. He'd already set my family altar on fire. I was sure he'd also set the shed on fire. How much more havoc could one ghost wreak?

I swallowed hard, and a throbbing ache spread through my head. A chill swept over me. I shivered and looked around. "Do you feel that?"

"Feel what?" Leon scanned the area and then, in a quick motion, grabbed his calligraphy brush from his bag. He brandished it like a weapon at the dumpsters beside us, and slowly backed up. "Get behind me."

Heart thudding, I scampered beside Leon and steadied myself. I'd kicked Henry's pasty ghost butt back to the Underworld once. I could do it again. I reached into my pocket for a paper talisman.

The lid of the dumpster flew open.

I sucked in a breath. "That's not Henry."

A ghost stood in the middle of the dumpster. It was lean, with dragging limbs, and it had a great yawning mouth, so dark it was like looking into a hole. Instead of hair, it had long, vicious black needles on top of its head. And its eyes . . . They seemed to pull me in. It wanted me closer to that bleak emptiness inside it.

"That's a zam mou gwai. Needle mouth ghost." Leon grabbed me by the arm. "What are you doing? Don't go any further."

I blinked. I'd advanced a few steps without realizing I'd even moved. Leon shot me another alarmed glance before swiping out several strokes with his calligraphy brush. The shimmering gold character hovered in the air for a brief moment before vanishing, and the zam mou gwai froze in place. It was like someone had paused reality over it.

"What'd you write?" I asked hoarsely.

"*Zam zyu—Stop.*" He wrote out the character again. "Come with me. It will only hold for a minute or so."

He started hurrying away, but I stood there, unable to tear my eyes from the zam mou gwai's head of sharp needles. "But my family—"

"It's only after you." He wrung his hands guiltily, like he thought he was to blame for all my problems. "I should have done a better job protecting you. The ghosts have been increasing around you for months, and with the Ghost Festival fast approaching . . ."

Dread dug its claws into me, but it wasn't as awful as seeing Leon berate himself for something that wasn't his fault. "Where are we going?"

A grim look settled onto his face. "To see the only person who might be able to help. Let's go."

A hair-raising shriek pierced the air, and I flinched. The zam mou gwai had broken free of the spell. It took a stumbling step towards us, mouth open in a silent scream as it pulled at the cruel needles on its head—and without thinking, I grabbed on to Leon's hand and we ran off into the night.

CHAPTER 7

We sprinted through downtown, keeping to the side streets as much as possible. A couple of people glanced at us as we ran by them in the dark, but we didn't slow—not until we reached the towering red Gate of Harmonious Interest of Chinatown. My heart beat erratically in my chest as we passed beneath the ornate entryway, and I dared a look over my shoulder. The shadowed trees behind us reached spindly branches towards the night sky, but nothing moved in the darkness.

"It's not following us anymore," Leon promised.

"Where'd it go?" I panted.

His eyes lit up at my question. "Back to the Underworld, most likely. Hungry ghosts do not possess enough spiritual energy to linger long in the mortal world."

He beamed at me, and I had the sudden urge to toss him a biscuit. Unlike me, Leon looked like he'd had a leisurely walk through the park. Even his hair still looked picture-perfect. I shook a rock out of my shoe, and we continued into Chinatown.

Our Chinatown was more of a China Street. A long

time ago it'd been larger than the two streets it currently encompassed, one of which we were walking down. Now it was an eclectic assortment of hipster juice shops and old Chinese restaurants, all under the same lantern-strewn sky. At night, the lanterns made the street feel otherworldly, like we'd stepped back in time. Red brick walls and wrought iron balconies. Busy storefronts with tea sets and cheap ice cream bars that Michelle and I liked to buy during the hottest days of summer. Then Leon and I passed by Fan Tan Alley, the narrow divide between two buildings, and I suppressed a shudder. People said it was haunted.

I checked the status of my head. No aching. The alley wasn't haunted.

For now.

I followed a few steps behind Leon. Wool peacoat aside, anybody would've instantly pegged him for a visitor. Something about the bright way he took in the neon signs and swaying silk lanterns above us. It would've been easy to mistake him for a tourist soaking in the sights.

And maybe that's what this was to him—just another day on the job for the immortal guy stuck doing ghost cleanup in the realm of shorter lifespans. Eventually, he'd forget all about the Wong family haunting. Maybe he'd laugh about it with his friends, and all that would be left was a story on the tip of his tongue.

Something about the thought was oddly comforting, and I straightened taller as I walked. We'd each do our part, and then go our separate ways. There'd be an end to this.

Leon paused outside a dilapidated brick building. My gaze roved up the four storeys, taking in the wrought iron railing around the balconies and the shuttered windows.

"You're not trying to murder me, are you?" I asked, only half joking.

Leon climbed the two steps to the building entrance. "My friend works here. She may be able to help us with your situation."

"You have a friend? *Here?*" In the dim glow of the street light, I squinted at the board of business names on the inner alcove of the entrance. More than half of the spots were missing. The rest of the name placards were held in place with rusty screws. "What is she, a crow?"

Leon's face blanched. "Please do not say that. She might hear."

He took out his calligraphy brush and scrawled a character on the handle in tiny, precise movements. The lock clicked open. I gulped. Running from ghosts was one thing—breaking into a building at night was a whole other level of wrong. I could just picture my family's upset faces if I showed up at my front door escorted by police. Mom would probably cry from the embarrassment. But if Leon's friend could help get rid of the ghosts, it'd be worth it.

I gave a quick nod, and we slipped inside.

The ancient wooden stairs creaked and groaned under our weight as we ascended. The steps sagged in the middle, and I had an awful feeling that if I stomped too hard, my foot would smash through. The building was old, and it smelled even older—musty, with more than a hint of dust.

At the top of the stairs was a blue door with a luxuriously elaborate etching of a chrysanthemum covering the glass panel. Leon grabbed the handle and swung the door open for me.

"After you," he said graciously.

I bit my lip and stepped through, unable to place the apprehension I was feeling.

The shop was full of glass jars, neatly spaced along rows of wooden shelving. Every jar had a label displayed on the front, with some more yellowed than others. I approached the wooden counter at the front. Some things I recognized, like the dried red dates and longan that I'd seen Mah Mah use in soups. Most of it, though, was as much of a mystery as the characters on the labels.

I tried to look past the curtained doorway behind the counter, but there was no sign of any movement. "There's no one here."

Leon nodded solemnly. "Be patient. She is coming."

And right on cue, a young woman came through the door we'd entered through.

She was carrying a stack of cardboard boxes so tall that the only part of her head that I could see was her hair. It'd been combed into an impossibly smooth black bun.

"Hello, Bo Liang," Leon said, dipping at the waist.

"Oh, Li Gwan! Good, you're here. Be a dear and come help me with these boxes." She peered around the stack of boxes in her arms and the smile disappeared from her face. "Ah. I see you've brought a little mortal girl into my shop."

Stunned, I could only watch as Leon dutifully took the boxes from her and set them on the counter. A million questions ran through my head. I hadn't heard anyone come up the stairs behind us. She barely looked a day older than sixteen, but she had the gall to stare down her nose at me like I was trying to steal from her parents' shop.

I swallowed down the nervousness in my throat and extended my hand. "Nice to meet you. I'm Emma Wong."

She brushed past me on feet so light she appeared to be floating and went behind the counter. With a delicate touch, she pushed the boxes to the side as if they weighed nothing.

Then, in front of me, her clothing instantly changed.

Her cashmere sweater and beige chinos transformed into a flowing robe the colour of a pale spring sky. Embroidered flowers and long-tailed swallows ran along the sides of her torso and up her drooping sleeves. She slid open a drawer under the counter and took out a gold filigree ornament studded with round cuts of brilliant green jade. With a surgeon's precision, she slid the ornament into the bun on top of her head, then lifted her chin.

"I greet you, Emma Wong," she said. "My name is Bo Liang Song, Lady of the Chrysanthemum Court and presiding member of the High Council in the Upper Realm." She tucked her hands into the opposite sleeves and sniffed. The ornament in her hair caught the overhead lights, and the brilliant shine forced me to squint in order to see her upturned nose. "Welcome to my medicine shop."

"... Thanks, I guess?"

"Mortals," she scoffed, dropping her hands from her sleeves and rolling her eyes. "You do them the honour of gracing them with your presence, and all they ever do is gawk like they've never seen an immortal before."

Leon cleared his throat, casting an apologetic wince my way. "Please pardon our intrusion, Bo Liang. We will not be long. There is an ... issue for which we would like your assistance."

"Of course. Give me a moment, won't you?" She patted the jade ornament in her hair. "If I don't put these peony roots into cold storage right away, the ghosts on this street might come and consume their energy, and my past three months of work in this wretched realm will be wasted." She shuddered delicately before picking up one of the boxes on the counter and heading behind the curtained partition to the back of the shop.

As soon as the partition stopped fluttering behind her, I whirled around to face Leon. "Okay, what in the world is going on? There are other immortals here?"

His eyebrows arched in innocent surprise. "Of course. Most prefer to stay in the Upper Realm, but there are still many who travel through the Three Realms for business and fun in the sun."

"No," I groaned. "Please don't say that ever again. Nobody says that."

Leon's shoulders sagged. "Fun in the sun? But I just learned it. It is a lovely idea."

"Just say business and pleasure. I promise, it's more normal." I shuddered. "Bo Liang has a store here in the Mortal Realm? Just conveniently in my city? And you know each other?"

He picked up a business card from the stand beside the cash register. "Bo Liang and I have known each other for decades. As for this shop, she took it over when the last owner passed away in the late 1930s. She changes her appearance every few years to prevent the residents here from becoming confused." He flipped the business card over, then handed it to me with both hands.

I took the card, not bothering to look it over before shoving it into my pocket. "But you think she'll be able to help me?"

The two halves of the curtained partition billowed outwards as Bo Liang stepped through, her sleeves fluttering behind her like gossamer wings. "Help with what?"

"Do you remember Lam Kai Ming?" Leon asked.

"Lam Kai Ming?" Her mouth crinkled into a displeased frown. "Oh. The ghost hunter?"

"Indeed." He drew in a deep breath. "He has taken a . . . particular interest in Emma and her family."

"He chased me out of my bedroom window," I added. "And set my ancestral altar on fire. Leon said you might be able to help get rid of him."

She wrinkled her nose like I'd suggested she go take

a swim in the sewer. She twisted off the top of the jar and grabbed a handful of the dried lily bulbs inside. "I'm afraid I really don't have the time. *Important* matters call for my attention at the Chrysanthemum Court."

My mouth fell open. A white heat flushed through me, but before I could say anything, Leon walked up to the counter.

"Bo Liang, I ask you for a favour," he said softly.

She paused in the middle of replacing the jar lid. "Anything—for *you*."

"I was tasked with protecting Emma's family." He cleared his throat again. "Emma *Wong*." He emphasized the last part of my name, and I suddenly got the uncomfortable feeling that I was missing something.

"Wong?" Interest flashed in Bo Liang's eyes as she peered past Leon, observing me with an uncomfortable scrutiny. "The Wong family of the Three Great Hunter Clans?"

I shot Leon a sharp look. "What Three Great Hunter Clans?"

Bo Liang laughed—a high, tinkling sound, like a chime in a summer breeze. "This silly mortal girl doesn't even know her own lineage."

I stiffened. Leon looked down at the ground, as if he'd been caught red-handed in a lie—which didn't seem to be far from the truth.

"The Three Great Hunter Clans were responsible for maintaining much of the spiritual balance here. They eliminated ghosts that were overstepping their bounds in the

Mortal Realm," he said. He raised his head. "Your family is one of them. There is also the Fung Clan, and the Lams."

Bo Liang sighed. "A pity the Lam Clan is nearly gone. It was like watching the Tang Dynasty fall."

My head spun. My family was descended from ghost hunters. Leon dug out his calligraphy brush and passed it to me, handle first. I took it. My hand shook, but I closed my fingers around it—and as soon as I did, a warmth spread up my arm. It coursed through my body like a river current returning to the ocean. I gasped and nearly dropped the brush when a sparkle of gold burst out from the brush head.

"That," he said quietly, "is proof of who you are. Children from the Three Great Hunter Clans innately know how to grasp their spiritual energy and put it to use. Outside these clans, it would take a mortal years of training to have the brush spark gold."

I turned the calligraphy brush over. It really did look like the calligraphy brushes from Chinese school. But there was no ink to write with.

"How does the brush work with no ink?" I asked.

Bo Liang waved her hand lazily. "The wielder's spiritual energy is the ink."

"Well, I guess my family being one of the Three Great Hunter Clans doesn't excuse the head ghost hunter of the Underworld from coming after us, huh?" I said tersely, passing the brush back to Leon. As soon as I did, the warmth it brought dissipated, and I almost regretted giving it back.

Bo Liang picked up a jagged leaf, brown and brittle, and examined it carefully. She pulled out a stone mortar and pestle from underneath the counter. "I must say, I hadn't expected to find your lot on this side of the ocean. I thought the last of the Wongs had all moved to the cities in Guangdong."

"My grandma immigrated here."

"Wong Lin Mui?"

"You know her?" I spluttered.

"I know *of* her." She turned back to the shelves behind her. Her fingers danced down the row of jars, lifting airtight lids with a pop and picking ingredients to throw into her bowl. "Her mother used to grow the most wonderful ginseng. It was well-known in the Upper Realm for its healing properties. She had two girls, if I remember correctly."

"My grandmother and her sister," I said, surprised.

"So you *do* know something of your lineage."

I looked down at my shoes. "My great-aunt passed away before I was born. I never knew her."

Bo Liang made a contemplative humming sound in her throat. "And so ends a prestigious family line. I'll miss that ginseng." She threw in small pieces of ingredients and got to work, grinding and scraping the contents against the bowl. "I'm afraid I cannot help you with your situation. It is forbidden for immortals to interfere with mortal affairs."

My mouth dropped, and I turned to Leon. "Is that true?"

His face flushed. "Well . . . I would not say forbidden . . ."

"You told me you were a guardian for my family!"

Bo Liang tutted. "There's no such thing as an immortal guardian—"

Leon coughed. Loudly. I narrowed my eyes at him.

"But I suppose there are always exceptions," she quickly added before turning back to her mortar and pestle. The oddly calming sound of grinding stone filled the silence in the shop. "Are there other ghosts tormenting the Wong family?"

Leon wrung his hands. "I would not say *tormenting*, but—"

"Tormenting," I agreed. "There was one that had fire in its mouth and another with needles on its head."

Bo Liang hummed. "And they have all been ngo gwai?"

"Hungry ghosts, yeah."

"If they've all been ngo gwai, then I can see why Li Gwan is helping you. Desperate times, desperate measures and all that. It'd be a pity to see the Wong Clan go the way of the Lams." She leaned her elbows on the counter and wove her slender fingers together. "Ngo gwai don't usually haunt a specific family they're unrelated to. Unless . . ."

"Unless they're being ordered to," Leon finished, his eyes wide. We exchanged a look. He was thinking the same thing I was: Henry was working for Tin Hong, a Ghost Lord of the Underworld. Henry wanted to bring me to the Underworld. What if Tin Hong was ordering him to?

My stomach turned. "What happened to the Lam Clan?"

"Oh, what usually happens to mortals who strive too hard to be something they're not," Bo Liang said with an aggrieved sigh.

What usually happened to mortals who tried to be something they weren't? A part of me wanted to know, but what really mattered was that my family didn't go the same way the Lams had. And in order to make sure of that, I had to do something. Something bigger than what I was already doing. Something more useful.

"I suppose you won't be needing anything from me now," Bo Liang continued airily.

I worked up enough patience to smile. "I guess not. Thank you, though—"

"Then if you will not be purchasing anything, I must ask you to leave. Trouble trails ghost hunters like vermin after rice grains, and I *finally* managed to clear out the ghosts in this building." She plunked another glass jar on the counter in front of her and shivered delicately. "I don't want to smell another lìguǐ for at least another hundred years."

"What's a lìguǐ?" I asked nervously.

"Oh, you'll know if one ever comes within a hundred li of you." She turned her attention back to the wall of jars. "Farewell, Emma of the Wong Hunter Clan."

CHAPTER 8

As soon as Leon and I left the medicine shop, I squared my stance. He pointedly avoided meeting my eyes as he started down the stairs. He was definitely keeping something from me. In fact, he seemed like he was keeping a lot of things from me. Why? I wanted to ask him, but I had the feeling that if I did, he'd fly away. I had to be careful if I wanted answers—but even more than that, I had to know how to protect my family.

"Teach me how to do magic," I said in one fast breath, grabbing on to his arm. "You said Henry works for Tin Hong, a Ghost Lord of the Underworld. Maybe he's ordering the ghosts to come after my family."

His expression froze. "What?"

"Please." I thought back to the warmth the calligraphy brush had brought me. "Holding the calligraphy brush felt . . . right. I need to know how to defend my family against ghosts if Henry is going to return."

"No." He shook his head and started back down the stairs in a rush. "No, no. I do not think that is a good idea."

"I'm really thankful," I continued more loudly, following him, "that you've been looking out for me, but you can't be my bodyguard forever. Besides, my parents would freak if they caught you with me. No offence, but you don't exactly pass for a classmate. You look like the right age, but they're going to wonder why I'm hanging out with a private school student."

And for the first time since I'd met him, his smile completely disappeared from his face. "No."

A twinge of annoyance shot through me. "Why not?"

"I have never taught anyone how to use syu fat mo before," he said. He shot the door to Bo Liang's medicine shop a pleading look. As if she was listening in on us, the click of a lock resounded through the stairwell. Leon pinched the bridge of his nose in frustration. "It would take years to properly train you."

"Then don't properly train me. There must be a crash course of basic spells you can teach."

He ran his fingers through the thick wave of hair hanging over his forehead, pushing it back. "Practising syu fat mo increases your spiritual energy. The greater your spiritual energy, the more danger it attracts. There are ghosts aside from Henry who would take your spiritual energy for their own."

I didn't like the idea of attracting more ghosts, but now I was truly scared. Regular ghosts were bad enough. A Ghost Lord? Yeah, no thanks. "My family's already in danger. I'm sorry, Leon, but you can't protect me forever."

I could see him mulling the idea over in his head. And maybe it was just the exhaustion getting to me, but he looked rather unhappy when he was deep in thought, like all those years of being immortal were finally catching up to him and he was deciding that he didn't like what he was doing after all.

"Okay," he finally said, relenting, and my heart leapt. "I will teach you a little syu fat mo. Just to protect yourself. But you must promise me something."

"What is it?"

"Don't try to engage with anything that you feel is too strong." He looked down at his hands and flexed his fingers. "Immortals live much longer than mortals, and some ghosts live even longer still. Time is strength, and you are young."

Done deal. I didn't fancy an early trip to the Underworld, or anything else that happened when ghosts got their nasty spectral hands on people. "Okay. It's a promise."

We reached the bottom of the stairs and opened the door back to the outside world. The cold wind rushed over me. I rubbed my arms to try to warm them.

"We'll start tomorrow?" I asked.

"Tomorrow," Leon agreed, with all the enthusiasm of being forced to drink Mah Mah's herbal remedies.

• • •

True to his word, Leon showed up the next day at my front door, armed with a calligraphy set. We took the bus to

Cadboro Bay beach, which was the last place I was hoping to go.

"What's wrong?" Leon asked with a frown when I took my time trudging over to the beach.

"Nothing."

"You look like you are upset."

"I don't have the best memories of this place," I admitted. My memory was fuzzy, but I was pretty sure I'd come here with Michelle when I was younger and something terrible had happened. I remembered cold water and Michelle's dad screaming.

"We don't have to be here," Leon said. "We could go to a different area with water. Perhaps a lake? What is that lake called on the highway? Moose Lake?"

"Elk Lake," I corrected. "And I'm fine. Let's go."

We set up Leon's calligraphy set at the far end of the beach. As Leon blathered on about proper stroke order for writing, I closed my eyes and imagined my first day of summer vacation, minus the uncomfortable memories. Summer vacations were ice cream and long bike rides and hanging out with Michelle under the stars. I'd finally be able to help Michelle and Nathan get DiverBot to work. They would scream, and I'd cheer them on at Nationals next year—

"No, no," Leon said, breaking my daydream. "Try again. Like this."

He dipped the long, silky hairs of his calligraphy brush into the ink and wrote the same character for *protect* that I'd just done, only his character looked like an elegant piece at an art auction while mine looked like a mangled root ball. He held up his piece of paper in the sunlight. The sheet was so thin I could see the shimmer of the ocean through it.

"That's what I've been doing," I forced out through clenched teeth. I swept a few pine needles off the short wooden table in front of me and placed a new square of paper on it. I wrote the character for *protect* and waited for the golden barrier light to appear.

Nothing happened.

I crumpled the paper into a ball and tossed it onto the sand beside me. The beach was nearly empty despite it being a Saturday. The wind was bitingly cold, and I had to sweep my hair out of my face for the hundredth time that hour. "Why does it feel like I'm in after-school Chinese class instead of learning to beat the crap out of ghosts?"

"Basics first." Leon picked up a black ink stick and began to grind it on his inkstone. An earthy cinnamon smell wafted up with every pass he made over the iron surface. "Syu fat mo is a written magic."

I groaned and re-inked my brush, shifting uncomfortably on the damp sand. Spread out before me was a stack of papers, a calligraphy brush stand, and an inkstone. There was also a small, flat box. The set-up was disappointingly normal. In fact, it looked almost exactly like my Chinese writing lessons with Mah Mah, complete with the posture-killing low writing table.

The only difference was that we were at Cadboro Bay beach, and my dreams of simply flicking out my calligraphy brush and crushing all my ghostly enemies were quickly disappearing the longer we spent copying out the same character over and over.

Leon leaned over and frowned. "No, your stroke here is too short. You need to make it longer."

"I thought you said that it didn't matter if my characters looked like crap," I groaned.

"Your characters don't look like . . . crap." He avoided looking at me as he picked up several wadded-up paper balls off the ground. "Most beginners struggle with intent and focus. Writing the strokes correctly will help you with both." His brow pinched together in worry. "You *are* focusing, right?"

"Bubble tea," I grumbled.

"Pardon?"

"I'm thinking about how I need to buy Michelle a bubble tea after volunteering at the community garden tomorrow."

"Emma," Leon said patiently. "That's not focusing. Come on, let's write the character for *teon* again."

I rested my brush on top of my paper and sighed. "Why are we even here, anyway?"

Leon gave me a patient look. "You said you wanted to learn magic. Water holds a great deal of spiritual energy. That is why people who do not have enough energy must use ink to channel their magic. Water is life, and the largest source of water is—"

"The ocean," I finished for him. I held up my hands.

"Leon, I stopped being able to feel my fingers half an hour ago. Maybe we should stop for now."

"One more try. It will happen. You simply need to concentrate. Watch."

He scanned the area to make sure no one was around, then he scrawled out the character for the barrier spell again. A golden light shimmered out in an orb around him—then, as quickly as it had formed, it vanished. He looked over at me. The hope in his eyes made my heart twinge. All the sharp words on the tip of my tongue faded away. I couldn't kick a puppy if—well, I just couldn't kick a puppy. So, I dipped my brush back into the ink and wrote out the nine strokes for *teon*. *Protect*.

For one brief second, a golden light flared up around the paper—and then it was gone. I exhaled slowly when what I really wanted to do was roll around in the sand, crying.

Leon's face lit up like I'd just written an entire poem in Chinese. "See? You are almost there."

I channelled all my incredulity into one hard-hitting stare. "Is there anything else you can teach me? Maybe something a little more . . . aggressive?"

"Perhaps a new spell would help," he admitted. He slid a fresh piece of paper over to me and picked up his brush. "Copy me, please."

I dipped my brush into the inkstone and stifled a sigh. There was only so much calligraphy practice I could take, and I was close to hitting my limit—but just when I thought he was going to jot down another hundred copies of the same character, he took his piece of paper and tore it down the middle. Then he ripped those in half, and the halves into smaller pieces still.

My jaw dropped. Leon was capable of destruction. I'd officially fallen into an alternate universe. I watched in mild horror as he crumpled the papers into little balls and threw them into the air. Before they fell back down, he sliced out a quick character with his brush.

The papers hung in mid-air for a split second—and then, as if manipulated by an invisible hand, they folded, creased, and bent into tiny paper animals.

Over our heads, a rabbit and a frog hopped along an invisible path. A heron soared around a lumbering bear. And above them all snaked a dragon, whiskers and all, lazily cutting figure eights beneath the winding red arms of the arbutus trees above us.

"All right," I breathed. "I believe you. That's real magic."

He held his finger out and the paper dragon drifted down, landing on it with an audible rustle. "This particular spell is an easy one. It can be adapted to many uses later on. Your paper creatures may not be able to move like mine at first, but the focus is on making them move."

As if on command, the paper creatures dropped down to the table and lay still. I picked up the rabbit and unfolded it. It had returned to being just a piece of paper and nothing more.

"Okay," I said. "Let's do this."

"Good. You will be a quick learner. I'm sure of it." Leon pointed his thumb towards me.

I squinted. "What are you doing?"

"I am encouraging you with a thumb-up."

A cackle escaped me before I could help it. "That's not how you do a thumbs-up. Here."

I demonstrated, and he studied my raised thumb before imitating it with precise movements of his own. Then he cracked a grin, and I laughed, and then he laughed louder, until we were both clutching our sides, rolling in the sand. It felt nice to be able to teach him something for once.

"I lied," I gasped out. "I can't practise anymore. I need a break."

"My thumbs-up was wasted on you." He held out his hand. "I'll need it back."

I sat up. "I have a better idea. Come with me to the community garden tomorrow."

His smile faded. "The community garden? But there will be people there."

I stood up and brushed the sand off my pants. "Exactly. People like Michelle. You should meet her. I think you two will get along. You're both . . ."

"Both what?"

"Effortlessly perfect." I blanched. "Forget I said that."

His mouth pulled down at the corners. "No one is perfect."

"I know." I started to pick up my mess of crumpled papers. "That's why I said to forget I said that. It was a weird thing to say."

I finished picking up the last piece of paper, and then

I put away all my calligraphy tools. Leon had been quiet for so long that I thought he was taking my advice to wipe his memory clean. But when I turned around, his gaze was lowered to the ground. He seemed stuck in place.

"Leon?" I whispered. "What's wrong?"

"I'm not perfect," he said, his voice hoarse. His fingers tightened around the piece of paper he held between his hands. "I have made a lot of mistakes. Ones I can never fix."

My mouth went dry. His eyes were watering.

"It's okay to make mistakes," I said.

"It's not." He drew back as if he was ashamed of even admitting it. "But I am doing my best to make it okay." He wiped a hand across his eyes, then smiled at me like nothing had happened. "I would be happy to meet your friend."

"Are you sure?" I asked. His eyes were still a little red, and I didn't know what else to say to make him feel better. "You don't have to if you're not comfortable—"

"I am," he said firmly. He picked up the calligraphy table. "What time tomorrow?"

"Our volunteer shift starts at eight."

He rewound his scarf around his neck. "I will meet you then."

An idea struck me. "I'll buy you bubble tea too."

His smile cracked open. "You might not want to after tomorrow."

"Why?"

"I will be testing you on what we learned today."

My mouth dropped open. "Wait, what?"

"Surely you did not think we were practising writing those characters today for fun." He shook his head in disappointment.

"You didn't tell me there would be any tests!" I yelped, but before I could say anything else, he laughed and transformed into a pigeon, calligraphy desk and all. I whipped around to see if anyone had noticed, but the beach was still empty. As he flew over the tops of the arbutus and pine trees, I could have sworn I heard a chuckle on the wind.

"I hate tests," I moaned to no one.

CHAPTER 9

The next day, I took the bus down to the Fairview Community Garden. No one was going to keep me away from it, even if it was summer vacation. The garden smelled heavenly. Wet, rich soil. Dewy fir needles. Fresh-sawn wood. It would've smelled even better if I could just get my barrier spell to work.

"Come on," I muttered under my breath, scrawling out the character for *protect*—*teon*—again. I looked at my spade. No golden light surrounded it.

I sighed, then scooped up some more fertilizer. Every time I shovelled out another spade of fertilizer, I practised writing out the character with the calligraphy brush Leon had lent me. The handle was made out of a cheap plastic, and the brush hairs were already starting to fray. I could have blamed my failure on the brush, but deep down, I knew it was all me.

Michelle sat her bag of bark mulch on the ground and arched her back like she was fifty. Maybe that's how old her soul was. She wasn't exactly an old soul, but sometimes I'd catch her looking wistfully out of windows or lingering too long at vintage clothing shops. The obvious answer was that she was a hipster, but I couldn't bring myself to condemn her like that.

"Can we trade?" she asked. She was wearing sunglasses even though the sky was brimming with a thick sludge of grey rain clouds. We were having the weirdest summer weather ever.

"Trade what?"

"Jobs." She caught the bag of mulch just as it started to topple over, her face twisted like she was caught in mid-sneeze. Her jacket wasn't zipped up, and I kept catching flashes of the angry corgi splashed across the front of her shirt. "I think I'm allergic to whatever's in this stuff."

"You mean the bark mulch?" I patted down the fertilizer around the newly seeded sunflowers. They'd only start to bloom in late summer with how cold the weather was being. "Just leave it for now. I'm almost done."

"If *I* was immortal, I bet I could just magick this whole area clean, and then we could get bubble tea."

I stifled a groan. Michelle hadn't stopped making snide remarks ever since I told her what had happened with Leon and the burning shed. Unsurprisingly, she had taken in my story with the sort of hunger that plagues gardeners when they hear about a seasonal plant sale.

"So when is Leon supposed to arrive again?" She rubbed her hands together like she was plotting something.

"An hour ago."

MISADVENTURES IN GHOSTHUNTING

The evil grin fell from her face. "I'm not going to be able to meet him before we finish our shift, will I?"

"No, but you might be able to help me." I withdrew my calligraphy brush from my pocket. "Come look at this."

Nervously, I aimed the calligraphy brush at the bag of fertilizer beside the pergola. I just had to concentrate. Visualize the barrier spreading its golden light out around the bag. A perfect circle, clean and without breaks.

Carefully, I wrote out the nine strokes for *teon*. For a brief moment, a shimmering cascade of gold flared out around the bag, and my heart leapt. It was better than nothing.

Her eyes became impossibly huge. "Hold on—Emma— you—"

I hunched my shoulders. "I know it's not very good, but I'm practising every spare minute. I was wondering if you could help me sometime when Leon's not around. It works better if someone else is with me."

"Are you kidding me?" she shrieked, punching me playfully on the shoulder. "That's amazing! What else can you do? Set your own fires? Levitate? Smash someone through a wall?"

"I'm also working on moving things— Wait, what?"

She hopped around me, clapping her hands together. "Just wait until the school talent show comes up next year. We're going to whup everyone's butt."

I winced. "You're going to have to keep this a secret. I'm not doing this for fun. Leon's teaching me how to defend myself against ghosts."

She covered her mouth with her hand. "Shoot. I'm sorry, Emma."

"There's nothing to be sorry about." I anxiously spun the calligraphy brush in my hand. "Have you heard of geoi hau gwai?"

"A *what*?"

"Geoi hau gwai." I dug my phone out of my pocket and swiped it open. I showed her the webpage I had open on hungry ghosts. "This is the type of ghost that burned down my family altar."

"Ohhhh, you mean a jùkkǒuguǐ" Michelle said. She walked over to the rickety table our backpacks were sitting on. I heard a zip and a thunk, and suddenly her laptop was flipped open. "Okay. Let's do this. Research time."

"But the bark mulch!" I said in dismay. It had started to drizzle, and little droplets were collecting on the plastic bag the bark mulch was in.

She rubbed her hands, and I didn't know if it was because she felt cold or was enjoying my plight way too much. "Oh, come on. We both know Leslie will finish tidying up if I don't get everything done. Besides, isn't this what you're doing? Trying to find out more information about ghosts? Seeing what you're up against?"

"Kind of? But Leslie's not going to be happy if she catches us."

Leslie Phuong was the lead volunteer at the Fairview Community Garden. The last time we'd met, she had a smile warmer than Mah Mah's black chicken soup. I had a sneaking suspicion she wouldn't be as happy if she caught us slacking off.

"Listen, Emma—don't take this away from me. All those years of torture in after-school Chinese classes are finally going to pay off." She paled and added, "Don't tell my parents that. They'd make me go back in a heartbeat if I ever admitted to finding the lessons useful, and there's no way I'm going to listen to another one of Sun Laŏshī's lessons on correct stroke order."

"Cross my heart," I promised. I glanced back down the gravel path. The rain had started in earnest now. "But if Leslie comes . . ."

"Excellent. Sun Laŏshī was a little too trigger-happy with assigning penalty lines. I swear she gave me future carpal tunnel." She flexed her fingers and opened up the search engine for Baidu. "You aren't going to find much on jùkkŏuguĭ on the English side of the web."

Resigned, I came up beside her. Raindrops ricocheted off the tin roof of the pergola as if the sky didn't approve of what we were doing during volunteer hours. "There's wi-fi here?"

"No, but the bakery across the road has a really long signal."

And fingers flying, she took off, typing in Chinese faster than I could type in English. Robotics Club had begged her to come back for a reason—she was the quickest programmer on the team. Even Nathan had happily taken a back seat when she'd taken over planning last year's national competition entry at our old middle school.

But if I was being honest, underneath my admiration was a tiny sliver of jealousy. Not for Michelle's programming skills, but for her ability to use Chinese. She had the advantage of living in a home where everyone spoke Mandarin. My parents and grandmother usually only spoke Cantonese to their friends or my relatives, leaving me with the vocabulary of a kindergartner and the listening comprehension of a dog—but a really smart, friendly one, as Michelle often consoled me.

I rested my head on her shoulder. "Have I told you how much I love you lately?"

"You might want to hold that thought." Michelle frowned at her computer screen. "Internet's not working."

"Guess the bakery decided to crack down on wi-fi thieves."

"It would've been easier to look this up on a bigger screen, but a phone will do." She pulled out her phone and tried typing something in. "Or not."

"No wi-fi?"

"No *anything*. Look." She flipped her phone towards me, and I caught the ominous *no signal* icon in the corner. I switched on my own phone. No signal, either.

"It was working just a few minutes ago. Is the power out?"

She gave a little sigh of dismay. "LTE is cell towers, not modems. We'd at least still have LTE if the power was out."

"I don't know what you just said, but maybe no internet is a sign we should finish up and head back."

She brightened. "Or maybe—"

"Don't say it."

"—it's a ghost?" she continued like I hadn't said anything.

"Ghosts can't mess with the internet. That's ridiculous." I slipped my phone back into my pocket and zipped it up. "They're all too busy haunting the old houses on Moss Street and hanging out in the Underworld."

"Underworld? You mean Dìyù, Chinese Hell?"

I'd meant it as a joke, so Michelle didn't have any right to look as serious as she did. My mouth went dry. "That's what Pigeon B—Leon said."

"Ten Lords of the Underworld and all that?"

"Yeah— Wait, *what*?" My fingers felt cold, and it had nothing to do with the chill in the air. "You know there's a classist hierarchy in the Underworld?"

"Oh, yeah. Learned about it in Chinese school. You don't mess with the Ten Lords of the Underworld." She stood up and closed her laptop. "That's what my mom says, anyway. She's convinced my great-uncle's never going to make it to reincarnation because he's probably annoying all the Ghost Lords with his complaining. I think he even yelled at the woodpeckers one time when he was visiting us. Can't imagine what he's up to in Dìyù."

"Probably yelling at ghost woodpeckers." I swallowed. "Do you know the names of the Ghost Lords? Like Tin Hong?"

"Is that Mandarin or Cantonese?"

"Canto, I guess."

"Then nope, I have no idea." Michelle tried typing on her phone some more, then she sighed. "I should probably head back in case Mom freaks out trying to get a hold of me. She's invited some of her book club friends over for dinner, and she needs my help getting ready."

My heart sank. "You go ahead. I'll catch up."

"But what about bubble tea?" Her eyes went glossy with hope. "And meeting Leon?"

"I don't think he's going to show up, and I'll treat you to two bubble teas next time."

She sighed and stuffed her phone back into her coat. "Done deal. Watch—as soon as I leave, Leon's going to show up."

I waved goodbye, despite the unease I was feeling. Out in the rain, every tree trunk was the unwavering silhouette of a watching spectre.

I'd dealt with ghosts my whole life. Another ghost story or two shouldn't spook me—and it wouldn't have, prior to the family altar burning to pieces. Now, everything felt cold and far away, like I was stuck behind a waterfall and I couldn't see what was on the other side. Well, I suppose I knew what was on the other side.

Tin Hong and his little ghost hunter crony Henry, a.k.a. the menace trying to destroy my life.

With a despondent sigh, I finished cinching off the top of the bag of bark mulch and shoved it beneath the pergola. I dusted off my hands then reached for my backpack, only to catch something out of the corner of my eye.

A person was walking up the path towards me. They had something on top of their head. It looked like a tall hat, but I couldn't tell through the downpour.

"Sorry, no tours are being offered today," I said. "You'll have to come back another day."

The person came into focus. It wasn't a hat on their head but a bush of needles, sticking out in every direction. My throat closed.

It wasn't a person at all. It was the zam mou gwai.

"I found you," the ghost croaked in a voice that sounded like rustling paper.

The words ricocheted around in my head. I shoved my hand into my coat pocket and pulled out the calligraphy brush Leon had given me. With my hand shaking, I slashed out the character for *teon*.

Nothing happened.

I tried again.

Zilch.

The ghost opened its mouth. Its shoulders shook. With a new sort of horror, I realized the zam mou gwai was *laughing* at me. Heat rose to my face.

It took a step towards me, and I finally ran.

In the distance, the yellow glow of the noon sun peeked through a cage of shadowed rain clouds. It would've been beautiful if I hadn't been running for my life. For the first time ever, I hated the rain. My sneakers slapped through puddles along the sidewalks. Dodged planter boxes of flowers. Skirted parked bikes. The zam mou gwai walked along the ground like any normal person would've, but every few seconds it would vanish and reappear several feet closer, propelled along by an unfelt wind.

I fled until the streets became more familiar, until I saw my neighbours' mailboxes, until I saw the garbage bins at the end of my driveway. The volunteer centre wasn't far from my house.

I unlocked the front door with shaking hands. Slammed the door shut behind me. I bent over, wheezing, then straightened as fast as I could.

"Mom? Dad?" I stumbled over to the light switch. Flicked it on. "Mah Mah?"

No answer. The house was empty, and I couldn't hear anything but the sound of my own breathing.

Heart pounding, I peered through the peephole in the front door.

The zam mou gwai stared back.

I ducked down, my hand clamped over my mouth, stifling the scream inside me.

My parents would be home from running errands soon. I couldn't risk letting them come into contact with that—thing. I needed a weapon. Something to hurt it with, or scare it away. I'd never heard of anyone exorcising a ghost with a kitchen knife, but I didn't have any other choice. I needed to do something.

I darted over to the kitchen and started pulling open the drawer with the knives, and then I noticed the long, narrow box of incense on the counter. Mah Mah always lit incense at the family altar. She said it drove away bad energy. Kept away evil spirits.

Maybe she'd been on to something this whole time.

Quickly, I grabbed the box and shook out a few red joss sticks. Lit them with the lighter on the counter. Slid open the drawer and grabbed a knife too—just in case I wasn't going crazy and it was actually a real, live person outside my door after all.

And very quietly, I tiptoed back over to the front door.

I peeked through the peephole, hoping the zam mou gwai had left. Maybe it had got tired, or—

Nope. It was still there. Now it was standing even closer. It stared straight ahead with those empty eyes like it could see me through the door.

My hand tightened around the handle of the knife. This was a bad idea. Really bad. It topped the list of things I shouldn't be doing. I was trying to ward off the spirit of a dead person with a few scrappy sticks and the knife Mom used to chop green onions.

But I couldn't let my family run into it.

I held my breath.

Gripped the handle—

and shoved open the door.

"Get lost, creep!" I shouted as I desperately waved my small bundle of incense at it.

The ghost reached towards me with its bony arm. I reared back, and before I could blink again, it vanished.

And behind where it'd been standing—

My mouth dropped open. "Mah Mah?"

My grandmother looked up at me, a weary look of resignation deepening the wrinkles around her eyes. She was dressed in a floral-patterned blouse. Her permed curls were a halo of soft clouds around her head. She looked every bit the picture of a sweet old granny.

Well, except for the slender dagger in her hands.

She closed her eyes and muttered something under her breath, and maybe it was because my Cantonese sucked, or the rain was too loud, or my brain was muddled because I'd just tried to confront an otherworldly entity, but it almost sounded like she was swearing.

CHAPTER 10

"Um," I said.

I didn't know who should've been more upset in this situation, but judging from the uncharacteristically deep lines dragging down Mah Mah's mouth, she looked like she needed a few more consoling words than I did. She fished out an iron sheath from her pants pocket and slid the blade into it. The dagger made a satisfying snick as it went in.

"Did you just kill a ghost?" I asked faintly.

"We go inside," she said, dropping the sheathed dagger into her wicker tote of gardening tools. "You want some tea?"

". . . Sure?"

On wooden legs, I followed Mah Mah into the kitchen. She took a tin canister of tea from the cupboard and spooned some leaves into a teapot. Awkwardly, I pulled out a chair at the dining table and sat down. I bit my lip. Chewed it, really. Like it was gum and the only thing keeping me stuck to this earth.

What. The. Heck. Was. Going. On?

When the tea was done, Mah Mah joined me at the kitchen table. Wisps of steam rose from the cups in front of us like frail apparitions. The ticking from the clock beside the fridge was painfully loud.

"Is it gone?" I blurted out.

"Yes."

"What'd you do to it?"

She took a sip from her cup. "Keoi gwai."

"Keoi gwai?"

"Make the ghost go away. Sometimes from inside people."

"You mean you exorcised them?" I squeaked. "Is that what you did to the . . . the thing out there?"

She nodded, even though I got the feeling that she didn't completely understand what I was asking. She only repeated, "Keoi gwai."

My head spun. My grandma exorcised ghosts. Other people's grandmas did normal stuff, like baking cookies or knitting. I mean, my grandma did that too. But she also keoi gwai'd ghosts.

"Did you give me the paper talismans because you knew I could see ghosts?" I asked. Suspicion rose inside me. "You said to hide them from Mom and Dad. That they'd only work if I used them."

She exhaled. It wasn't quite a sigh, more like a long release of a pressure that had built up inside for years. "When I was young, everyone in Wong family can see ghosts." She smiled wistfully, as if, against everything she'd taught me, people being able to see ghosts was a good thing. "Now Seeing gone.

No more. Just me now." She took another sip of her tea. "And you, Ah Ling. Yes, talisman only work for you."

Mah Mah was the only person who called me by my Chinese name, Yan Ling. Usually, I liked hearing her call me by that name. It felt like a secret between us. Now it reminded me that all families had secrets, and they weren't all good. I stared down into the amber surface of my teacup. I'd already encountered ghosts five different times this week, and that was five encounters too many. She was being so nonchalant about everything. As if she'd never told me to hide what I could see when I was younger.

"Why did you never tell me you could see them?" I asked, my voice small. "Why didn't you tell me what the paper talismans were really for?"

She reached out and grasped my hand in hers. Her hand was sun-spotted. Warm. "I left Hong Kong to start new life here. New country. No ghosts. No more."

"No more what?"

"Hunting." She poured more tea into my cup. "We not do anymore. You can see ghosts, but don't touch them. Don't speak to them. If you see one, pretend you don't see."

And that was just it—my whole life, my family had taught me to hide what wasn't acceptable. My ability to see ghosts. My low test scores. But hiding problems was a chore in itself. It made me into someone I wasn't. Someone I couldn't be.

Despite the tea, my mouth felt dry. "I can't do that, Mah Mah. I can't keep hiding what I can see."

She leaned back in her chair, and all of a sudden I was looking at a stranger. She looked exactly like my grandmother, but there was a hardness to her that I hadn't noticed before. A force that stared down everything that I wanted to say.

"One of my uncles was a ghost hunter," she said quietly in Cantonese. "Too confident. He tried to fight off a ghost, but the ghost was stronger. His body was alive, but his hei was gone. It was impossible to bring it back." She shook her head and poured some more tea into my cup before refilling her own. "His wife and children cried for so long, we worried they would become ghosts too."

I shifted uneasily in my chair. "*Hei*? You mean like spiritual energy? Qi?"

"Energy, yes. Everyone has inside. Some people have stronger," she said, switching back to English. She coughed and drank another sip of tea, and my chest clenched. "You can see ghosts because your hei is strong. But ghost hunting needs tools. Power. You don't have. If you have trouble with ghost, you can't escape."

"But you're still hunting them. You have a dagger."

Her hand tightened around her cup, and she closed her eyes briefly before opening them again. "My sister's. She die a long time ago." She bent down and fished around inside her bag of gardening tools. She placed the sheathed dagger on the table, but she didn't extend it to me. The iron sheath was decorated with a phoenix that arched into the sky, its tail flared majestically. On the hilt, the same phoenix wound around the narrow body, creating shadowed ridges and curves that gave the creature a semblance of life.

"She was smart and strong, but sometimes the ghosts are smarter. Stronger. We were both lucky today, Ah Ling. I am old now. I cannot protect you all the time. My hei isn't strong enough." She patted her chest as if all her spiritual energy was concentrated in that one spot. "Don't go near ghosts. Run. You are fast."

Despite the calm in her voice, her fingers trembled—only slightly, and I wouldn't have seen them quivering at all if I hadn't been looking, but I didn't know where else to look. So I pushed down my frustration, my disappointment, my embarrassment, and all the rest of the questions I wanted to ask—and instead gave a small nod. "Okay, Mah Mah."

Her face softened, and she was my grandma again. "Gwai ah. You're a good girl. Be careful."

She raised her teacup to her mouth, and just like that, it was as if the ghost had never happened.

. . .

When people talked about family secrets, they usually didn't mean the ancient art of punting a ghost back to the Underworld.

I paced back and forth across my bedroom floor, gnawing on my thumbnail. It was a bad habit that I'd carried with me all the way until fifth grade, when Michelle had accidentally commented about it in front of my mom. After that, I reserved my nail biting for the most incomprehensible of moments, and this situation definitely called for it.

Of *course* there were ghost hunters. There were deer hunters, after all, and moose hunters too. And it made total sense that my family hunted ghosts. My ancestors needed something to do in their spare time, so why not go for a good game of hunting terrifying spectres from the Underworld?

I forced my thumb back down and pulled out my phone, wanting to message Michelle. I needed to tell her what had happened. She was going to explode. Then I remembered she was helping her mom entertain the book club, so I just left her a short message:

IMPORTANT!!!! msg me back when you see this

I paused, then wrote another one:

seriously msg me right away. I really need to talk

She didn't reply.

MICHELLE PLEASSSE

I sighed, then tossed my phone onto the bed. Mah Mah had made it pretty clear she didn't want me involved in any paranormal business, but I had a bad feeling that wasn't the last ghost I was going to see. Thankfully, I had someone I could count on: Leon.

I mean, so what if he was also a bird? I wasn't going to discriminate. And okay, so maybe he never appeared when I needed him most, and he sounded exactly the way my dad did when he really got into different types of building materials, but right now, he was the best guide to getting me out of this mess.

But where was he?

I went up to my window, reached behind my row of succulents, and shoved the window open. I'd been keeping it unlatched ever since the Henry incident in case I needed to make another quick escape. The sun had ducked back behind the rain clouds. Even though the rain had stopped for now, the air felt heavy with moisture.

"Leon?" I tested in a whisper. "Are you there?"

The breeze ghosted past me, and I shivered before shutting the window again. It was silly of me to think he was just hanging around outside my house. I hoped he was okay.

I dug into my pocket for the calligraphy brush he'd lent me. The bristles were even more frayed than before. Experimentally, I tried writing out the character for *teon*— *protect*. I held my breath as the last stroke shimmered into gold existence. It spluttered and sparked and the whole character vanished.

My heart dropped. How was I supposed to protect my family if I couldn't even make a simple spell work?

Something tapped at the window. When I looked up, I caught sight of a grey wing. A pigeon fluttered down onto the outer sill. Its orange eyes stared at me, unblinking, and relief washed through me.

I threw open the window again. "You're here!"

The pigeon hopped inside, and in a split second it was gone—Leon stood in its place. He was still wearing his wool peacoat, but his scarf was ragged and carelessly looped around his neck. His hair was a mess. Strands of it flopped over his eyes. It was the first time I'd seen him be anything less than perfect. His cheeks were sunken, but he managed to summon up a smile as he nodded at the calligraphy brush in my hand. "You have been practising."

"Are you okay?" I asked as he wavered on his feet. "You look like you got eaten by a dragon." I paused. "Wait. Did you? Did it spit you back out? Do immortals taste bad?"

His brow pinched in confusion. "Immortals don't eat other immortals."

"Dragons exist?" I squeaked.

"Certainly," he said, like it was the most obvious thing in the world. "Although most masquerade as snakes nowadays. Mortals no longer consider giant, slithering beings in the sky to be auspicious."

"So, you're really okay?" I looked him over, but he did seem okay, other than being tired and dishevelled. "What happened? You were supposed to meet me and Michelle at the community garden this morning."

He winced. "I ran into some trouble while I was trying to find out more about the ghosts haunting your family."

The heat drained from my face. "Did you run into—?"

"Tin Hong?" He whacked the back of his shoulder like he'd pulled a muscle. "No. Ghost Lords do not leave the Underworld. They are bound to their specific courts."

"Here. Come sit." I pointed at my computer chair. For a moment it seemed he was about to refuse, but then his shoulders slumped and he dragged himself over. He sat down with a plop, his eyes widening in surprise. He did a cautious twirl in the chair, and his tired smile was replaced by a genuine one.

"It moves!"

"Of course it moves. It's better for working at a desk." My mouth dropped open. "Wait a second. Have you never sat in a computer chair before?"

He clasped his hands together on top of my desk and said seriously, "We do not have moving chairs in the Upper Realm. Good posture is instrumental for a long and healthy life."

"Okay." I sank down on the edge of my bed. "It's probably a good thing you weren't at the community garden, anyway. A ghost showed up."

Instead of freaking out as I expected him to, he stayed quiet. He tapped the desk with a finger, then seemed to realize what he was doing and drew his hands together again. His knuckles were white. "The best thing you can do right now is continue to practise your syu fat mo."

My gut churned unpleasantly. "I'm trying, but . . ."

"I could try teaching you a different spell if you would like."

"It's not that." I looked down at the calligraphy brush in my hand. "What if I'm just not good at syu fat mo?"

His eyes softened in understanding. "You come from a prestigious lineage of ghost hunters. The Wong Clan was very respected for centuries, both for their healing remedies and for their calligraphy."

"*Was.*"

"Pardon?"

"You said *was*." I tried to keep my tone light, but insidious thoughts were starting to niggle at my mind. "That's because the Sight has faded from the family line, right? No more Seeing ghosts, no more hunting ghosts. My grandma told me."

"She did?" he asked, horrified.

"I know," I said glumly. "I'm the only person in the world whose grandma shanks ghosts with a dagger."

"No, it isn't that." He wrung his hands together. "Although I suppose it *is* a tad unusual."

"Right?" I cried. "What if the ghosts are targeting my family because my grandma and I can see them?"

Then a thought hit me. I went cold.

"What if *I'm* the problem?"

The rate at which he was wringing his hands increased twofold. "Emma, don't think that way."

"But it would make sense, wouldn't it?" I shot up from my bed and paced around the room. "You said the ghosts are after me. That they'd follow me. *Me*. Not my parents. Not my grandma."

"It was just a theory I had. I don't know if that is truly the case."

"But maybe we could test it."

He stepped in front of me. All the colour had leached from his face. "No. That is a terrible idea."

"Well, what ideas do you have, then?"

He ran a hand through his hair anxiously. "I simply need more time to find out what is going on."

"You mean you're going to try to talk to Tin Hong," I said flatly. "A Ghost Lord recluse who never leaves his musty room in the Underworld."

He shook his head. "He will not entertain a request from a random immortal. I need to ask other immortals if they have any information."

"And in the meantime, more and more ghosts are going to be coming after me and my family." I swallowed, but it didn't make the awful pit in my stomach go away. "My grandma's involved now, Leon. It's time to put a stop to it."

He closed his eyes. I had the feeling he was trying to think of a way to convince me to keep practising what he'd taught me. To give him more time. But giving him more time meant giving the ghosts more time to harm my family.

"We catch a ghost," I said.

A long, drawn-out sigh escaped him, and he opened his eyes. "Oh dear."

"Think about it. The ghosts want me." My hand tightened around the handle of the calligraphy brush. "Henry said he was going to take me to the Underworld."

"And that is exactly why this is a horrible idea." He unwound his scarf from around his neck, then straightened it properly. "You're mortal."

"No need to rub in your immortal superiority over me," I grumbled.

"You do not understand. Only the dead live in the Underworld."

Cold prickled the back of my neck like icy fingers had hold of it. "We're only trying to lure in a ghost."

"If anything happens, and you do go to the Underworld, you won't be mortal anymore." He pointed at my calligraphy brush. "This won't protect you. You will be dead. A ghost yourself." He lifted his gaze. There was an emptiness in it that I'd never noticed before.

"You don't know what the Underworld is like," he continued hollowly. "It's a realm just as dead as its residents. Life there is paper-thin. A meaningless copy. It slips from your fingers before you can fully grasp it. Ghost Lords are the least of what you must fear in the Underworld."

I shifted under the weight of his uncomfortable stare. "We won't let anything happen." He shook his head, and I raised my voice. "I promise. I'll be really careful, okay?"

He stepped back. "Give me a few days."

"For what?"

With a small poof, he transformed back into his pigeon form. Its head bobbed and ducked away from me.

"Are you ignoring me?" I said incredulously as he took to the air. "Hey! Don't just fly away—"

Before I could slam the window shut again, he shot out and vanished into the night. That sneaky little—

I slammed the window shut anyway. Fine. If he didn't want me to talk to him, I wouldn't. I didn't need his help. I'd already sent a ghost back to the Underworld. I could take care of myself.

My phone dinged, and my heart soared. Michelle had finally returned my message.

is it a ghost

are you dead

do I have to plan your funeral

Quickly, I started typing.

wth why is that your first thought—

Then I stopped.

Michelle had never shied away from any of the paranormal misfortunes plaguing my life. If Leon wouldn't help me, then maybe she could.

You free tomorrow night? I messaged.

Does DiverBot dive? Don't answer that.

I grinned and furiously messaged back: *Meet me at the park near my house.*

CHAPTER 11

"So, you want me to lay out the salt in a zigzag path?"

Michelle shook her box of table salt at me. I traced out the path in the air again. It was Sunday evening and my family thought I was working on DiverBot with Michelle at her house. Technically, a third of that was true.

The park near my house was dimly lit in the dusty grey haze of another strangely cloudy evening. The air felt damp. Michelle was half-cast in shadows. She was wearing a T-shirt with an angry-looking bear on it, its arms crossed below the words BEARER OF BAD NEWS. I was already shivering in my hoodie, but she never seemed to be cold.

"With as many sharp corners as you can make," I said. "Ghosts can only travel in straight lines, so the corners will stop them from getting to us."

Hopefully.

The day had passed quickly and now I was having some serious second thoughts while we worked on setting out our trap in the shaded coverage of the Douglas firs. The trees shook their boughs at us in disapproval. We'd bought out all the boxes of table salt from Soonshine Market. I would've bought some of the containers of Himalayan pink salt too, just in case it did a better job. But one bottle would have cost me an entire week of allowance, so whatever ghost we summoned would just have to make do with normal table salt like the rest of us.

I swallowed, though the lump of worry in my throat didn't budge. "You don't have to do this, you know. It could get dangerous."

Her eyes watered as she finished sprinkling out the last of the salt path. She had her hair in short, twin braids today, and she swept one of them off her shoulder. "Emma, I'm so proud of you."

"Huh?"

She clapped a hand onto my shoulder. Her eyes glistened. "You have a life outside your plants."

"What's wrong with my plants?"

"You have no idea how worried I was after that tenth succulent you bought." She wiped away an imaginary tear with her finger. "I thought I was going to have to stage an intervention."

"I'm going to put chili flakes into your bubble tea," I threatened.

"Oooh, make it extra spicy for me, okay?" She tossed the box into the pile under one of the Douglas firs. Then she flipped her hood over her head. "Seriously, though. I'm totally fine." She peered at me from under her hood, and that sneaky smile was back. "Are you?"

I stood back and surveyed the path we'd created with nine boxes of table salt. The path zigzagged through the small clearing in the middle of the trees. One of the ends was completely enclosed. That was the end where I'd stand and hope I wasn't making a massive mistake. I slipped my hand into my coat pocket for my calligraphy brush. The smooth, cool handle brought me a tiny bit of comfort.

"I'm ready," I said nervously, moving towards the end of the path, still holding on to my calligraphy brush.

She rubbed her hands together gleefully just as the street lights flickered on. "Do you think I'll be able to see the ghost?"

"I wouldn't count on it. Just stay outside the pathway. If anything goes wrong . . ."

The humour vanished from her face, replaced with a solemn understanding. "I'll get your grandma."

I nodded, too tense to say anything. We'd purposely picked the park because not only was it dead quiet most days, it was also close enough to my house that Michelle could run there and get my grandma if things didn't go according to plan.

At the end of the salt pathway, I took a careful look around, ears open, eyes wide. The park was empty. Dark. It was the perfect time to break one of Mah Mah's superstitions.

I started whistling.

Michelle scrunched up her face. "Maybe you should let me whistle instead."

I paused to suck in another breath. "Too dangerous.

Grandma said whistling at night will attract bad luck." I was starting to realize that *bad luck* was really her code word for ghosts and evil spirits.

"What's dangerous is your lack of melody."

I pointed my calligraphy brush defensively at her. "I'm trying to call a ghost, not join a K-pop group."

She drew her hood down more and tugged on the strings. "At this rate you're going to call up Linglun's ghost. He's going to yell at you for ruining music."

"Who's Linglun?"

She scoffed. "Only the legendary creator of music. He even made a flute that sounds like a phoenix's song."

"You're distracting me," I said. "On purpose."

She shrugged, but before I could whistle louder to spite her, my head started pounding, and the note died on my lips. I held my breath. Even Michelle seemed to notice something was amiss, because she turned her wide eyes to me.

A gust of wind shot by, whipping my hair to the side, and I adjusted my sweaty grip on my calligraphy brush.

Something poofed into existence in front of me. I jerked back—but it wasn't a ghost.

It was Leon.

And he looked *really* upset.

He straightened the lapels of his coat. He had another scarf on, but this time it was sitka-spruce green and carefully coiled around his neck. His polished oxfords were perfectly shiny. He took in the salt pathway around us, and his hand tightened around the strap of his leather messenger bag.

"Emma," he said in a strained voice. "Please tell me this is not what I think it is."

I cleared my throat. "It's not what you think it is."

"I told you to wait."

"You ignored me."

His mouth thinned. "I only needed a few more days."

"You've been saying that this whole time," I said. "Also, you *ignored* me. You literally just flew off. Who even does that? No one."

"I am sorry. Truly. I just . . ."

Suddenly, I felt as awkward as he looked. He lowered his head and I looked up to the sky. Why couldn't a ghost have shown up? Why did it have to be Leon?

"I am concerned," he said hoarsely. "I feel I am making the wrong decisions."

I kicked a pine cone. "Yeah, well, we all make mistakes."

He pinched the bridge of his nose. "Did your grandmother teach you to make the salt pathway?"

"No." I still felt frustrated, but I continued, "I'd read that salt was purifying. A lot of cultures use it to drive away evil spirits."

"I cannot dissuade you, can I?"

I thought hard. I really did. But before I could answer, Michelle cheerfully said, "Nope."

She was standing under the coverage of one of the pine trees. The expression on her face said that she was entirely unimpressed with our whole conversation. She stuck out her tongue at Leon and rolled her eyes. Thankfully, he either didn't notice or didn't care.

"Good afternoon," he said, extending his hand to her. "You must be Michelle."

She shuffled away from his outstretched hand. "You suck at apologies."

He winced like she'd struck him in the heart. "I *am* sorry. If there is something else I should be doing—"

"Help us out," I quickly intervened, because Michelle looked like she was going to erupt.

He mussed his hair then tried to sweep it off his forehead, but it didn't settle and it ended up making him look like a panicked spider plant. "I still think this is a terrible idea. If anything happens to you, I'll never be forgiven."

"By who?"

Leon cleared his throat. "I believe you mean by *whom*—"

"You said you'll never be forgiven. Usually that means somebody would need to forgive you." I crossed my arms. "Unless you mean you'll never forgive yourself?"

He seemed to draw into himself. "The latter."

I uncrossed my arms. The expression he wore was a mix of guilt and dismay, and I had a good idea who it was directed towards. It made me want to give him a comforting hug. "You're really hard on yourself, you know."

His face clouded. "I have reason to be."

"Well, are you going to tell us the reason?" Michelle asked. She was giving him a peevish glower, as if she'd finished scrutinizing him and found him lacking. Which was weird, because Michelle didn't dislike anyone until they did something she didn't agree with. Hmm. Actually, maybe her reaction wasn't so strange after all.

Leon flushed, the pink tinge spreading all the way up to his ears. "Sorry. Let us focus on the task at hand."

He started whistling. Clear, high notes, as crisp as the early evening air. The sound cut through the quiet, slicing through my apprehension and warming my ears.

"Are you bad at *anything*?" I groaned.

He stopped whistling like he was going to reply to me, but as soon as he did, my head rang in alarm—and a second later, a crescendo of nausea whupped me in the gut.

I hunched over, but before I could find a tree to steady myself against, I slipped on the loose dirt and tumbled down a path that had newly opened up before me. I crumpled into a heap amongst the ferns and salal bushes, curling up as the nausea turned to pain. Blearily, I looked up, only to find that the small wood around me had stretched out impossibly large. Dozens of pine trees filled the space, clustered into dense forest. They blotted out the rest of the park.

"Michelle?" I said shakily. "Leon?"

A loud hum vibrated through the ground, strong enough that it rumbled through my body. I jolted up. Twigs dug into my hands, sharp enough to cut. I scampered back as the space in front of me darkened.

And kept darkening.

The darkness became a mass that was a deeper black than the bottom of the ocean, so dark that it swallowed what little light was left. I couldn't see past it. I couldn't even see into the middle of it. The darkness was so deep that it was almost tangible.

Out of the darkness, a hand reached for me. It was skeletal and weathered, and its papery skin was ashen. Panic swept over me, cold and hot at the same time. I patted the ground. Where was my calligraphy brush?

The hand lurched out, and I dodged it. Barely. I scrambled to my feet. My calligraphy brush was nowhere in sight.

"Emma!" someone called, but their voice was faint, an echo of an echo.

I flinched back as the hand grabbed for me again. I tripped and fell out of the darkness. A golden barrier went up around me.

For one exhilarating moment, I thought I'd thrown up the barrier—and then I spotted Leon tearing through the dark underbrush towards me.

"Stay down!" he shouted, skidding onto the path. He whipped out his calligraphy brush and wrote something in the air before him. Another barrier went up, this time around him.

The dark mass stretched and ebbed. It condensed into three distinct forms. Human forms.

Terror gnawed at me with sharp teeth when I recognized what they were. The geoi hau gwai yawned its mouth open, revealing the molten core. Even at this distance, I could feel the heat from that ball of fire. Beside it was the zam mou gwai. It dragged its spindly fingers through its scalp of needles. Two hungry ghosts, one made of fire and the other of needles.

And behind them was Henry, head ghost hunter of the Underworld.

"It didn't have to be this hard," he said frostily, stepping forward. "You could have just accepted Lord Tin Hong's initial invitation to go to the Underworld. Now you've dragged everyone else into it."

My head thudded—not in pain but in annoyance. "I'm not just going to go with you to the Underworld. Didn't your parents ever teach you about stranger danger?"

"My parents," he gritted out, "are dead."

My stomach flipped. Oh. His gaze flicked to Leon, then back to me. "Lord Tin Hong requests your presence."

"Why?" Leon asked tensely. "It is against the laws of the Three Realms to take a mortal to the Underworld before their time."

He shrugged. "Not if it's to make reparations for damage caused by this girl's family. You're all about upholding the balance of the Three Realms, Li Gwan. Even you should understand that mortals messing with Underworld business tips the balance. The girl comes with me."

I took a step backwards, and the barrier followed my movement. Leon whirled out another character, one with so many strokes I couldn't follow all of them—yet Henry could.

His eyes followed the movement, and his hand reached for his own brush—

"I'll come!" I yelled.

Henry's hand halted. His eyes narrowed suspiciously. "Really?"

"No." I held my breath as a bright gold light shot from my brush towards Henry. It was going to hit him—but at the last second, the geoi hau gwai darted in front. The light hit it in the chest. It crumpled to the ground.

Henry slid his glare to it. "Get up."

He reached into the black drawstring pouch at his side and withdrew a short stick. He gave it a twirl, and the stick elongated until it was as tall as he was. A vicious, fanged silver blade sat at the top. A red tassel hung off a notch in the blade, and it swung forward as he pointed the blade—not at us but at the ghost at his feet. It dragged itself up on shaking limbs while Leon inched closer to me.

"When I say so, grab your friend and run," he muttered.

Dread filled me. I looked around for Michelle, but she was nowhere in sight. I couldn't see past the edges of the strange forest that had engulfed us. "Why?"

"I cannot exorcise the geoi hau gwai back to the Underworld," he continued in a low voice. "Henry is sustaining it with his own spiritual energy. They're too strong for syu fat mo spells, and I don't have any ghost hunting tools on me."

My mouth went dry. "What about you?"

He grimaced. "I will hold them off as long as I can."

My eyes didn't leave the sharp blade of Henry's weapon. If Leon got run through with that, he'd be toast. We'd all be toast. Burnt and best left to the compost. Or the Underworld.

I gulped. "Okay."

He steadied himself. Henry scowled. "You're making this a lot harder than it needs to be. I can keep this up all day. But you?" He lifted his chin and shot Leon a disgusted sneer. "Your spiritual energy is already waning. Those beginner spells are taking a lot out of you, aren't they?"

"Try it, jerkface!" Michelle shouted.

I tensed and turned around. Michelle was trudging through a thicket of salal bushes, panting. She had a box of salt in her hand.

Panicked, I called out, "Wait—"

She threw the box at Henry. Salt sprayed out like glittering snow. It dusted his hair. His clothes. The box fell to the ground with a thud. He stared at it. A snarl twisted his mouth. He dragged his icy glare to Michelle.

My stomach dropped and a strange energy zinged up me.

She placed her hands on her hips. "That's right, you nasty spirit. Get lost. The Underworld needs your ugly face back."

Fury filled his expression and Henry lifted his blade. As he did, I caught a flash of a long white string of spiritual energy. It was connected to his chest and trailed off into a place I couldn't reach. I blinked, and it vanished. I raced towards him, the energy inside me humming and restless— but Leon beat me. He dove in front of me. The blade sunk into his chest.

"Leon!" I screamed.

Henry whipped his blade back out, and Leon fell backwards. The energy soared through me. Darted into the tip of my pointer finger—and without thinking, I slashed my finger down, and a blinding gold light flared up around Leon.

I ground my teeth. Spun around. Slashed out two more characters for *teon*—*protect*. Gold orbs flickered into existence, surrounding me and Michelle. Henry stopped outside Michelle's, hatred etched on his face. He lifted his blade again, but the tip of it only skidded off the edge of the barrier, sending sparks flying. He turned that hate-filled glare to me, and a grin spread across my face before I could stop it.

"You have nothing to be proud of," he said. "Your family disrupted the balance of the Three Realms. Now you need to fix it."

And then he and the ngo gwai vanished, leaving nothing behind but a cold breeze.

CHAPTER 12

I felt sick, and it had nothing to do with the ngo gwai. Leon groaned and sat up, rubbing his chest where the blade had sunk in. The gold of our barriers shimmered beneath the pine trees, illuminating the canopy of branches and leaves above us.

"Emma," Leon wheezed. "Ignore him—"

"Sure," I said. "Let me just pretend I didn't hear that my family *disrupted the balance of the Three Realms*. What does that even mean?" I rubbed my temples. "Actually, forget that. Are you two okay?"

"I will be," he croaked, sounding like death warmed over. "Soon."

"You just got *stabbed*," I protested. "With some ancient Chinese weapon. Maybe we should go to the hospital."

He waved away my concern weakly. "His gwandou is a ghost hunting weapon. It does not injure immortals."

"Much," Michelle said drily. She pointed at his chest. "Unless you're just clutching your ribs because you're about to faint. You aren't, are you? Because I don't do well with unconscious people. Gives me the creeps."

Leon sat up, trying to act like he wasn't in pain but failing miserably. Things were beyond bad, but we couldn't stay here. I'd lied and told my parents I'd eat dinner at Michelle's house, but it was way past dinnertime. They were going to start blowing up my phone if I didn't return home soon. I took a single step forward—and smacked into the barrier around me.

"Am I supposed to be stuck in here?" I asked.

Leon's face paled. He took a step forward and examined the golden light with the same kind of scrutinizing intensity that Mom gave my report cards. "Try again, but pretend that the barrier does not exist. Move through it like it is water."

I tried again, imagining I was one with the universe, and that I didn't have a Ghost Lord coming after me and my family. Nothing happened.

He rested the palm of his hand against the barrier I'd created—and then his hand went straight through, causing me to jerk back. "Your spiritual energy must have created an erratic barrier. You will need to focus on releasing the energy. You must guide it back into yourself. Find your connection to this moment."

I stared at him in disbelief. "Are you really pulling this meditation crap on me?"

He pinched the bridge of his nose. "Try closing your eyes. It helps."

I closed my eyes.

Concentrated.

I didn't know what I was looking for, but—

My eyes flew open. "I felt something. Like a string dangling in front of me."

Leon frowned in puzzlement. "A string?"

"Yeah, like . . ." I tried to remember what else I'd felt, but the memory was quickly fading. "Like the string was there, but I wasn't able to reach it."

"Maybe you need to pull on it," Michelle piped up. "Give it a really hard tug."

"That is . . . unusual," Leon said. "Most people sense a calm pool of water, or perhaps a circle with four gates opening to a hole at the centre."

I closed my eyes, and there it was again—a small string. I tried following it in my mind's eye.

"One more time," Leon urged. "I saw it flicker."

Biting back a sigh, I closed my eyes again. This time, I found the string much more quickly. I felt the tug, felt it rooting me to this earth, to the space around me—and instead of trying to break it, I sank into it. I let myself flow down into that single string.

When I opened my eyes again, the barrier was gone. Michelle wore a strange look on her face.

"It worked," she said.

"I thought I was going to be stuck in there forever," I grumbled. I turned to Leon. "Can you transform into a pigeon? I'll put you in my backpack. There's medicine and bandages at my house."

He straightened with another groan. "Immortals heal quickly."

"How quickly?" I asked skeptically. He looked like he'd been run over by a horde of angry ghosts, which wasn't far from the truth.

He rubbed his chest again, wincing. "I suppose some medicine would help."

He morphed into his pigeon form and I scooped him up. He was so small in my hands, and barely heavier than a peony bulb. He closed his orange eyes and drew up a grey wing over his face, like he didn't want me seeing how fragile he was. I sighed and carefully placed him into my backpack.

"You should come back to my place too," I said to Michelle.

"Okay," she replied immediately, flattening the last of the table salt boxes and packing them into her backpack for recycling.

"Yeah, but we almost got wiped out by angry ghosts— Wait, what'd you say?"

She shrugged. "I said okay. The ghosts were . . . different than what I expected."

As Michelle stuffed the last box into her backpack, her shoulders tight and high to her ears, a flutter of guilt went through me. I really shouldn't have dragged her into my issues. She'd always listened to my ghost stories, but now things felt more real. More dangerous. I couldn't pretend ghosts didn't exist any longer. They lived out here in the real world, where they could hurt us.

"Hey," I said. I looped my arm through hers. "You'll be okay. Okay?"

She nodded and gave my arm a squeeze. We hurried back to my place, huddled together like every shadow had claws. When I stepped up onto my porch, I tried to do so as gently as possible to prevent Leon from jostling around in my backpack. I didn't know if immortal pigeons got motion sickness, and I didn't want to find out.

Before I could open the door, it swung open. Mah Mah stood in front of us, clad in a plaid apron and wielding a pair of chopsticks in her hand. I stiffened when she frowned at me. Could she sense Leon inside my backpack? Did she know we'd just snuck around the park, dodging ngo gwai? But then she spotted Michelle, and her frown broke into a smile.

"Come, come," she said, coaxing her into the house with a hand on her back. "Are you hungry? Eat dinner with us."

Michelle shot me a look. *If I pig out on your grandma's food, am I going to blow our cover? Your parents think we ate at my place, right?*

I aimed a look back at her. *No.* It'd be more concerning if we *didn't* eat anything. My family thought everyone had a bottomless stomach.

Michelle brightened. "Is that curry I smell?"

"Ga lei ngau lam," Mah Mah confirmed with a swish of her chopsticks. "Big pot. Lots."

Michelle wiped a string of drool from her mouth. "You know, I had a dream about your curry beef brisket the other day . . ."

While Mah Mah happily led Michelle into the kitchen, both of them chattering away, I raced upstairs and slammed my bedroom door shut before unzipping my backpack, exhaling in relief when I saw that Leon was still in one piece. He gave himself a small shake and hopped out of my backpack. One poof later, he was sprawled out in his human form on my bedroom floor, limbs akimbo.

"You are not a smooth runner," he complained, rubbing his head.

"Just be glad I didn't accidentally crush you between my textbooks." I drew my curtains closed, just in case my parents were out in the backyard and wondering why I was talking to my floor. "What do you need? Bandages? Tylenol?"

"No bandages." He pulled himself upright and peered down the collar of his shirt. The skin beneath it was miraculously unmarred. He tentatively touched his collarbone and winced. "Perhaps some jin wu sok?"

It wasn't a word I recognized. "Um . . . I don't think we have that. What about Advil?"

He flopped back down and closed his eyes. "I simply need some rest. I cannot travel back to the Upper Realm until my spiritual energy is regenerated. Henry's gwandou damaged it."

Someone knocked on my bedroom door. Frantically, I looked around for something to throw over Leon. He poofed back into his pigeon form, and I'd just finished tossing a blanket over him when Mom opened the door.

She glanced at the blanket. I could tell she wanted to say something about it being on the floor, but Michelle popped around the door frame.

"I promise we'll be down in a few minutes, Mrs. Wong," she said cheerily. "We just really need to finish these last few questions on our homework."

Mom's face blossomed into warmth. "You're such a good influence. I hope Emma can become like you one day."

She closed the door once Michelle was in the room. As soon as she did, Michelle pressed her back against the door.

"Yikes," she said.

"I know," I said, rubbing my temples, thinking of what my family must have done to anger a Ghost Lord. "This is such a huge mess."

"No, I meant your mom," she said, giving me a strange look. "I should've said something."

"Don't worry about it. And don't crush Leon. He's under the blanket."

Right on cue, the blanket fluttered up as Leon transformed back into his human form. "My mother often compared me to my older brother. I stole his wooden horse carving out of spice once."

"Spice?" Michelle asked, confused.

"He means spite," I explained. "Anyway, I can't believe you threw a box of salt at the head ghost hunter of the Underworld. Did you see Henry's face?"

"Oh, yeah," she said smugly. "Like I whacked him with a bag of dog poo? I'll be dreaming about that for ages."

I worried my bottom lip. We were all lucky that we were okay. It would've been easy for any of the ghosts to hurt her—

"Wait a second," I said. "You could see the ghosts?"

A flicker of confusion crossed her face, and she pursed her lips. "Huh. Guess I could. Kind of lacklustre. I was expecting a lot more floating. Maybe some transparent bodies."

Leon buried his head into his hands. "Not good. If mere mortals without the Sight can see ngo gwai, that means the ghosts' spiritual energy is increasing."

"Yeah, but did you see what Emma did?" Michelle gushed. She slashed out her arm and did a roundhouse kick, nearly knocking over my cactus on the windowsill. "Bam! Gold magic everywhere! You were amazing."

Heat crept up onto my cheeks. After so many failed practice sessions, it *was* kind of amazing. It'd be even better if I could figure out how to work the magic all the time, but I was starting to realize that being terrible at syu fat mo was the least of my problems. "Forget that. How do I get in touch with Tin Hong?"

Leon sank back down to the ground with a weary sigh. "You do not. He cannot leave the Underworld."

"But he's sending ghosts after my family, so he has some sort of connection here."

He drew the blanket up over himself. "Let us get some

rest for now," he said, muffled beneath the quilted cover. "If we are fortunate, the ngo gwai will not return for at least a few hours."

I lifted the blanket. His eyes were closed, like he thought he could make me go away just by ignoring me. "Can't we at least try?" I prodded. "Is there some sort of special Ghost Lord tune we can whistle to summon him?"

He rolled over onto his side, his back towards me. "Ghost Lords cannot be summoned. And whistling requires energy, which I do not have."

I let out a loud huff and dropped the blanket. Michelle jabbed a finger at Leon's prone form and rolled her eyes. I didn't want to say anything, but Leon was being *really* pessimistic. Maybe that's what a long life did to you—you got stuck in one way of thinking, believing you'd already seen everything the world had to offer. But just because Leon was telling me his way of doing things didn't mean I needed to follow it.

"You know what? I think I'll see if we have any . . ." I scrunched up my face. "What did you want again?"

"Jin wu sok?" Leon offered helpfully from beneath the blanket.

I nodded enthusiastically. "Right. I'll go see if we have any."

"I'll help look," Michelle announced, giving me a wink.

The Leon blanket bundle shifted with a contented sigh. "Thank you. I will recover my spiritual energy here."

Michelle and I crept out of the room and shut the

door behind us. As soon as we reached the top of the stairs, Michelle grabbed me by the shoulders.

"*Please* don't make me go back in there with him," she said. "Send the ghosts after me instead. They're way more fun."

"He's just worried," I said. "You don't need to talk to him. I'll handle it."

"I don't think you should trust him."

"He's not *that* bad."

She shot a nervous glance back at my bedroom door. "Seriously, Emma. I . . . I just don't get a good feeling about him. What do you really know about him?"

I opened my mouth to reply, but hesitation pulled me up short. Michelle had been right about Clarissa, who'd been caught stealing stationery from the homeroom teacher's desk last year. She had her own sixth sense for these things.

What *did* I know about Leon? He'd told me he was immortal and that he was responsible for protecting my family. But Bo Liang had mentioned that immortals weren't supposed to interfere with mortal lives.

Maybe I needed to do some digging of my own.

Dad and Mah Mah were in the kitchen, preparing the last of dinner. We usually ate late on weekends because everyone was busy running errands. Dad was scooping rice into bowls, and Mah Mah was stirring around a big pot on the stove, adding dashes of white pepper. She'd warned me to not get involved with any more ghost business, but I was getting desperate. She would understand—wouldn't she?

I tried to casually sneak in beside my grandma, but Dad passed a bowl to Michelle and then another to me.

"How's DiverBot coming along?" he asked.

Michelle and I exchanged glances. "Great," I said, taking the bowl of rice. It was hot in my hands, and fragrant steam puffed off the top. "We're making lots of progress on the user manual. It'll probably place in Nationals next year." I wasn't exaggerating. DiverBot really would make it to Nationals with Michelle on the team.

"Michelle's parents must be happy to hear that." He chuckled, then said to Michelle, "I can give you a ride home after dinner."

I cleared my throat, and Michelle jumped into action. "Thanks for the offer, Mr. Wong. You know, I was meaning to ask you about your work. You're a building inspector, right? Do you think any of your clients need a diving robot?"

While Michelle talked to my dad, I inched up close to my grandma and whispered, "Mah Mah—"

"Emma, Michelle! Come sit, come sit." Beaming, Mom shoved in beside us and ladled a spoonful of ga lei ngau lam into Michelle's bowl. "Eat as much as you want."

I bit back a groan as we were shepherded to the dinner table. I'd just have to ask Mah Mah about Tin Hong later. I plunked down, and Mom placed a piece of broccoli in my bowl. And another. I used my chopsticks to fend off another piece of broccoli. "Mom, I can't get to my rice."

"You need to eat more veggies." She tutted in disapproval and put the piece into Dad's bowl instead. "You're getting fat."

I flushed. Michelle was suddenly extremely interested in the mushroom in her bowl. "I'm the same weight I was last year," I protested. "I've literally gained nothing." If I wasn't fat, then I was too skinny. It never ended.

"Emma's not fat."

I looked up at my dad in surprise—and hope. He never backed me up.

"Just a little chubby. Baby fat. I didn't lose mine until I was in my twenties." He chuckled, and my heart fell.

"You still have it." Mom sighed, then wagged a finger at me. "Maybe you should not have quit track and field. You should join again. Just ask the teacher nicely. I'm sure he'll let you back in if you're polite about it."

I put my chopsticks down. "The whole reason I left is because you guys didn't want me to do it anymore. You can't just suddenly change your mind."

Mom leaned back like she had been slapped. "I'm not changing my mind. I'm just saying to eat more vegetables. Too much sugar and even exercise won't save you. Look at Michelle. She's so skinny I bet you eat plenty of vegetables, don't you?"

Michelle cast a terrified look my way. "Um, Mrs. Wong—"

"Don't fight," Mah Mah said quietly. She placed a piece of broccoli in Mom's bowl.

I shut my mouth—for Mah Mah's sake. Dad had fallen silent. He munched on a piece of beef brisket, pulling a slice of ginger out of his mouth with his chopsticks. Michelle got up from the table and flipped open the rice cooker, releasing a billow of steam.

Mah Mah tapped my hand under the dinner table. I looked at her, confused, then looked down. She had a White Rabbit candy in her hand. Just seeing the white, red, and blue wrapper made my mouth water.

I took it from her and whispered, "Thanks, Mah Mah."

She smiled softly. "Mm sai geng."

I unwrapped the White Rabbit candy and stuffed it into my mouth. The sweet, milky flavour did help clear away some of my worries, but not all of them. Mom was worried that I was getting fat. I was worried that a ghost would end the entire family line. A ghost like Henry could do it, too. I had little doubt he'd be back again with more ghost goons. Plus, he was a little nuts. He'd basically broken into my house. Speared Leon like he was a piece of meat. Threatened me, chased me, and tried to coerce me into touching a pocket mirror to what was probably my death. If that wasn't a felony, then I didn't know what was.

What had he called me again?

Lin Wai. That was it.

Henry had been convinced I was her, which meant that either he was severely delusional . . . or I looked like her. And if I looked like her, then maybe that meant we were related. Henry was a ghost hunter. My ancestors were ghost hunters. It wasn't too far-fetched.

"Mah Mah," I said. "Do you know anyone named Lam Kai Ming?"

She chewed her mouthful of food slowly. "No."

"What about Lin Wai?"

The table fell silent. Even Michelle dug into her rice with a nervous flinch.

"How you know that name?" Mah Mah's voice was low and terse.

"I saw it in the family photo album," I lied. "On the back of a photo."

Dad gave me a confused look. "That's impossible. I don't think there are any photos of Mah Mah's sister."

My heart stuttered.

Lin Wai was Mah Mah's sister?

Mah Mah put her bowl down. I thought she was going to say something—but instead, she walked out of the room without another word.

Stunned, I rested my chopsticks on top of my bowl. Mah Mah had never left the table in the middle of dinner before.

"Soooo," Michelle drawled out. "Maybe I should get going?"

"I'm sorry," I said to her as I sprang to my feet. I needed to talk to Mah Mah. It wasn't what good Chinese-Canadian kids did, but if I was going to protect our family, I needed answers.

CHAPTER 13

Mah Mah was in her bedroom upstairs. It was on the same side of the hallway as mine, but at the very end. The door was ajar just enough for yellow light to spill out into the hallway like a slice of sunshine.

Hesitantly, I pushed open the door. "Mah Mah?"

The air was perfumed with the delicate fragrance of orange blossoms from the tree at the window. She was brushing the fallen white petals into a dustpan. I wanted to help. I'd done it a thousand times. Leaned against her shoulder. Played with the jade animal figures on her vanity. Curled up beside her when I was sick. Dug up secret treasures from her closet before she chased me out. She'd never been far away, but right now, the space between us hung at a standstill. I had nothing to offer her—nothing to bridge the distance. No apples. No good report card. I didn't even have the language to say what I wanted.

Being the descendant of ghost hunters sucked. All I seemed to be able to do so far was make my family upset while I ran from the ngo gwai plaguing our household.

I slid the calligraphy brush out from my pocket. The plastic handle was smooth and glossy. I twirled it between my fingers. Then, slowly, with precise movements, I wrote out the character for *teon* in front of me. The gold strokes hovered in the air like wisps of cloud.

A soft golden light flared out around my grandma's still form. Not as bright as the first barrier I'd created, but more solid. More complete.

Her small shoulders stiffened—and the barrier fizzled out. My heart sank.

In a very quiet voice, Mah Mah said, "You make good teon."

"You don't need to lie," I said, embarrassed. "I know it's bad."

"Not bad." She stood up and walked over to me. No matter how much taller I was, she always felt like the bigger person. "Show me."

"Sure." I swallowed, suddenly nervous. But I lifted my brush and wrote out *teon* again. A barrier shimmered out around the orange blossom tree.

She took the calligraphy brush from my hand. Her fingers were soft against my skin. "You need to make this stroke sharper at the end," she continued in Cantonese. "Like you are wielding a sword, not a brush." She traced the same character over my arm. The word sank into my body, and a warmth travelled through me, as soothing as a cup of hot tea.

I held my breath as I tried writing out the character once more. This time, the barrier flared around the tree with a dazzling light. My mouth dropped. "My syu fat mo was bad because I wasn't writing the character right?"

"No, you were just more confident the second time." She gave my arm a small pat. Her warm brown eyes drifted up to meet mine, and there was a hint of sadness in them. "You know about my sister."

"I only know her name. Someone else knows her." A lump formed in my throat. "Knew her, anyway."

"Who?"

"A ngo gwai."

Her face fell.

"Come," she said, switching to English. She sat down on the edge of her bed and patted the space beside her. "Sit."

I squeezed my hands together, but I sat down.

And we talked.

I told her about Leon and the ghost at Soonshine Market and everything after that. What I knew about syu fat mo. Henry. The Ghost Lord, Tin Hong. Every now and then she would ask me a question, wanting either more details or to clarify something I had said. Mostly she just listened.

"You work hard to protect our family," she said when I was finished.

I shook my head. "It's not enough."

She held up my calligraphy brush, examining it with tired eyes before handing it back to me. "My sister say the same thing. She always want to do more."

I watched her fold and unfold her hands in her lap. Dad did the same thing when he didn't know what to say, and sometimes I'd catch myself doing it too. Finally, she rested her hands in her lap.

"Wong Lin Wai was three years older than me," she said, switching back to Cantonese. "She was born in the year of the dragon. After she was born, Ah Ba and Ah Ma went to the fortune teller. The woman told them my sister would grow up and be the best. Smart and strong."

"Gifted," I marvelled.

Mah Mah smiled. "Yes. Gifted. Ah Ba and Ah Ma were very happy. They had a big celebration for her one hundred days after she was born. Many people in the village—" She shook her head in disapproval. "She was the first girl in the family to have this big celebration."

"Usually it was only for boys, right?" I remembered that Mom had told me about it before—a party to celebrate the baby's good health.

"Yes. At that time, it was only for boys. But the fortune teller was right. My sister was gifted. She had a good instinct for ghosts and spirits, and she learned fast. But she was also not careful. Too much fire." Mah Mah placed her hand over her heart, held it there.

"When my sister was fifteen, she begged to be engaged to a kind boy in the village. His name was Gwang Sam. He liked learning about medicine and was studying to become an herbalist. He often bought candies for my sister from the British sweets shops in Hong Kong. He came by on his bicycle and they shared a chocolate bar under the persim-mon tree in front of our house. They gave some to me if I saw them." She smiled, a faraway look in her eyes. "Gold words, purple paper. Heavy paper. Different from now."

"Cadbury?" I asked, surprised. "Cadbury was around back then?"

"For a long time," Mah Mah said. "It was very special back then."

My hands twisted in my lap. It was difficult to picture my grandmother as a small girl, eating chocolate with a sister I'd never met. I wondered if they ever had to worry about ghosts in the same way I had to worry about them. If their family embraced what they could see, and didn't dampen it with turning heads and hushed voices.

"Because they weren't married yet, Gwang Sam didn't know about keoi gwai. It was the family rule. New family members weren't informed until a year had passed since joining the family."

"Why?"

The lines along Mah Mah's forehead deepened. "Safety. Sometimes we couldn't trust people to keep secrets."

"Oh." I rolled the edge of the bedsheet. "What happened when Gwang Sam found out about the family business?"

"He didn't."

"The family didn't tell him?"

"No. A few weeks before they planned to go see the fortune teller to choose an auspicious date for the wedding, he died. He fell down the temple stairs and hit his head." She stared straight ahead, like she was looking at her own ghosts—ones I couldn't see.

"He was a good boy," she said quietly. "Everyone tried to tell my sister it was an accident, but she thought Gwang Sam died because she'd made a ghost angry. I saw her talking to Ah Ba, Ah Ma, everyone in the family. She tried to remember what she did, which ghost, when."

Cold crept along my back. Mah Mah's fingers quivered, and I wanted to wrap my own around hers, yet mine felt too stiff to move.

Lin Wai had thought the death of her fiancé was an act of revenge.

Was it?

"Late one night," Mah Mah continued in English, "I went to the toilet. I saw the light in my sister's room. Heard her crying. I thought I should say some kind words. But I not go inside. I want to go in, but everything I want to say was too small. So, I wait outside her door." Mah Mah paused and switched languages again. "For many years after, I always wondered what would have happened if I went inside."

"You were young too, Mah Mah," I said softly. I would've done the exact same thing.

Her hands tightened around each other and she continued in Cantonese. "Ai, but I should've been smarter. My sister was holding her red wedding clothes in both hands. Her eyes were wet. I felt like a stranger, so I went back to my room. I thought she needed more time by herself. And I needed time alone too. Gwang Sam had already become like my brother."

And suddenly, I saw her—the young girl that my grandmother had been. Scared and unsure. Mah Mah and her sister sitting under a persimmon tree. A young man riding up on a bicycle.

A young man, dead.

"In the morning, the house was very noisy. Many people: aunts, uncles, cousins, friends. They were preparing to go up the mountain. They had found a letter in my sister's room. The letter said she knew a way to make Gwang Sam come back, but she needed to be fast." Mah Mah's voice wavered. "She also said she was sorry and to please forgive her."

A part of me didn't want to hear the end—and yet a louder part did. I knew how the story was going to end, but it was Mah Mah's story. My family's story.

"Ah Ba and Ah Ma couldn't stop me. I ran up the mountain. I knew where she was. We had played on the cliff many times. And I was right. Her wedding clothes were in the leftover fire, all black. She had burned paper copies of her weapons and tools. She tried to burn her real ones too, but of course she only burned the wood part. The metal was singed.

"Gwang Sam was gone. My sister was gone. My parents didn't know what to do. For a long time, no one came to our house. They were afraid we'd been cursed. When your grandfather passed, I thought maybe it was true. I came to Canada to escape my past. To protect the rest of my family."

"Mah Mah—"

She looked down into her lap. "Now I see I couldn't protect you at all."

My throat swelled with emotion. "That's not true, Mah Mah."

Her sun-spotted fingers closed around mine. Her gaze was warm, but there was also a sadness in it. "I shouldn't have hidden what you could do from you. I thought I was keeping you safe. I was wrong."

My mouth felt stuck. I knew what to tell her—that it was okay. But it wasn't. Not really. Thinking I was alone for all those years had left scars I couldn't erase. "Do you think your sister managed to save Gwang Sam?"

She shook her head gently. "The dead do not leave Deiyuk."

Deiyuk. The Underworld. A terrible idea struck me, and I stiffened.

"Can ghosts really curse people?"

She gave my hand another pat. "Yes."

I stood up and started pacing. "How would you know? Is there a way to tell if you've been cursed?"

She followed my movements with wary eyes. "Many unlucky things will happen."

"Mah Mah," I said, stopping in front of her. "What if your sister did manage to go to the Underworld? What if she broke the rules to do so, and it made a Ghost Lord angry? Angry enough to curse our family?"

"Lord?" she asked quizzically.

"Oh, uh . . ." I tried to recall the word for lord, but all I could think of was king. "Gwai Wong?"

"Gwai Wong?" To my shock, she started to laugh. Not

149

just a small laugh, either—a full one that came from deep inside her belly. "Gwai Wong don't curse people. They don't need to."

"Right. Because they only stay in the Underworld," I said with a sigh.

"No," she said, her laughter quieting. "Because Gwai Wong can send ghosts instead."

CHAPTER 14

I nearly smacked into Michelle as I rushed out into the hall-way.

"What are you still doing here?" I whispered frantically. "Didn't you go home?"

"I thought about it, but I figured you might need me, so I snuck by your parents." She squinted at my face. "Good news or bad news?"

"Bad," I said. "Definitely really bad."

She wrinkled her nose in disappointment. "Guess your grandma didn't know how to contact Tin Hong either?"

"Stand back," I said, marching up to my bedroom door. "What—"

I laid my hand on the doorknob. A sliver of unease crawled through me. Maybe Leon didn't know that Ghost Lords could leave the Underworld. Maybe he was worried that if I managed to talk to one of the ghosts, they'd hurt me. Maybe he already knew that my family was cursed but he didn't know how to bring it up to me.

Maybe, maybe, maybe.

All I knew was that the ngo gwai had started showing up at the same time he did, and instead of going away, they were getting worse. Stronger. Deadlier.

I shoved open the door. My blanket was neatly folded on my bed.

The room was empty.

Michelle pushed my curtains to the side and peered out the window. It was open, and the night breeze was slipping through, rustling the leaves of the plants crowded on my desk.

"Guess he recovered enough of his spiritual energy," she said.

I grabbed my coat off the back of my computer chair. "I need to find him."

"Now? It's almost ten thirty!"

I shoved my arms through the sleeves, fully expecting to have to argue my way into leaving, but Michelle merely grabbed her backpack and grinned mischievously. Uh-oh.

"I'll tell my parents I'm sleeping over," she said, and whipped out her phone.

I tried to grab her phone, but she whirled around, typing faster than I could stop her.

"You are *not* coming with me. Remember Henry? Dead ghost hunter guy with the gwandou? You threw salt at him. If he sees you, you're screwed."

"Hey, I take offence to that. Who says I can't handle a ghost or two?"

"Me!" I whispered. "You couldn't see them until today!"

"Yeah, but that was *earlier*. Now I can see them." She pressed the Enter button on her last message and slid her phone back into her pocket triumphantly. "There. Where are we going?"

I wanted to flick her forehead so bad. Her bangs were parted in the middle, so it would've been easy to press my finger against my thumb, go up to that smooth expanse of skin, and give it a really good flick. The issue was that I didn't think anything I did would knock any sense back into her. She still had that maniacal grin on her face, and now she was bouncing lightly on her heels, revving up like she was about to jump out the window herself. I shuddered. The last time she had that grin was when she spent ten hours straight beating every single high score at Quazar's Arcade, then was promptly banned for life for "cheating."

She was doomed. We were all doomed if I couldn't find Leon.

She pulled me in for a side hug. "Emma, I'm not going to leave you to fight off some ghosts by yourself. I can be backup. I'll call your grandma if anything happens, okay?"

I hugged her back, then turned off my bedroom light and bunched up my blankets. If my family came in, hopefully they'd think I was just sleeping. "You have to promise me you'll leave if it gets bad."

She snorted and flipped her hood over her head. "How much damage can a pigeon possibly do?"

I didn't want to think about that, so I pushed the window up all the way. My stomach flipped. The last time I'd gone through, it was because a ghost had tried to drag me to the Underworld. Falling had *really* hurt.

"Let me go first," Michelle said, clearing my precious succulents off the windowsill. She nearly dropped one, but I managed to catch it before it teetered off the edge. By the time I stood back up, she was already outside. She crouched down and held out her hand, and I wondered how upset she'd be if I dragged her back through the window and called her mom. Probably pretty upset. Cold-shoulder-for-days upset.

"Thanks," I breathed gratefully, grabbing on to her as I stepped out of the window.

"You were totally thinking about locking me in your room, weren't you?"

"Of course not," I lied.

"Liar."

The night sky was painted in strokes of cloud wisps. The moon was barely a sliver, but so near it felt like I could touch it if I reached out far enough. We inched our way along the asphalt shingles and shimmied down to the next level when the roof dipped. When we reached the edge of the roof, we hopped off. The landing was much softer this time.

"Do you think he's a ghost?" Michelle asked once we were back on solid ground.

"I don't know," I said, but I was quickly running out of reasons why he wasn't.

"I could whistle and see if it calls him. Emphasis on *I*."

"He's not going to show up when he just left my house. I want to talk to someone who knows him."

Even in the dark, I could see her roll her eyes. "Are they just as bad as he is?"

"Her name is Bo Liang," I said, ignoring her jibe as we slunk along the fence to the front. "She runs a traditional medicine shop in Chinatown."

We headed towards the bus stop. I tried to walk quickly, only daring a look back at my house once. Thankfully, no one had noticed we were missing. Yet. As we walked in the darkness, I couldn't shake the feeling that we were being watched. I shivered, but I didn't have to worry long. The bus pulled up and we hopped on. Fifteen minutes later, we were in front of the red Gate of Harmonious Interest, the entrance to Chinatown.

"It's spooky here at night," Michelle said, keeping close to me as we walked past dark, narrow stretches of alleyway to Bo Liang's shop.

It was kind of creepy, and that feeling of being watched was back. But when I looked around, no one was paying any attention to us. There were a couple of people milling up and down the street, and the restaurants were busy, but a thick quiet hung in the evening air. All the souvenir stores and tourist attractions had long since closed for the day. Overhead, the fabric lanterns flickered in the wind.

"Don't look down Fan Tan Alley," I said when we passed by it.

She squeezed closer to me. "There's a ghost, isn't there? I knew that place was haunted—"

"No, there's a raccoon. I don't want to give it any ideas."

By the time we got to the building where Bo Liang's shop was, my stomach was a mess.

"I'll just ask her some questions and then we'll go home." Tentatively, I pushed the door, and it opened. Encouraging shouts from the late night spin class on the ground floor broke the quiet.

"What if she's on Leon's side?" Michelle asked.

"She knew my great-grandmother. When I met her last time, it didn't seem like she wanted my whole family to be wiped out."

She'd also said immortals weren't supposed to interfere with mortal affairs, but I conveniently forgot to tell Michelle that as we reached the top of the stairs. I knocked on the blue door with its chrysanthemum etching on the glass. Light shone through it.

"Bo Liang?" I called out. "It's me, Emma."

No answer.

Michelle pressed her ear against the door. "Maybe she's closed for the day."

I tried the door handle. Locked.

"What's the character for *move*?" I asked, pulling out my calligraphy brush. "In Cantonese, it's *yuk*."

"*Move*?" Her face scrunched up. "There are a ton of words for *move*."

"And I don't know any of them. I can't remember what Leon taught me."

"Maybe try *yí*. Like this." She slowly wrote it out with

her finger, and I copied each stroke with my brush. A click sounded.

"It worked!" I squealed. "You're a genius."

"Does this mean I get to be an honorary ghost hunter now?"

"No."

We slipped inside the shop and closed the door behind us. The lights were all on, but no one was inside. The counter was swept clean of everything. Behind it, the door had its curtain drawn closed. A snap cracked the silence in the shop, and both Michelle and I jumped.

"What was *that*?" she squeaked.

"Bo Liang?" I tried again. When no one replied, I edged around the counter. "It sounded like it came from the back room."

As if someone heard me, shuffling and whispering noises started up from behind the curtained doorway. I held my breath, checking in with my head and stomach. A thudding was echoing behind my ears, and my stomach was swimming in circles like one of the pickle boats in the Inner Harbour.

A ghost.

I met Michelle's eyes. Hers were wide with more anticipation than fright. I swallowed, then cautiously drew back the curtain.

A pigeon was fluttering around on the floor.

"Leon?" I said in disbelief.

In a flash, it was up on its feet. The feathers on its left wing were ruffled. Several grey feathers were scattered on the floor. It looked . . . injured.

And then it whizzed by me and shot out through the open shop door.

"Leon, wait!" I shouted, but he was already gone.

"I knew he was suspicious!" Michelle yelled as we raced down the stairs. The pigeon knocked into one of the walls on its way down, but it righted itself quickly just as a stream of people left the spin class.

"Watch out!" one of them shrieked. "There's a bird in here!"

"C'mon, let it out!"

"Wait," I cried, just as a woman grappled with the handle of the building's main door.

We reached the bottom of the stairs just as the door flew open and the pigeon zipped outside. We chased it down the street, but even with its injured wing, it outpaced us. It darted down a dark alleyway and we followed, only to jerk to an abrupt halt.

"I can't see anything," Michelle whispered.

I looked over my shoulder. The sign for Fan Tan Alley hung off the street light at the entrance, but it was the only thing visible. All the light from the lanterns had vanished. The dark surrounded us, and a stifling heaviness settled over my skin. I thought I caught flickers of faces—a pair of glowing eyes, a mouth too large for its head, long, jutting needles for hair—but the apparitions vanished as quickly as they came.

"We should leave," I said. My own voice sounded distant. I fumbled to turn on my phone light. It shone out, a thin beam of light in that unending darkness.

I turned around, sweeping my light down the length of the alley.

Michelle was gone.

"Michelle?" I whispered.

No one replied.

I hurried over to the entrance to the alley, but the darkness seemed to continue forever, stretching the length of the alley. The street light with its sign seemed so close, but every time I thought I was about to touch it, the dark slipped out in front of me.

I'd just got my best friend kidnapped by ghosts.

At least, that's what I thought had happened. The ngo gwai wouldn't do anything to her . . . would they?

"All right," I said, only a tiny bit scared. With shaking hands, I clutched my phone like a weapon. "Bring it."

Instead of walking towards the street light again, I turned in the opposite direction. The brick walls of Fan Tan Alley seemed to close in around me in a constricting tightness. But then I blinked, and the walls were back in place. Something brushed past me, and a scream rose in my throat, only to die when I spotted an open door along the wall.

It was a black, wrought iron door, with chipped bricks framing its entry. The door was slightly ajar, and a glowing red light seeped out. Tentatively, I pushed it open.

Inside was a single room, with no other doors along its

cobwebbed walls. Unease prickled at my scalp, and I swept my light along the ground.

There was an entire, huge hole in the ground.

It definitely hadn't been there a moment earlier. It was about a metre squared, and when I crept over to look down, I was met with a darkness that stretched past my light. A pungent dampness filled my lungs, as if I'd sunk my hands into soil and brought up something I hadn't wanted to find.

My heavy breathing filled the room. I'd seen enough horror movies to know where this was going. Girl finds a hole in the ground in some weird, haunted alleyway.

Girl goes in.

Girl doesn't come back out.

"Emma!"

I startled, tripping over my own feet and falling backwards. My heart pounded.

"Michelle?"

It sounded exactly like her. Her voice echoed down in the hole below, but I couldn't make out what she was saying. The words sounded distorted, as if she was deep underground. I swallowed hard, then peered again over the edge of the hole.

Darkness.

With fumbling fingers, I grabbed my phone. Light filled the hole. There were no stairs leading down. There wasn't even a ladder. But the distance to the next level down wasn't that far.

"Are you down there?" I asked shakily.

I thought I heard her voice again—and then, soft sobbing. Panic swirled inside me. What were the ngo gwai doing to her?

Shakily, I sat down at the edge of the hole. My feet dangled down far enough that my shoes disappeared into the darkness. I clicked my light off and tucked my phone into my coat pocket.

Trying hard not to think about what I was doing with my life, I let myself fall.

CHAPTER 15

A huge cloud of dust puffed up when I landed. I coughed, waving my hand to clear it away. I clambered to my feet. A soundless hum vibrated around me and sank into my bones like a breath of fresh air.

Spiritual energy.

The place was full of it. I fished my phone back out and switched on the light.

A long, empty tunnel stretched out before me. The darkness gnawed at the edges of my circle of light like it wanted to swallow it whole. The farther I walked, the more nervous I got. Each sound echoed back into my heart. With each pang, the feeling grew that I was no longer beneath Chinatown. It might've had something to do with the increasing amount of concrete in the dirt walls, or the faint glow of light at the fork up ahead.

Forked pathways were for people who had a sense of direction. For me, though, the two concrete-lined pathways at the fork looked exactly the same. I hesitated, wondering if I should've brought a bag full of bread crumbs with me, then turned down the left branch. Farther down the tunnel, graffiti decorated the sides in jagged sprawls of paint.

I turned another corner.

Above me, dusty beams of purple light shone through glass tiles in the ceiling. Shadows pressed into the glass, accompanied by a soft thudding—the footsteps of people who had no idea that a girl was just below them.

A door was embedded in the side of the tunnel. I swung my light behind me, just in case, before I pointed it at the ominous-looking entryway. The door was made of steel, with large screws set into the thick hinges. A fine film of grime covered it, but the handle shone under my phone light, like it was clean.

Like someone had used it recently.

I stared at the handle, and then something shiny on the ground caught my attention.

Michelle's phone.

Fingers shaking, I picked it up and swiped it open. Nothing was on the screen, and it was password-locked. An awful feeling swept over me. She was here, and I needed to find her.

I yanked the door open. The tunnel in this new section was wider and taller than the ones I'd left—so much so that it barely qualified as a tunnel anymore.

And it wasn't empty.

Doors and windows lined the sides of the walls. Shop placards hung from wooden posts buried deep into the ground. Crumbling brick. Broken glass. I stepped out into the tunnel and into a half-sunken city.

Old Victoria.

The city had been a fort once, with trading posts and supply stores for gold rush miners. Then the original street level of the city had been covered by a layer of scaffolding and concrete, and a new city had been built on top. It was strange to know that whole streets had just disappeared from sight, and even stranger to see the tops of the buildings poke up through the ground. It was as if they'd been buried by a lazy grave keeper, and I was standing in their cemetery.

"Interesting place, although it's not really my style."

I jumped so high my chest actually hurt.

Henry Lam was sauntering up to me in his black bomber jacket, charcoal shirt, and cloth-laced boots. His hands were in his pockets, and he looked for all the world like he was just out for a casual stroll. Underground. In an abandoned city. Where a well of spiritual energy pulsated so strongly it was almost suffocating.

"What are you doing here?" I demanded.

Henry arched one dark eyebrow. "I should be asking you that. If this is your idea of summer break fun, I don't want to see what your weekends are like."

I gritted my teeth. "I'm not here for fun. You know exactly why I'm here."

He paused. "Yeah?"

"You took Michelle. Where is she?"

"I've got enough pets. I don't need to entice one more into joining the menagerie. However, now that you mention it . . ."

He pulled out a wooden stick from his side. I watched as it extended into his gwandou—a long polearm with a blade that was sharp and curved at the top. I swallowed nervously. Our last meeting flashed across my thoughts. If Leon hadn't shown up in time, I probably would've got sucked into Ghost Hunter Hell.

"I might've seen some ngo gwai with her," he said mildly.

I whipped my phone at him. It flew through the air—and landed cleanly in his outstretched hand.

He looked down at my phone in disgust. "I wasn't offering to trade. Also, this model is three years old. It's worth nothing, let alone a mortal life."

Heat rushed to my face. Suddenly, more than anything, I wanted to be buried face down. Of *course* I'd get the snarkiest ghost in existence trying to do me in. He tossed the phone to the side, where it bounced against a wall and fell flat outside a shop door. Immediately, the light disappeared.

And then, a second later, a warm yellow glow enveloped the tunnel, giving me a clear view of the frustratingly smug look on Henry's face—and the calligraphy brush in his opposite hand. Flickers of silver followed it.

"Let Michelle go," I said shakily, drawing out my own calligraphy brush. "She's done nothing to you or Tin Hong."

He stood his weapon up. The blade had a notched piece that stuck out like a fang, and attached to it was that decorative red tassel. The tassel swung as he leaned the polearm against his shoulder. A flicker of something crossed his expression, and it wasn't amusement.

"Hold on," he said slowly. "You think I took Michelle?"

"You didn't?" I backed up, a horrible realization crashing down on me. "Then where is she?"

He hunched over. His shoulders shook like he was—crying?

No. Oh no. I wasn't equipped to deal with a crying ghost, let alone one that was trying to murder my family. He ran a finger along his eye, and I froze. A terrible feeling swept over me. He wasn't crying.

He was *laughing*.

I caught the side of a white-toothed smile behind his hand before he straightened and gave his weapon an expert twirl. He slammed the end of it down into the ground, and I flinched. Any traces of mirth had vanished from his face.

"I didn't take her, and I don't know where she is."

I took a step back. "I heard her calling for help down here. You've been following Tin Hong's orders all this time. I'm sure he'd be happy if you used her to get to my family—"

"Don't confuse me with that da ba gwai," he said coolly. "I have my reasons for working for Tin Hong, but it doesn't mean we have anything in common. And I don't need Michelle to get to your family. I have other ways."

I bristled even as dread cascaded over me. "Just because my ancestors used to be ghost hunters doesn't mean my family's inherited their problems."

He shrank his weapon down. "You know, maybe you're right," he said in a suspiciously cavalier tone. "I don't need to bother your family. Not your whole family."

I tightened my grip on my brush. I didn't like where this was going.

"Tin Hong never told me to bring your parents to the Underworld." His footsteps echoed off the half-buried buildings as he took a step towards me. "It seems the ghost hunter bloodline skipped your father, but your grand-mother—"

I raised my brush. "Don't you dare lay a hand on her."

His mouth tilted upwards into a nauseating grin.

"Dou ze sai," he said. Faster than I could follow, he scrawled a character into the air, silver light dripping from each stroke.

And right before my eyes, he transformed into . . .

Me.

"I'm not going to bother Po Po. I'm sure you give her enough trouble already." Henry raised his arm—*my* arm—and let it fall back limply to his side. My voice rose out of him, scathing and foreign. It was at that moment that I fully regretted not pummelling Henry back into the void as soon as he appeared in the tunnels.

"What the hell are you doing with my body?" I seethed. My feet shuffled back of their own accord, like I was stand-ing too close to a mirror and my body knew it.

"What do you think?" He flipped his long hair—my hair—over his shoulder and smirked. My stomach roiled in disgust. "Luring Cheung out, of course. I saw that pesky pigeon dart into the tunnels. He's up to something."

My heart sped up. So Leon *was* down here. "He's not going to fall for that."

"I wouldn't be so sure about that." He clasped his hands together and sent his gaze skywards. "Oh, no, *Leon*. Please help me get away from that big, scary ghost!"

"I've never said that!" I spluttered. "Not ever!"

"Really?" The grin vanished from his face and an unsettling coldness spread across his—*my*—face. "You might say it now."

A prickle crept along my scalp as he pointedly looked past me.

I wasn't going to look behind me. I wasn't.

I looked behind me.

A geoi hau gwai stood a few feet away. Pale as bone, with a bulging stomach. It had a slit for a mouth, and something was wrong with its skin. Mottled and creased, it wrapped around its thin, dragging limbs like aged paper.

Henry let out a short, humourless chuckle. It sounded wrong coming from my mouth. "Try not to ruin your family's reputation too much."

The ghost jerked towards me, and I could've sworn I heard its body rustle. I jabbed my brush in its direction. The tip of it shook with each heaving breath I took, but the handle felt as heavy as lead.

"Oh, sure," I said, backing up. "Get another ghost to do your dirty work for you."

The geoi hau gwai slammed into me. I hit the ground, hands scraping along the concrete. I scrambled to my feet. My palms burned. The ghost rolled back up to its full height, wavering like the last leaf on a dying branch. It opened its mouth. Inside it was a single crimson ember. No teeth. No tongue.

Just a ball of molten fire inside a mouth.

I couldn't move. The air around me prickled with heat. I flung up a barrier—only to remember, too late, that my barriers were faulty in the worst way possible. I backed away, chest heaving, as the ghost yawned open its flaming mouth—and it leapt for me.

Skeletal joints, pressing into me. Fingers grappling for my face, pulling at my mouth, my ears. Its hollowed face loomed in and out of focus through waves of heat. I tried to shove the ghost away, but it didn't budge. The energy surrounding it was disorienting—sickening. I bent my knee, gave a hard kick upwards. But it grasped the sides of my head with long fingers.

I couldn't breathe. Couldn't breathe—couldn't—the eyes—they were so black. Consuming. Two endless holes, sucking me in. The fire from its mouth fanned against my nose. My cheeks. In a daze, I flung my arm out, trying to give one last shove—*and that's when I felt it.*

A line of spiritual energy, hanging from the ghost's chest. Like a piece of thread, so skinny it was barely there. Like a string to follow. I closed my eyes. Its fingers pressed into my head. Pain jolted through my temple—had to focus.

Focus.

I drew the string towards me. Enticed it closer. Felt the energy of it seep into my body, like it was returning home.

And when I opened my eyes again, the ghost was gone.

Henry's eyes were wide. He uncrossed his arms. "How did you do that? Where did its spiritual energy go?"

Panting, I struggled to my feet. My legs felt like jelly, but my head was clear. "Why don't you find out, Ghost Boy?"

His expression darkened. He spat out a curse as he brandished his calligraphy brush at me—but before he had time to write anything, a rumble sounded in the tunnel behind us.

A ngo gwai stepped through the doorway.

And then another came through.

And another.

I stumbled backwards as a whole crowd of them pushed through, crowding around us. Some had necks that were too long, with heads that towered over the rest. Several had the same bloated belly as the geoi hau gwai I'd just exorcised. All of them had papery, mottled skin.

"This is going to give me nightmares," I muttered under my breath.

"About time," Henry said to the ngo gwai, with a hint of exasperation. He flipped his hair—*my* hair—over his shoulder again. "Grab the mortal."

The ngo gwai closest to him let out a low hiss—but instead of grabbing me, it latched its skeletal fingers onto him.

CHAPTER 16

"What are you doing?" Henry asked angrily. In an instant, he reverted back to his original form. "It's me, you fool. Release me!"

"Hei Nga said you are too slow," the ngo gwai hissed. "Why have you not brought the mortal to the Underworld yet?"

Slowly, I backed up. I thought Tin Hong was trying to bring me to the Underworld. Who was Hei Nga?

"It would go a lot faster if you helped me instead of getting in my way," Henry spat. "Now *move!*"

He flung off the ngo gwai's hold, but as soon as he did, several more clustered around him.

"Return to the Underworld. Lord Tin Hong will speak with you, gwai lip yan."

Henry's face steeled and he steadied his stance. As more ngo gwai surrounded him, an opening appeared in the crowd. The doorway I'd entered through was straight ahead. Nervously, I looked back at Henry, but the ngo gwai had swarmed him. He was hidden behind their skeletal bodies.

This was my chance.

I slipped between the ngo gwai, shivering as I brushed against their bloated stomachs and papery skin. The door was so close. I was almost there when a hand clapped down on my shoulder.

I looked up at the ngo gwai who'd caught hold of me. Way, way up.

It had its long fingers wrapped tightly around my shoulder. Its head bobbed along on a skinny, elongated neck. It snaked its head towards me, close enough that I could see the sickly purple veins criss-crossing the whites of its eyes.

"Come, mortal," it whispered into my ear, so quiet I could barely hear it. "It is time to go to the Underworld."

I held up my calligraphy brush, only to remember what I'd done to the other ngo gwai. I took a deep breath and closed my eyes, searching for its string of spiritual energy in the darkness. When I found it, it hummed, as if it was calling to me in a forbidden song. Like the other ngo gwai's energy, it was a long, skinny white string. I gave it a tug. The ngo gwai hissed out a harsh, windy gasp and released its hold on me.

Behind me, more shrieks rang out, sounding like a storm of wind gusts. I turned just in time to see Henry whipping his gwandou through several more ngo gwai. Their bodies scattered to dust.

"Report back to Lord Tin Hong," he said angrily, aiming the tip of his blade at the closest ngo gwai. "He has overstepped the contract he holds with me."

"We do not answer to you, gwai lip yan—"

Ghost hunter. For some reason I didn't understand, the title bothered Henry enough that his face tightened with anger.

"Don't call me that!" he roared. He ran his weapon through the ngo gwai. Instantly, it vanished like ash in the wind.

I gulped. Between the horde of ngo gwai and Henry, I didn't know which was worse. I didn't have long to ponder, because another ghost latched on to me. This time, I didn't hesitate. I closed my eyes, found its string of spiritual energy, and pulled. It spun towards me, and when I opened my eyes again, it had disappeared, just like the geoi hau gwai.

"Stand back," I warned the rest, the thrill of the ngo gwai's spiritual energy coiling around inside me. "Unless you also want to get sucked up like spaghetti."

All the ngo gwai paused at my words—and then they crowded in around me, pushing me back. Fear speared through me. I gritted my teeth in determination. If I didn't stop them, they'd keep coming after my family. I closed my eyes again. I searched for the closest string, and I pulled on it. This time I opened my eyes just in time to catch it fading to dust—and Henry was right behind it, gwandou held defensively like he'd been warding it off. His mouth was agape.

"I know what it looks like," I said archly. "But I didn't mean to save you."

"Whatever," he bit back, his face snapping back to its usual cold look. "Just keep doing whatever you're doing and maybe we'll both get out of here."

The last thing I wanted to do was leave the tunnels with the ghost who kept harassing my family, but I didn't have much choice in who I fought right now. Henry's movements were smooth, his weapon twirling fluidly despite the unwieldy length, slicing through the ngo gwai that surrounded us. We fell into a weird rhythm of tackling the ghosts, and before I knew it, I'd spun the spiritual energy of the last ngo gwai into me.

Henry's harsh gasps filled the empty space. He stood his gwandou up. "Your technique needs work. You were a split second too slow on most of them."

"You're breathing too loud. Do you actually need to breathe?" I retorted. "Pretty sure dead people don't."

His cheeks flushed an interesting shade of pink. "It's none of your business how I choose to live my afterlife."

I felt too much like throwing up to care. All that spiritual energy sloshed around in me like a rotten plate of pasta. I clenched my jaw shut and dragged myself over to the tunnel door.

He popped up in front of me, his arms crossed. "Where are you going?"

"What does it matter? Are you going to stop me?"

He froze, and then his eyes narrowed. "I could."

"Okay."

I stood there for a few seconds, fully ready to take his spiritual energy if he tried anything. When he finally looked away, my jaw dropped. "You can't do anything, can you?"

He huffed, then spun his gwandou around, the red tassel

fluttering off the fang, and it shrank back down into a short stick. "I can do whatever I want."

"You got injured during the fight." I felt for his spiritual energy. Unlike before, the string had shrivelled to a few threads wound together. "You're hurt. You're *weak*. You couldn't even drag a rat to the Underworld—"

"Quiet," he snapped, even though that interesting shade of begonia pink was coming back over his cheeks. "I'll keep an eye on you for now."

"Or I could take your spiritual energy like I did with the other ngo gwai," I said casually.

His hand dipped into the pouch hanging off his belt.

"But I won't," I finished before he could withdraw anything from his pouch. "The spiritual energy from you ngo gwai gives me a stomach ache."

His shoulders slumped in relief. I turned away, biting my lower lip. I really didn't feel good with all that spiritual energy swirling around in me, but sucking up a ngo gwai was also kind of . . . murder. Even if he was trying to do my family in, I couldn't stoop as low as him. At least the other ngo gwai had looked like monsters. Henry looked human, like a boy who could've been in my classes at school.

"Of course you feel sick. The spiritual energy you took has upset the balance inside you," he said harshly. "There's a reason why taking a ngo gwai's energy as your own is forbidden."

Cold swept over me. "It is?"

"You think you're the first to see the strings of spiritual

energy inside a ngo gwai? The Three Great Hunter Clans forbade the technique after a few hunters died from taking in too much."

"How much energy did they take before . . . ?"

He smirked. "Probably a little more than you did today."

Oh. That seemed bad. The spiritual energy I'd taken refused to settle inside me. I wondered if I could throw it up, but what if that made things even worse? Instead, I marched towards the tunnel door.

"Do what you want," I said. "But I'm going to find Michelle."

He didn't say anything, so I took that as my cue to head back into the tunnels. My footsteps echoed off the curved walls, but Henry's were soundless. He stayed several feet behind me. He seemed to be doing his best to make it seem like he wasn't there, and I had to check back over my shoulder more than once to see if he still was. Unfortunately, he was, trailing me like a particularly nasty shadow. After several minutes, I finally came back to the fork.

"Are you really going to follow me the whole way?" I complained, shining my phone light at him.

He bared his teeth in a menacing imitation of a smile. "You could get rid of me if you don't mind dying. It'd be a quick trip back to the Underworld for me, but it'd be much more permanent for you."

I huffed, but slowed as I rounded the corner. Down the tunnel, the faint outline of a door was barely visible.

I would've spun around and gone back the other way if Henry hadn't been blocking the path behind me.

I was really starting to hate doors. I wouldn't be able to handle another fight again so quickly. I scanned the area behind me. One long, dark maw. No ghosts. Well, except for Henry. He wore a smug look on his face, like he knew something I didn't.

"What?" I demanded.

"What *what*?"

"What have you done?"

"Nothing," he said, shrugging innocently. "Yet."

The same red glow from Fan Tan Alley slipped out beneath the bottom of the door—and so did the sound of a girl's crying. My mouth went dry.

"Michelle?"

I wrenched the door open.

It wasn't another tunnel. It was a cavern. Against the back of it were faded red pillars, tall and imposing like fangs in a lion's mouth, stretched up to a tiled roof. Tasselled lanterns dripped along its edge to curved corners. Their flames cast flickering, blood-red shadows down stone steps. And beneath those lanterns, tucked away in the protection of the darkness, stood a pair of closed doors, large enough to swallow a god.

A temple, right beneath the city.

"Michelle?" I called out, my voice wavering. The crying increased in volume. It sounded as if it was coming from behind the closed temple doors. I forced one foot forward, then the other, and with every step the pit of nerves inside my gut grew deeper. The air sat heavy around me, thick with spiritual energy. Like the last den of a forgotten beast, the rugged walls of the cavern stretched wide around the temple.

A figure stepped out from around one of the temple pillars, looking it up and down like he was searching for something. I ducked behind a pillar. My heart beat loudly in my chest. The figure came closer—and then I saw who it was.

Leon.

I sucked in a sharp breath. What was he doing here? I pressed myself against the pillar, but as I did, my shoe squeaked against the concrete floor.

Taking his calligraphy brush from his pocket, Leon wrote a character in the air before him. I jumped when the door to the cavern swung shut with a soft thud.

"You need to return to the surface," Leon said urgently. "It's not safe here."

I stepped out from behind the pillar. He didn't seem surprised to see me, and now that he was right in front of me, I realized that I wasn't really surprised to see him here beneath the city, either. But I should've been surprised—and *that's* what was weird. He was always popping up right when I needed him. It was awfully suspicious. I no longer believed he was only trying to help my family. He was up to something. He always had been. Everything he'd done—every time he'd appeared—had been too convenient.

"Why did you fly away from us?" I asked carefully, trying

to keep as much distance as possible between the two of us. I tested the air—he wasn't a ghost, but the blanket of spiritual energy felt off. If he wasn't a ghost, then what was he?

He darted another cautious look around. "Pardon?"

"We saw you at Bo Liang's shop in the back room in your pigeon form. You flew away and led us down Fan Tan Alley."

"I did no such thing." His face paled, and he whirled around, holding his calligraphy brush out. "The ghost hunter, Henry. Where is he?"

"He's right—"

I looked behind me. Henry wasn't there.

Leon opened his mouth to say something, then fell silent. His brown eyes searched my face. I refused to look away. He must not have liked what he found there, though, because his jaw squared. "You are suspicious of me."

"No," I said, but the lie fell flat on my tongue. "Okay, yes."

"Why?"

"You've been really helpful."

He patiently continued, "As I explained, it is my job—"

"Too helpful." My mouth was working faster than my brain was, and I couldn't stop it. "You show up right after a ghost sets my family altar on fire. You teach me how to do syu fat mo. You know my family, and you knew that they were ghost hunters, yet you didn't tell me."

His face pinched in concern, but I didn't know if it was for me or for himself. "I did tell you—"

"I can't tell what you want, either."

His hand tightened around the strap of his messenger bag, and I had the sudden, uneasy feeling that I was stepping into an unknown biome. "I have told you what I want. I made a promise to protect your family."

"No, that's what you said you're doing. But why are you doing it? Is it out of some sense of honour? Do you feel guilty? Because I can't tell. It's like—"

I snapped my mouth shut.

"Go on," he said quietly.

If I had nothing nice to say, then I shouldn't say it at all. Mom had always told me that. But deep below the city, in an underground tunnel with no one to help me, who was I trying to protect? Because it definitely wasn't Leon, and it wasn't even my family. Not at that moment.

I took a deep breath. "It's like you're empty on the inside."

And for just one moment, his face went perfectly blank. All the warmth drained from me.

"I see," he said.

He lifted the flap of his bag and pulled out a string-bound book. The cover was pale blue. Faded, like hydrangeas after a long summer. He opened the cover and pulled out a piece of paper. He glanced at it briefly before handing it to me.

A photo. Black and white. Wrinkled at the corner.

I took it with cold fingers.

A young woman sat on a narrow chair. She was wearing a plain cheongsam, more loosely shaped than what I was used to seeing. Her hands were folded demurely over her lap, but there was a stiffness to her expression, like she wasn't used to having her picture taken. Behind her stretched the slender branches of a tree with white blossoms.

There was something familiar about the young woman in the photo. Her nose. The way her forehead had a single crease in it, as Mah Mah's did when she was uncomfortable.

And it hit me—hard.

"You're Lin Wai's fiancé?" I squeaked. "The one who died?"

Leon stared down at the photo, as if looking at it long enough would call it to life. "A photographer came to the village the month before we were to be engaged. He took our picture for a meal. She loved that persimmon tree." The corners of his mouth curved up. He swept gentle fingertips over the surface of the photo. "She came to the Underworld to find me. We were supposed to ascend to immortality together, but the ritual went wrong. It was only I who ascended." Tin Hong was furious. The dead aren't meant to return to life. We'd defied the natural order of things, and by doing so, we'd defied him.

I wanted to sit down. My head spun. Leon did have an ulterior motive for helping my family, but it wasn't what I'd thought. My great-aunt, Mah Mah's sister. The one who'd burned her ghost hunter tools and gone to the Underworld to try to bring back her fiancé—that's who was in the picture.

"What happened to her?" I whispered.

"Nothing she deserved." A shadow passed across his face. "During the immortality ritual, she died the final death. She was removed from the Cycle of Death and Rebirth. Gone forever. So, I made her a promise."

My mouth was dry. "What promise?"

He exhaled heavily and tucked the photo back into his book. "I'm going to protect your family, Emma. I'll spend the rest of my immortal life stopping Tin Hong from getting his revenge. I couldn't save her, but I can save you. And to do that, you need to return to the surface."

"No," I said, louder than I meant to. "Not until I find Michelle."

He frowned in confusion. "I have not sensed any other mortals here."

I moved towards the temple, fighting against my instincts to run from the pulse of spiritual energy emanating from its closed doors. "Didn't you hear her crying? It was coming from the temple doors. We need to check there. She might be hurt—"

Leon ran up to me in alarm. "It's a trick, Emma. Someone has created a bridge between the Underworld and the Mortal Realm through the temple. The energy will lend strength to even the hungriest of ghosts. It only becomes stronger the closer we get to the Ghost Festival."

"Then where is she?" I cried. "She was with me in Fan Tan Alley, and then she vanished, just like a—"

"A ghost?" Henry murmured from behind me.

The hair on the back of my neck stood on end when I realized he was right at my back, gwandou in hand. Cold radiated off him.

Something whistled through the air. Leon collapsed on the ground. His messenger bag fell open and the pale-blue cover of his book peeked out. The photo of my great-aunt had fallen out onto the ground beside him.

"Leon?" My voice was far away.

I dropped to my knees. Reached out.

He didn't move. His chest rose and fell—and sticking out of the middle of it was something white. Something as long as the length of my hand. Slender as a needle. It looked like a thin leaf of paper, folded over itself.

I spun around. The pulse in my ears was a roar. "What did you do?"

But Henry wasn't looking at me. His glower was locked onto the darkness of the temple entrance. I scrambled to my feet, and the room spun—

"He didn't do anything."

Michelle laid the palm of her hand against the temple pillar. In her other hand was a calligraphy brush. It had a brilliant jade handle. Its brush head was silky white.

"I did," she finished, and she grinned.

CHAPTER 17

"Oooh," she said, stepping down from the temple entrance, giving her brush a twirl. "This is sort of awkward. Kai Ming *really* should have finished with you by now."

The light shining out from the red lanterns framed her in an ethereal glow, making her seem otherworldly. Her face was serene—only Michelle never looked serene. She was always eager for the next thing. A shudder went down my back. Even her smile looked wrong—lips tilted up in a bodhisattva's merciful expression. Only she wasn't a bodhisattva or a god. She was just a girl, like me.

Wasn't she?

With measured steps, she walked up to me. I backed up. Stepped on something soft. Looked down. Leon was still on the floor behind me. Still breathing. Still alive.

Henry lowered his gwandou. "I brought her as you instructed, Hei Nga."

She stopped a few feet away. So close I could see the mole on the side of her nose, so near I could touch her. But she wasn't looking at me. She was looking past me. At Henry.

"You've earned your payment," she said to him. "But you were slow. You've already had weeks to bring her to Lord Tin Hong. That means a deduction's in order. You'll be paid your one month of offerings when you return to the Underworld."

"I was promised two months on the contract I signed," he said through clenched teeth. He caught sight of me, then promptly flicked his gaze away. If I didn't know any better, I would've thought he looked guilty.

She lifted her chin and said in a chilling tone, "Three weeks. And no more. You wouldn't have been stalling, would you? I told Tin Hong the previous first son of the Lam Hunter Clan couldn't be trusted. You always had a tender spot for mortals."

Terror slithered up through my chest. "You're not Michelle. Stop wearing her face."

She waved my suggestion away with a careless hand. "Oh, no. That's Kai Ming's trick, not mine. Besides, I'd never let him use my appearance. Let me guess—he got you to speak to him of your own free will? Pfft, that's an amateur mistake. Everyone knows you're not supposed to speak to ngo gwai."

My head spun. "Is that what you are? A hungry ghost?"

She tilted her head to the side, considering. "I never did like that name, you know. Always rubbed me the wrong way. Like we were cursed to be hungry right from the start."

Her face began to shift, twitching with jerky movements. Terror cemented me to the spot. Her smile grew larger and larger until her jaw extended midway down her chest. The rest of the room blurred. The lanterns melted into the temple walls. All I could see were the sharp white tips that filled her mouth.

Shiny tips. Hundreds of them. Triangular. Little fangs, jagged and not human—

Then her face snapped back into place. The girl in front of me was the Michelle I'd always known. Short hair, tied back into twin braids. A nose that was just a little too sharp for the rest of her soft features. Blue bands on her braces. The only difference was that her warmth had been replaced by a repulsion so strong I could feel it on the backs of my arms.

I should have been running. I knew it. My body knew it. But this was my friend, not a monster. Not a ghost.

Not Michelle.

"I know you," I croaked out. "I know your family. We go to school together. We—"

"I go to school with you because that's where I was instructed to go," she said flippantly.

My vision blurred. "We grew up together."

"Don't you remember, Emma?" She stepped closer, but there was nowhere else for me to go when Leon's body was right behind me. "Second grade? You went swimming in the ocean with Michelle. She went under, and by the time anybody had noticed, it was too late."

"That's wrong," I said, but as soon as the words left my mouth, I knew that I was the one who was wrong.

Because I did remember.

I remembered that day—fragments of it, anyway. We were both seven. Michelle and I had been playing at the beach. She went out too far into the water. Her head sank below the white waves. Her father rushed out to grab her. He thought he was too late, and he'd cried when her eyes fluttered open.

She hadn't been breathing. Not for at least ten minutes, Mom had said, or maybe it was longer. Too long for someone to come back to life.

"That day—was that the day you died?" I asked, my voice thin in my throat.

She tapped her finger impatiently against her chin. "No, that was the day *Michelle* died. I was never Michelle. I've been a ghost for decades, way before your great-aunt screwed things up in the Underworld. Tin Hong needed someone to keep an eye on the Wong family while he tried to restore the balance, and I volunteered."

I watched as she tucked a braid behind her ear, just as I'd seen her do a hundred times. A thousand times. I felt sick.

"I was lucky that the Zhang girl died when she did. It was the perfect opportunity to get close to your family, so with Tin Hong's help, I took over her body. We cut it pretty close. The blood flow to her brain had been cut off for so long that we weren't sure if I could even get the body moving again."

My vision tunnelled.

My best friend was a ghost.

"But I guess you never suspected a thing," she continued.

"I did a pretty good job, huh? All that waiting paid off in the end when you told me you could see that little ghost girl on the playground. I went home after and celebrated, you know. Ate a whole bag of White Rabbit candy. Then, I made a quick trip back to the Underworld to tell Tin Hong he could put the rest of his plan into action. We'd been so close to giving up. We thought the Sight had died with your grandmother's generation. No Sight, no spiritual energy. No key to immortality."

Her grin slipped. I needed to move. To do something. But I was standing in the middle of a waterfall of memories, and it was pinning me to the spot. To move was to see Michelle for who she really was. Who she'd been this entire time, only I had never put the pieces together.

"Was all of it a lie?" I asked quietly. "We were never really friends?"

She ran her finger down a red pillar, rubbing away dust only she could see. "Wish I could say I was sorry, but I'm not."

Her words hit me like a punch to the stomach. She raised her calligraphy brush. Quickly, I created a barrier. The golden light shimmered down over me. Michelle snorted.

"That won't help you." She scrawled something in the air before her. The character hung, silvery and glowing, before it dissipated. Immediately, a flutter of yellowed papers slipped out from beneath her jacket. They flew out in a coiling line, wrapping around her in a tornado.

"Your family's already used their spiritual energy to help

a ghost ascend to immortality," she said in the midst of that wind of paper. "Tin Hong just wants to chat with him."

My stomach plummeted.

Leon.

"Don't touch him," I said.

Michelle—not Michelle, *not* Michelle—raised her brush, and the papers folded into tiny birds with sharp beaks. She slashed her arm down and they dove towards us. Hurriedly, I raised my brush to make another barrier around Leon. I wasn't going to make it—

Several of the birds fell to the ground, sliced in half.

My chest heaved. Henry had his gwandou out, blade flat in front of us as if he'd blocked them. He lowered his weapon and walked past me. Clapped a hand down onto Michelle's shoulder. Hard.

"Don't play around," he said in a low voice. "Tin Hong is waiting. He expects the immortal to be in one piece, unless you want a cut to *your* contractual offerings."

She threw his hand off with a scowl. She turned towards me to say, "If I were you, I'd be checking up on the rest of the family right about now."

My pulse soared. "What did you do?"

She tilted her chin up in defiance. "Oh, I can't take credit for Lord Tin Hong's curses."

My mind went blank.

I rushed forward. Grabbed her by the arm.

And I saw it.

A string, dangling there in my mind's eye. White and

long. Unravelling at one end. I couldn't see the other end, but something about it seemed oddly enticing, like it was a hideous, ripe fruit on the tip of a branch.

I reached out to pull it—

Michelle tore herself out of my grip, a strange look on her face. "Li Gwan will do for now. If Lord Tin Hong's plan works, no ghost will ever have to die the final death ever again."

The paper birds surrounded Leon in a flurry of movement. Helpless, I watched as they lifted his limp body into the air. They followed Michelle as she walked over to the temple doors. They opened for her, and a gust of spiritual energy blew over me.

I needed to stop her from taking Leon, but Michelle's threat about my family ricocheted around in my head.

"I'm sorry, Leon," I whispered, and I sprinted back into the tunnels.

CHAPTER 18

My footsteps echoed off the tunnel walls as I ran back towards the hole I'd jumped into. When I reached the spot, despair crashed through me. Had the drop really been that far? The hole towered above me by a good couple of feet.

"Come on," I pleaded desperately, stretching on the tips of my toes. I jumped, and my fingers skidded the side of the hole.

A breeze whispered past me, chilling the back of my neck. Startled, I looked behind me. The tunnel was dark and empty.

"Hello?" I said hesitantly, but when no one replied, I turned back to the side of the hole in annoyance. "Fine. Be that way. I don't even care anymore. At least I don't lie, trick, and hurt people—"

My voice cracked. I was so tired of ghosts.

I bent my knees, steadied myself, then bounced up. I fumbled to grasp the edge of the hole with both hands—and then I was being pulled up. I landed unceremoniously on the hard, tiled ground of a souvenir and trinket shop.

Wait. A souvenir shop?

Confused, I took in the shelves of paper fans and tea sets. I glanced back down to the floor, but the hole had disappeared. Flat, square tiles covered the space. I wrung my hands together. They were warm despite the frigid air. It felt like someone had grabbed hold of them and pulled me up.

I shook my head to clear the thought. A ngo gwai would sooner set my house on fire—or harm my family—than help me. Maybe Michelle was lying. Even if she was a ghost, she'd never stoop so low.

Right?

I pulled out my phone to call my parents—and my head emptied.

Fifty-six messages.

Twenty missed phone calls.

Come home

Where are you???

Come home right now Emma

There's something wrong with Mah Mah

I nearly dropped my phone. I tightened my grip around it. My breaths came shallow.

Emma come to the hospital.

• • •

Bright white lights. A steady beep. The stinging aroma of soap and antiseptic and flowers too cold to bloom. Mah Mah's small frame, flat beneath the thin hospital blanket.

Dad's hand, smoothing the sheet over her. Brushing her curls away from her forehead.

Mom paced back and forth beside Mah Mah's hospital bed. Puffy bags lined her eyes. "The doctor said she's stable. They don't know why she isn't waking up, so they're monitoring her for now." Her fist was tucked against her mouth, as if keeping it there would stop everything from rushing out. She muttered something beneath her breath in Cantonese, but I didn't catch what she said.

I kicked off my shoes and tucked my feet under me. The seat was warm, but my fingers were frozen, and so were my feet. The bus had taken twenty minutes to come. The same question kept repeating itself in my head the whole ride over:

Why?

My family had never done anything to deserve this. I felt angry—with Tin Hong. Michelle. Henry. All the ngo gwai who couldn't just leave us in peace. Even with my great-aunt, Lin Wai. None of this was fair.

The line on the monitor zigzagged up and down. Mah Mah's eyes stayed closed.

If I traced back my steps—recounted every action I took, everything I said—would I be able to pinpoint the exact moment things started to fall apart? I wrapped my arms around my knees. Mah Mah's chest rose and fell.

"I thought she was taking a nap." Mom made a sound between laughing and sobbing. "She was tired after breakfast. Yesterday, too."

"It's not your fault, Mom," I whispered. I rubbed at my dry eyes. Everything that I wanted to say died on my lips. Nothing was enough. "Here, just—sit down, okay?" I slid the metal chair with its forget-me-not-blue seat over for her, but she shook her head.

"No. You take it. I'm not tired." Her fingers tapped against her arm. "When we get home, we need to talk about where you were. You weren't in your room. We were so worried. We thought . . ."

She pressed her hand to her face again. I should have felt nervous, but all I said was, "Okay."

A curse from Tin Hong, Ghost Lord of the Underworld.

Mah Mah had spoken of a curse. She hadn't been wrong. Only she hadn't known where the curse was coming from. None of us had. It'd come out of the dark to wrap around us. I no longer knew which way to look. I could've said a million things to console myself, but here was the truth:

I'd gone out too far into the ocean, and the current was swelling over me. I thought I could protect my grandmother. All of us. But I was a single drop, and the ocean was vaster and deeper than I'd ever thought possible.

How did you win a fight against something when you couldn't even swim out to meet it?

"Mah Mah." The lump in my throat grew bigger. "I'm sorry."

Dad wrapped his arm around my shoulder. He'd been silent the whole time, sitting by Mah Mah, rubbing his thumb over her knuckles. Now he hugged me close. "You didn't do anything, Emma."

I rested my head against him, listened to the beating in his chest. I wished, more than anything else at that moment, that Mom and Dad could see ghosts too. That I could tell them what was going on. That I could own up to every-thing, even that big red D written at the top of my math exam. But I couldn't. I'd never forgive myself if Mom and Dad got hurt because of me.

I took Mah Mah's hand in mine and rubbed my thumb over her knuckles the way Dad had, over the calluses on her palm. I rubbed my thumb over them again and again and again, until the beeping of the heart monitor faded away, and there was only the sound of our breathing. The four of us, together, in one small room.

Alive.

For now.

CHAPTER 19

Nobody said anything on the drive back home the next day. It was almost noon, but the sky was dreary and grey. I tried not to look at the empty space beside me, the one Mah Mah would've been in if she were with us.

Once we reached our house, Mom carefully hung up her purse on the coat rack. She adjusted it until the straps were even on either side. Finally, she exhaled heavily.

"Pack some clothes for Mah Mah," she said. "We'll drop it off during visiting hours later."

Dad's face was lined with weariness. "And a couple of her gardening magazines for when she wakes up. She'll like that."

"Yeah," I said, my voice tight. "Yeah, okay. I'll get that."

I watched the two of them go their separate ways down the hall, leaving me alone at the front door. My brain had switched off long ago. I had a phantom's body, a spectre's heartbeat.

For a long moment, I let my house's quiet murmurs sink into me. There was the scratching of the Japanese maple at the living room window. The low humming of the refrigerator seeping out from the kitchen. The faint smell of burnt wood that still lingered, even though we'd got rid of the old family altar a couple of weeks ago. A new one stood in its place now—one that hadn't yet become ours despite our having set it up in the same way as the previous one. The incense burned the same, but it left trails in the air that were unfamiliar.

Upstairs, I walked down the hallway and pushed open the door to Mah Mah's bedroom. The smell of orange blossoms wafted out. Her gardening hats on hooks along the wall, the jade animals on her dresser, and even the carpet beneath my feet—all of it felt like it had continued on with her life in her absence.

"I need to do this, Mah Mah," I whispered to the empty space.

I pulled open her closet, and even now, when everything was falling apart, it felt wrong—as if I was looking through a diary I wasn't supposed to. For so many years, my grandmother had kept secrets I hadn't known about.

But I knew where she stored her secrets.

I rummaged through the stacked boxes, lifting lids and unpacking newspaper-wrapped memories. Finally, I pulled out a box at the very back of the closet. The edges of the box were tattered, barely held together by a crumbling layer of yellowed packing tape. Inside was a bundle of black fabric. I unrolled it, layer by layer, peeling away until I could see the dagger in its entirety, with its embossed bronze hilt. A single lotus adorned the end of the hilt.

I removed the sheath. The blade was unusually thin and narrow. It almost seemed more like a decoration than a weapon, but the weight was heavy and the metal had a deadly shine where it wasn't covered in scorch marks.

"I'm coming for you, Tin Hong," I muttered, and I could've sworn a coldness breathed along the back of my neck. I shook it off before slipping my great-aunt's dagger into my coat pocket.

I needed to find Henry.

He was going to take me to the Underworld. I'd rescue Leon. Together, we'd put a stop to Tin Hong.

• • •

A loud clacking came from the kitchen. Mom stood at the kitchen sink, her back towards me as she rolled chopsticks against each other in sudsy water, cleaning them. For the first time in a long time, her bobbed hair stuck out in flyaway strands instead of careful swoops around her small face. Her apron was tied in a lopsided bow at the back. The mellow fragrance of steamed rice drifted out into the hallway.

"Lunch is almost ready," she said.

I hurried towards the front door. "I'm not hungry." My stomach was tearing itself apart, but it wasn't because of hunger.

"You need to eat something." Mom stepped out of the kitchen. She had a piece of black bean chicken between the chopsticks in her hand. "Here, try this."

I yanked on my boots, hands fumbling with the laces. "I will. Later."

"Come, try it," she insisted.

She shoved the chicken into my mouth. I bit down.

"It's good," I mumbled, even though I couldn't taste anything beyond the salt. For some reason, I felt like crying.

Her gaze drifted down to my boots. "Are you going somewhere?"

I swallowed down the lump in my throat. "I need to check on Mah Mah's garden."

"You can do that later. Family should eat together."

"I'll eat with you after. I promise."

She clicked her tongue in annoyance. "What's so urgent with the garden that you need to do it now? We just got back. We're all tired. Eat."

I inhaled deeply. Filled my chest with as much calm as I could muster, then, in an even voice, said, "Mom, just give me ten minutes. Please. This is really important to me."

She lowered her chopsticks and scrutinized my outfit. "Are you hiding something?"

My face exploded into heat. "What are you talking about?"

"You never told us where you were yesterday night."

"I was with Michelle."

"Don't lie to me!" she cried. "I called Michelle's mom and you two weren't there. So where were you?"

I swallowed nervously. There was no way I could tell her we were downtown, getting sucked into some crazy alternate ghost universe where the laws of physics didn't apply.

"We were so worried," she continued, waving the chopsticks at me in exasperation. "We went up to your room and you weren't there. It was eleven at night! You've been sneaking behind our backs, lying to us—"

"No."

"You don't care about us. You could have gotten hurt—"

A tremor started at my temple. "Mom, I'm sorry, okay?"

"Sorry? You're sorry?" She loomed closer, her face red. "No, you need to stop! We didn't raise you to be this way. What happened? What did we do wrong? We try to teach you—"

"I'm trying my best!" I shouted, whirling towards the door.

"Don't ignore me!" Mom cried out, her slippered feet slapping against the hardwood floor of the hallway. "You're grounded. Right now. Go to your room."

I spun back around. "You don't know why Mah Mah's hurt, but I do. I have to stop them before they do anything else. You don't understand, but you need to trust me. Please, Mom."

Her face went ashen. "What are you talking about? If you keep lying—if you keep making these bad decisions—"

"I'm not making bad decisions," I said, my voice wavering. "I'm just making decisions you don't like. And I'm going to keep doing it, too. Like my final math exam. Guess what I got on it?"

Her expression changed, not quite into her Disappointed Mom™ frown, but something close to it. "Emma—"

"I got a D." My stomach fluttered unpleasantly. "Okay? And I hid it from you and Dad, because you always do this— you never understand, and you never try to."

Her mouth fell open. My eyes burned. I wrenched open the door and took off under the cold sunshine.

I flew down the road, past the open windows of my neighbours' houses, not caring if they saw me. I ran until I came to the forest at the back of the park. The grass leading to the Garry oaks was soft beneath my shoes. The last time I'd been here had been with Leon . . . and Michelle.

Angrily, I wiped away the tears in my eyes. For the first time, I felt truly alone.

Mah Mah was in the hospital. My best friend was a ghost—and not just any ghost, but one that was helping a Ghost Lord hurt my family. She'd taken Leon, the only person who'd been helping me.

Life sucked. True fact.

To say that it was more awful than usual would be putting it lightly. I could've given myself a pep talk. Told myself that when the going got tough, you got tougher. Or if you fell down ten times, you got up eleven, just to show fate who was really the boss.

But the only thing that kept me going was the thought that I needed to find the Ghost Lord responsible for putting my family through the wringer.

I had no idea where he was, other than that he was chilling in his safe and happy home in the Underworld. Probably hanging out with Michelle. Even though I felt like crap, I had to find him. Stop him, because he wasn't going to stop until he dragged my family to their deaths. Mah Mah was proof of that.

I sniffed loudly, then started walking again. The forest behind the park stretched out for several acres. I passed by several Garry oaks, dodging their low-hanging branches and gnarled trunks. There used to be a house in the middle of the lot, but it had been torn down years ago, just before I entered middle school. Nobody came here now, and even when they did, it was to go traipsing in the small stream that ran through the land. It was the closest body of water to my house.

Leon had said water was a conduit for syu fat mo. If I was going to trick Henry, I needed all the help I could get.

I stepped through the layers of rotten branches and underbrush, avoiding the hidden puddles as best I could. Overhead, the canopy of fir, heavy with fragrant needles, blocked out the sky. Soon, I heard the telltale shushing of the stream. It lay ahead, hidden behind the thinning trees. I came to the edge of the tree line and sucked in a breath.

In every inch of my body, I felt the unmistakable presence of a ghost nearby.

And this one felt big.

The instinct rippled through my body, tensing my muscles for a fight.

I shoved my right hand into my pocket. My fingers curled around Lin Wai's dagger. My thumb pressed down on the metal sheath, ready to flick it off. I'd never used a ghost hunting weapon before, but somehow it felt *right*. Like the cold metal belonged against the warmth of my skin, the two melding into one.

On stiff legs, I left the safety of the tree line, dagger tight in my hand. The stream rolled past in snaking rivulets and quick shimmers. It was almost narrow enough to cross if I took a running jump. Beyond it lay more trees, denser than I could see through. The wind rustled through the tall sprigs of grass at the water's edge.

I tensed.

Waiting.

Listening.

And then I started whistling.

Almost immediately, there was a scuffle of movement beside me, too fast for my eyes to follow. I caught a blur of something dark, and a chill set into my bones.

"You called?" Henry whispered beside me.

I flinched away—just as something whacked into the back of my hand and I dropped the dagger.

"Ow!" I cried.

"You were supposed to dodge that!" Henry shouted.

"How the heck am I supposed to dodge something I can barely see?" I yelled back, grabbing the dagger again.

"You were perfectly fine back in the tunnels. Your ancestors are going to pretend they don't know you when you go to the Underworld."

I gritted my teeth. Planted my feet. Whirled around, dagger out, and sliced through something soft and yielding.

Henry yelped loudly—and he materialized. He looked *really* upset. A little thread of guilt wormed its way through me.

"Sorry—"

"There's something called spatial awareness. Maybe you should learn about it," he said, seething. He brought his hand up to his cheek, wiping away a drop of blood with two fingers. "You know how many offerings I'm going to have to eat to make up for this?"

My guilt vanished. If looks could kill, I hoped mine immolated him into oblivion. "None if you get stabbed again."

He stared down at the smear of blood on his fingers, perplexed. "That dagger you used—that's a ghost hunter weapon. Where did you get a hunter weapon?"

"None of your business," I snipped. "I'm here to take you up on your previous offer."

"What offer?"

I breathed in. "Take me to the Underworld."

Without removing his eyes from mine, Henry reached into the black pouch at his side and withdrew his calligraphy brush. I tensed, but he only tossed it up into the air.

"No," he said. "You're planning something, and Lord Tin Hong hasn't called for you yet. He's busy with the immortal pigeon. Probably roasting him. Maybe grilling him over an open fire—"

My stomach turned. The sooner I could get to the Underworld, the sooner I could rescue Leon. An idea struck me. "Help me, or go away while I summon up a *better* ghost."

Henry stiffened. "What does that mean?"

"You know, one who can actually haunt someone properly," I said nonchalantly. "You had so many chances to get me to go with you to the Underworld. Now you just feel embarrassed, so you won't take me. I think that means you're bad at your job."

His eyes narrowed dangerously. "What did you say, mortal?"

I shrugged, feeling dangerous myself. "It's okay, I understand. Everyone's bad at something. Like me—well, you know what I'm bad at. Math—"

"I shouldn't have helped you out of the tunnels," he eked out between clenched teeth.

I squinted at him, trying to figure out what his game was. Then it hit me. "That was you who lifted me out of the hole?"

"The second-biggest mistake of my afterlife."

"Geez, I'd hate to know how terrible your biggest mistake was."

He maliciously jabbed his calligraphy brush in my direction. "My biggest mistake was letting Lin Wai help Li Gwan ascend to immortality. It took a year's stockpile of offerings in the First Court of the Underworld to give Li Gwan enough spiritual energy for the ritual. We had to ration offerings for years after. Many ngo gwai vanished forever because of that. If I'd known what she was up to, I never would have helped her—"

"Wait," I said in disbelief. "You helped my great-aunt? That's why you thought I was her? How come Leon didn't recognize you?"

He sealed his mouth shut, his face scarlet as if he'd let slip a secret. Sheepishly, he said, "He never saw me. He just left the Underworld in a mess. Didn't even bother to fix anything."

"So now you're helping Tin Hong destroy my family."

"He's not going to *destroy* your family. He seeks to repair the balance of the Three Realms with your family's assistance." He looked down, then continued quietly, "I just never thought he'd hurt your grandmother to do it."

Henry actually looked . . . sad. Really sad, not fake sad. It softened his face and erased the smugness he usually carried. He raised his gaze to meet mine, and my face went hot. Flustered, I snapped, "Well, he has, which is why I need your help going to the Underworld."

He frowned. "Like I said, no."

I squared my stance. I didn't want to have to do it, but I reached out for that white string of his spiritual energy and *pulled*.

He twitched—then tried to pull back. He didn't get very far. It was like he was frozen in place. I pulled on the energy string again, and he flinched.

"Wong," he warned, but he was wary now. He lowered his brush.

"Please, Henry," I pleaded. "Tin Hong's not going to stop at hurting my grandmother."

He shifted uneasily. I tugged on his energy again. Hard. He paled like I was choking him.

"You wouldn't," he said.

"What do you think happened to that ghost you tried to kill me with?"

"That was a ngo gwai."

"You're one too."

He flushed. "I'm not *just* a ngo gwai. I'm a ghost hunter, the first-born son of the Lam Hunter Clan, prodigy of the family, pride of my parents! I'd vanquished a hundred ghosts in my mortal life, and I've vanquished hundreds more since dying—"

I jerked on his energy. He stopped talking. "And you'll be the ninth ghost I exorcise unless you show me how to get to the Underworld. *Now.*"

His eyes searched my face. I could feel his gaze taking in all of me, and I wondered how desperate I looked to him. Did I look as ragged as I felt? Did I look like I had nothing to lose?

"Fine," he forced out. "Give me paper."

"Why?" I asked tensely.

"You don't have any, do you?"

I stayed silent. Because I didn't.

"Figures," he said with a scowl. "No one's ever properly prepared anymore."

He dug into the cloth pouch at his side and took out a small stack of square papers, each with a piece of silver foil in the middle.

"Can't believe I'm using my spirit money for this," he grumbled. He fanned the papers out and scribbled something in the air before him.

The spirit money rose up into a spiral and started slotting together. The papers creased and folded, interlocking with sharp corners until Henry snatched the mass out of the air. He turned it over, adding one more paper here, some colour there, all with deft swipes of his finger, as if he was an artist putting the final touches on a piece he was already bored with. One by one, piece by piece—until I realized I was looking at a boat.

The paper boat was about the size of a textbook, and its three red sails were made of paper so thin they were almost translucent. Tiny pieces of paper roping connected the sails to even smaller masts.

"Your carriage awaits," he intoned, shaking the boat at me.

I gritted my teeth and got ready to tug on his string of energy again, but as soon as I grazed it, he threw his hands up in exasperation.

"It'll take you to the Underworld. You just need to burn it near water."

"Then burn it."

"Burn it yourself," he bit back. "Unless—"

I stood there, fuming, as realization dawned on him.

"You don't know how to create fire?" A chuckle bubbled out of him. "It's a beginner spell. What has the pigeon been teaching you?"

"Give me the boat," I gritted out.

The humour slipped from his face—and before I could react, he tore the boat in half. And then in half again. And again, until there were only ribbons floating down, and all I

208

could think was that on top of everything else, this jerk had *littered*.

When he was done, he casually said, "I made you the paper boat like you asked."

I shot over to him, arm back, hand clenched in a fist. I'd never punched anyone before, but if it was going to be Henry, it was going to feel extremely satisfying.

He tried to dodge me. And he did—just enough that, instead of my fist landing squarely in his chest, it crashed into his arm instead. Pain reverbated up through my clenched hand.

The scowl on his face was mixed with shock and something I couldn't place.

"You hit me," he said, flabbergasted.

"Wish I could've hit you harder." I stared straight ahead, so that I was looking at the top of his head. In actuality, though, I was pulling out my calligraphy brush and focusing on the slips of shredded paper behind him. Behind my back, I frantically wrote out the character for *move*.

His scowl deepened. "This isn't a game. I could kill you if I wanted."

"Okay," I said. The papers swirled in the air behind him, coming together, flattening and folding—

"What are you doing?" he asked suddenly.

Before he could turn around, I darted past him and grabbed the paper boat out of the air.

"Burn the boat," I said, "and I'll give you a year of offerings."

He narrowed his eyes suspiciously. "You don't even know what that means."

"Yes, I do." I crossed my arms in defence. "Oranges and incense and things like that, right? I've seen my—my grandma make offerings. And I heard what you and Michelle were talking about. Ngo gwai need to eat regular offerings, or . . ."

I hesitated, not sure how to continue. What happened to ngo gwai that didn't receive enough offerings? Did they starve? Henry didn't look as if he was starving. In fact, he looked wary, like I'd stripped away a layer and discovered he was made of something soft and perishable.

"Or we vanish from the Cycle of Death and Rebirth." He raised his calligraphy brush and pointed the tip at me. Oh, shoot. I scrambled to tighten my hold on his spiritual energy.

"Siu yuk," he said.

"What?"

"Roast pork," he translated. "That has to be a regular offering. At least once a week. And pomelos."

My heart sped up. "Siu yuk and pomelos. Got it."

"And no fish. I hate fish. Tastes like rotting ngo gwai."

My nose wrinkled. "You're wrong, but fine. No fish."

"For a year?" he asked again.

"A full year," I confirmed, already mourning the loss of all the allowance money needed to sustain a full year of siu yuk and pomelos. Those things didn't come cheap. Snobby jerk.

But I held my breath as he flipped his calligraphy brush between his fingers like it was a pencil. His jaw worked back and forth like there was more he wanted to say. But instead of saying anything, he raised his calligraphy brush and wrote out a quick few strokes in front of him.

"Hey!" I yelped when the boat caught fire. "I was holding that!"

"Oops," he said with a smirk, and shoved his calligraphy brush back into his pocket.

From up the stream, a large boat sailed towards us. Its three sails were a vivid crimson, parting through the cloudy wisps like a lighthouse beacon guiding wayward souls. I eyed it warily. It felt—wrong. As it came closer, a faint rustling accompanied it, like fallen leaves whispering against the scuffle of footsteps.

The entire boat was made out of paper.

A sharp unease ran down my back. Aside from being completely constructed out of paper and rope, it could have passed for a perfect replica of a junk ship, albeit smaller than any I'd seen before. The hull was just wide enough that it took up the width of the stream. It swayed gently from side to side as it sailed towards us—an unmanned ship against the current.

It slowed to a stop in the water, like it was inviting us on.

Gulping down my hesitation, I stalked to the edge of the stream. An unusual fog crept along the water, sweeping along the bottom of the hull like a second layer of hungry water. When I reached the boat, I gave it a tentative poke with my calligraphy brush. The boat lit up with an unseen light source, and I shivered. The faintest whiff of incense curled inside my nose.

This was my chance to finally put an end to things.

I jumped onto the boat, and I held out my hand to Henry. "Come on, before the boat leaves."

CHAPTER 20

Henry stared at my outstretched hand with a look of revulsion. The fog around the boat swelled to cover his legs. "I'm not holding your puny mortal appendages."

"Fine," I snapped. "But you're coming with me."

"You've got to be kidding me. I'm not going with you. Lord Tin Hong will already have my undead head if he finds out I made this boat for you."

"I'll probably die," I pointed out.

"In the Underworld?" His lips lifted in a pleased smile. "There is a chance of that happening."

"And if it does, guess how many offerings you'll be getting? *Zeeerooo*—"

His face fell. With a look as if he was about to trudge through a thicket of thorny blackberry bushes, he took a running start through the fog and jumped onto the boat beside me. I stumbled back. The boat dipped with my movement, but not with his.

"Wa mui need to be part of the offerings," he hissed. "The extra-sour kind."

"Deal." I paused. "What's wa mui?"

"Seriously? How can you not know about the greatest snack in existence? Are you sure you're a Wong?"

Heat shot to my face. "Well, maybe if you told me what it is in English, then I'd recognize it. Just because I can't understand everything you're saying doesn't mean I'm beneath you. It's low to pick on someone's language abilities."

If I hadn't known any better, I would've thought he looked almost apologetic before his gaze darted away from me.

"It's salty dried plum," he muttered, heading towards the lantern-lit bow. "And we're going straight to Lord Tin Hong. No sightseeing. No pit stops. If any ngo gwai approach you, pretend they don't exist."

His words stung.

"Don't worry," I said, looking away. "I'm really good at that."

The vessel began to move in reverse, drifting back the way it had come. I swallowed, trying to quell the see-saw of nerves in my stomach. The paper railing was as solid as any wood, just like the floorboards beneath my feet. The sails waved overhead in a non-existent breeze. At the tip of the bow, a single lantern swayed at the end of a pole. It too was made of paper, but save for the brilliant orange orb within it, its mandala of curved petals was unmistakable—a lotus in full bloom. The light from it didn't reach far, yet the whole boat seemed to glow from within.

"What does Tin Hong need my family for?" I asked.

He crossed his arms and shrugged. "Tin Hong keeps his own secrets behind locked doors. I only know that he does a lot of boring paperwork to try to fix the disturbance your great-aunt created. Ever since Li Gwan ascended and offerings had to be rationed, the ngo gwai in the First Court of the Underworld have demanded a stable and plentiful store of offerings."

Uneasiness crawled along my skin. "Don't you think that it's weird a Ghost Lord wants a mortal family to fix something in the Underworld?"

"I have been wondering," he admitted. "But a ghost doesn't question Lord Tin Hong. Besides, the other nine lords of the Underworld keep him in check. He wouldn't be able to do anything that affects more than the First Court of the Underworld without their approval."

"What if he's hiding things from them?"

He gave me a sharp look. "That would be a crime."

"Kind of like what you're doing?"

He snorted. "The real crime here is your whistling, ban dan."

For one short moment, I thought about pushing him off the ship before I remembered that he was a ghost, and pushing him off would only make him more annoyed. Henry muttered something under his breath that sounded an awful lot like "ban dan" again, which was really rude, since it meant he was calling me an idiot.

The fog around the boat darkened—and kept darkening until all daylight had been replaced by an impenetrable mist that made me want to run. Ahead of us, the fog coalesced into a thick, black emptiness, like the mouth of an ancient and hungry beast.

And we were headed straight towards it.

As we passed through the darkness, a pale red light flooded over the ship, and my breath caught in my chest.

A river spread wide before us, its gentle waters lapping at the barren banks. In the distance was a sprawl of grey mountains, towering and blank. The red earth was dotted with empty birch trees and a flat layer of stone huts with tiled roofs. Many were clustered along the river's edge. Everything looked like it was covered in a fine layer of dust, muting colours and blurring details. Even the air tasted stale. Each breath stuck in my throat, chalky and dry.

"Don't fall into the Scoi Dang River," Henry warned.

My gut tightened. "Will I be stuck in the Underworld forever?"

"No, you'll be soaking wet." He darted a glance over at me, and his mouth split into a lopsided grin. "But maybe if I wish hard enough, you'll stay stuck in the river."

I reached out for his spiritual energy and gave a hard tug on it, which he ignored by turning around. The Seoi Dang River had a dock on either side. A forest of skeletal birch trees stood to the left of the river, and a small village lay to the right. I squinted at the dock on the right. "Why is there an ox standing on its hind legs and wearing armour?"

"Pok gai," Henry swore. He pushed away from the bow, and this time the boat swayed with each step he took, as if he had substance here that he hadn't had in the Mortal Realm. "That's Ngau Tau, one of the King of the Underworld's messengers. He escorts the dead to their appropriate place in the Underworld."

"But I'm not dead!" I protested.

"Yeah, you've got at least sixty more mortal years on you." He grimaced in displeasure. "Ngau Tau shouldn't be here. This isn't the typical way for mortals to enter."

"Lam Kai Ming," Ngau Tau boomed as we drifted closer on the boat. He held a steel trident in one hand, and his powerful arms were crossed against his thick chest. "You know the rules. Why have you brought a living mortal to the Underworld?" His large, velvety ears perked up. "Oooh, let me guess—is she your girlfriend?"

Henry's face went scarlet at the same time I made a gagging sound.

"No!" he shouted. "Why would you even think that?"

Ngau Tau's ears flopped back down. "You know how worried Ma Min and I get about you. You've already been in the Underworld for so long. You don't even have any friends—"

"I I do!" Henry sputtered. "And I haven't been here *that* long. It only feels long because you and Ma Min are old—"

In a panic, I ducked beneath the railing of the ship. Mah Mah had told me stories about Ngau Tau and his guardian partner, Ma Min. He wouldn't harm me, but he was dutiful. "Don't tell him why I'm here," I whispered to Henry. "He'll send me back to the Mortal Realm."

"I have to tell him," Henry hissed back, his cheeks still pink. "Defying Ngau Tau is like going against the King of the Underworld himself."

"Then lie."

He paled. "And say that you're my girlfriend?"

"Gross, of course not." I straightened above the railing. "Hi. I'm sorry to intrude, but one of my ancestors called me here."

Ngau Tau smacked the end of his trident into the ground. "Who?"

"My great-aunt."

"I will fetch her for you!" he shouted, plopping down cross-legged onto the dusty ground of the riverbank. He pulled an enormous book out of his sleeve. It was larger than his head, and it had to have at least ten thousand pages. "What is her full name?"

"Um . . ." I met Henry's eyes, desperately hoping no one would name their kid after a salty dried plum. "Wong Wa Mui?"

"Wong Wa Mui . . ." Ngau Tau muttered, running his large finger down page after page. "Wong Wa Mui . . ."

As Ngau Tau flipped through the pages of his book, I asked Henry, "How far away is Tin Hong?"

"Half a day of travel." He pointed towards the dock on the right where Ngau Tau was standing. "That way."

"Are you sure she hasn't been reincarnated already?" Ngau Tau yelled.

"I'm sure!" I said, drawing my calligraphy brush. But before I could write anything, Henry's hand clapped down onto the handle. His eyes darted to Ngau Tau, still leafing through his massive book of names.

"What are you trying to do?" he asked.

"I'm moving the boat to the opposite dock."

"You can't run from Ngau Tau. That's—"

"Illegal. I get it." I tugged my calligraphy brush out of his grip. "Please. I've already come so far. My grandmother's life depends on me finding Tin Hong. I'm not asking you to defy Ngau Tau. You can leave. I'll still pay you your year of offerings."

Henry's face pinched in surprise. "Why?"

"You helped me get to the Underworld. I mean, you could have made it a lot easier, but I'll take what I can get. I don't go back on my promises."

His face went funny. "You're being nice. You don't need to be nice to me."

"Yep," I said. "I don't."

He went quiet. I took it as a sign that he wouldn't stop me. Sure enough, when I wrote the first few strokes for *move*, he didn't try to grab for my brush again.

The ship drifted towards the other side of the river, where the birch trees stood evenly spaced, as if someone had marked them out in a perfect grid. When the hull of the ship bumped against the dock, I stole a quick look back at Henry before I leapt out onto the shore. He had his back to me as he leaned against the railing. It didn't feel right to leave without saying goodbye, but he'd also tried to do my family in. I had standards.

I hit the ground with a soft thump. A puff of red dust rose and fell around my shoes.

The tops of the mountains in the distance weren't capped with white like the ones I was used to. They were great, hulking forms, the colour of lunaria seed pods burnt by the sun, reaching high and spreading along the blurry horizon. There was no green in sight. All around me was brown and grey and beige—the colours of the earth without the life.

"I can't find any Wong Wa Mui!" Ngau Tau bellowed from all the way across the river, his voice deep and rumbling. "Can you tell me the spelling?"

I took a deep breath. "W-O-N-G—"

"Let's go." From out of nowhere, Henry grabbed my hand and pulled me up the slope of the riverbank. "Before I *really* regret helping you."

"I said you didn't have to!"

"And I decided I would," he said with an odd sort of finality. "Now come on. I don't see Ma Min, and Ngau Tau and Ma Min always travel as a pair."

CHAPTER 21

We ran into the bone-white forest, where the sun shone crimson through leafless branches. The straight white trunks of the birch trees were disorientingly similar. Behind me, Henry crunched across the dust and broken twigs of the forest.

"Are we lost?" I asked once we had slowed to a brisk walk. I glanced over my shoulder for what seemed like the hundredth time, but Ngau Tau hadn't followed us across the river.

"Of course not. I know this part of the Underworld like the blade of my gwandou." He cracked a branch in half as he marched over it. "The Seoi Dang River cuts through the whole of the First Court of the Underworld. We'll find another spot to cross once we're far enough away from Ngau Tau."

He snapped through another twig. His movements made noise here—and *why* was he so noisy for someone who was supposed to be the leader of a ghost hunting clan? Nervously, I scanned the forest again for any sign that we were being followed.

"Can't you walk a little quieter?" I complained.

"Nope." He stomped through another branch, and the resounding crack echoed through the silence.

I glared at the back of his head. "You did that on purpose. Someone's going to hear us."

"No one would dare bother me," Henry boasted. "I've dispersed many a troublesome ngo gwai in this region." He pulled the short form of his gwandou out of his pouch and flung it up into the air, where it lengthened into its sharp-tipped blade and red tassel. He caught it in one hand and flashed me a smug grin. "Feel free to name-drop me if you ever get in any trouble. My name is pretty much magic—"

In the distance, something snapped. Like a twig breaking under someone's foot.

"Quiet," I said, looking around.

"It's Lam Kai Ming. Here, I'll write it for you. Lam, like forest—"

"No, seriously. Be quiet," I whispered. "I heard something."

Another snap rang out in the forest. It sounded closer this time.

We ducked behind a tree trunk as Ma Min stopped on the path we'd been on a split second ago. I held my breath as he turned his horse head in our direction, his ears flicking. Like his partner, he wore a full outfit of armour, and he carried a wickedly curved polearm. Henry cursed beneath his breath.

"We can't go to the river," he whispered as Ma Min walked down the path towards us. "We'll be caught."

"Lam Kai Ming," Ma Min called. "Is that the red tassel of your gwandou I see there?"

"Run!" I shrieked, shooting to my feet.

Ma Min shouted for us to wait, but we didn't stop. He thundered after us on his two feet, angry steam puffing out of his nostrils. We wound through the forest until Henry sprinted off to the side, where the trees clustered together in a dense thicket.

"This way!" Henry yelled.

We pushed through the trees until they thinned and we stumbled into a clearing.

Huts spread out before us, pockmarking the land like dry scabs. The huts were made of knotted wood and sunken beams, with thickly thatched straw for roofs. An abandoned well jutted out from the centre of the settlement in a tangle of yellowed vines. I peered into the window of one of the huts as we walked by. The opening was covered with a slitted cloth. The makeshift curtain moved, and a sallow face peeked out at me.

I bit back a gasp and whipped out the dagger in my pocket. "Did you see that? There are people here!"

Henry rolled his eyes. "Of course there are people here. This is a ghost village. But the ghosts here are too weak to do anything, even to a mortal, so put that away."

Reluctantly, I sheathed the dagger and slid it back into my pocket. "Do all the ngo gwai here look so . . . sick?"

"They didn't used to," Henry said as we walked towards the middle of the clearing. "Most ghosts don't have much in the Underworld unless their families burn luxuries for them. The ghosts here are sick because they haven't had enough offerings since the Year of Loss."

"The Year of Loss?"

"The year that Li Gwan ascended to immortality and wiped out an entire year of offerings during the Ghost Festival. This region of the Underworld has never fully recovered since then."

Guilt spiked inside me for no good reason. Lin Wai had caused the Year of Loss, not me—so why did I feel partially responsible?

Henry slowed in the middle of the clearing and looked around. He started walking again before stopping once more. He started to walk forward. Stopped. Turned around.

"Uh-oh," I said.

He spun around, gwandou out. "What?"

"You're *actually* lost now, aren't you?"

He flushed. "I'm just getting a sense of my bearings."

"That sounds like lost to me." I pointed at a spot in the forest ahead where the trees parted around a tall wooden gate. "That looks like a path over there. Maybe it'll lead us to somewhere where we can hide."

"You shouldn't follow unknown paths in the Underworld," he said. "Or the Mortal Realm, for that matter."

"What other choice do we have? Ngau Tau and Ma Min are guarding the Seoi Dang River, and I don't see any other path leading out of here. You're welcome to leave."

Henry groaned. "I can't."

"I'll tell Ngau Tau and Ma Min I forced you to help me."

"No, it's not that." His face screwed up like he'd been forced to eat a whole basket of lemons. "Well, it's half the reason. But I think I'm also having . . . fun."

"Escaping from demon guardians is fun for you?" I asked, flabbergasted.

He glowered at me. "Yeah. It reminds me of my mortal life, okay? I used to run circles around ngo gwai while keeping whole villages of people safe. This is nothing for me."

He shoved his hands into his pockets but started walking towards the pathway—and it suddenly struck me that he wasn't just angry all the time. His shoulders were hunched like he was fighting his own internal ghosts. It reminded me of how tight and small I made myself when I had to show my parents an exam score I knew they would be disappointed in.

I jogged up beside him. "Do you miss that life?"

"Doesn't matter. I can't go back to it." He shrugged. "I'm dead, remember? It's only a matter of time before my offerings run out or I get reincarnated into my next life. The Underworld is only a waiting room. Time stops here. You either get out or you don't."

I waited for him to say more, but he simply continued walking through the clearing. I took a deep breath and said, "Let's see what other ghosts and demons we can find."

• • •

The farther we walked along the pathway, the more dense the clusters of huts became, until there was a clear row of houses and shops lining a straight road. We passed by a few stalls showcasing wrinkly carrots and shrivelled lo bak in straw baskets. The ghosts moped around in drab tunics and thread-worn pants, lingering outside quiet buildings. They stared as we passed. One ghost even dropped the clay jug he was holding, and it shattered on the dry ground.

"Hold on," Henry said, stopping beside a pottery stall. "Give me your hand."

"I thought you didn't want to hold my *puny mortal appendages*," I said in my best imitation of his voice.

"Don't be difficult," he grumbled, but he simply stood there, hand out, waiting for me to reach out. "I'm going to disguise your mortal signature. Everyone can tell you're a ghost hunter."

"I'm not a ghost hunter."

"Your spiritual energy says differently."

Reluctantly, I held my hand out, feeling weirdly embarrassed when he took it. He flipped my hand over so that my palm faced up. His grip was surprisingly warm. With his pointer finger, he wrote a character on the palm of my hand, his touch light against my skin.

"Don't go around smacking random ngo gwai and you'll be fine," he announced when he was done.

My hand still felt warm where he had traced his finger. "Thanks—I think."

A pink tinge spread across his cheeks. "This doesn't mean we're friends, okay?"

"Definitely not," I quickly agreed, even though my own cheeks were warm.

He nodded. "Good. Best to stay away. I don't want to get your short lifespan all over me."

We walked the rest of the street without any stares. He stopped in front of a squat wooden building. Rattan blinds covered the smattering of windows on its front. Its appearance was just as uninspiring as the rest of the town, but Henry cast a surreptitious glance over his shoulder before pulling open the wooden door and motioning me inside.

I stepped in hesitantly.

A middle-aged woman balanced atop a short, rickety ladder. Her long sleeves were tied farther up her arms with a narrow ribbon of cloth, and she was tying a yellow paper lantern to a ceiling beam. Several more lanterns were scattered around her, all in varying colours and sizes.

Without turning around, she pointed towards a narrow staircase that had a pile of stools precariously stacked beside it. "Go on up, then."

"Thanks," Henry said. "And if Ngau Tau and Ma Min show up . . ."

"Yes, yes. You were never here," the woman said, waving us away. Henry had insisted he had friends, but she didn't seem like one. Were Ngau Tau and Ma Min his friends? Thinking about someone being alone in the Underworld was awful.

We walked up the steep, dark stairs. When we reached the top, my jaw dropped.

The second floor was a restaurant. Ngo gwai clustered around tables on rickety wooden stools. Several tables had games of mahjong in progress, and the tiles clacked noisily amidst tea being poured and dishes clattering. The air was hazy with red dust, and in the dim lighting from the fabric lanterns overhead, the corners of the restaurant seemed to fade into never-ending shadows.

Henry strolled over to a table and sank onto the stool with a contented sigh.

I dove into the stool across from him and leaned forward. "You're kidding me. You want to eat? Now? While we're running from Ngau Tau and Ma Min? Is this also on the list of things you miss from your mortal life?"

"It's been a long day." There was a teapot and two cups on the side of the table. He flipped the cups over and poured yellow tea into them. "And we can hide out here. Ngau Tau and Ma Min will eventually leave. We'll stay here until they do."

He passed me a teacup, and I sniffed the steam curling up. "This tea doesn't smell like anything."

"All the food here is like that." He took a swig of his own cup. "If you get really fresh offerings, then you can almost taste the memory of them."

"How long do you think it'll take for Ngau Tau and Ma Min to leave?"

He shrugged. "Could be a day. Could be a week."

I projectile-spat out my tea. "A week?"

Henry scowled and wiped my tea off his face. "You're *disgusting*. And yes, a week. They're persistent. I once saw them interrogate a newly arrived ghost for a month because he couldn't keep his story straight about his life. They couldn't figure out which of the ten courts of the Underworld to send him to."

"I can't stay here that long." I pushed away my teacup, suddenly nauseous. "Tin Hong might do something else to my family in that time. And sorry about the tea."

"It's fine," he said gruffly. "Do you want anything to eat?"

"I'm not hungry." I rested my forehead on the table. I was the complete opposite of hungry. One of the ngo gwai at the table behind us roared with laughter and slammed a mahjong tile down. I didn't even flinch.

What was I going to do? My family was counting on me, even if they didn't know it. Their mortal lives rested on me talking to Tin Hong in time.

I needed to figure out how to get away.

"And don't even think about sneaking out some back door," Henry said after he flagged down a server and placed an order. "If you get caught by Ngau Tau and Ma Min, I'm done for. They're experts at getting information they need."

"I'd never think about sneaking away," I lied.

"Good, because I've been thinking about what you said earlier." He refilled my teacup even though I'd only taken a sip. "About Tin Hong needing your family. I can't figure

229

out why he'd call you to the Underworld. At first, I thought it was just to warn you against committing the same crime as your great-aunt, but why would he kidnap Li Gwan as well?"

"I don't even know how to make someone immortal," I insisted. "Is that common knowledge? Maybe my grandmother has the information hidden somewhere."

Henry shook his head. "Aside from Lin Wai, no one's ever been able to return a ghost to the land of the living, let alone gift them immortality. The most a ghost can do is inhabit a body, but it takes a lot of spiritual energy to stay for any length of time. I doubt your grandmother knows how. It took Lin Wai a lot of trial and error."

Unease spiked through me. "What did she do?"

"I don't know. I only know it took an enormous amount of spiritual energy to do it."

A terrible thought struck me. I leaned across the table and hissed, "That's why Michelle took Leon. Tin Hong thinks Leon knows how to give someone immortal life."

Henry tried to pour more tea into his cup, but only drops came out. He set the lid askew and pushed the teapot to the end of the table. "Even if he did, he'd never act on it. It's against—"

"The rules?" I prompted. "Maybe it's just me, but Tin Hong doesn't seem like the rule-following type. He's been sending ngo gwai after my family *and* he kidnapped Leon. I thought Ghost Lords and immortals weren't supposed to interfere with mortal life."

"They're not."

Henry and I both stared at each other.

"Lay low here," he said. "I'll wait for Ngau Tau and Ma Min to leave, and then I'll find Li Gwan. He might know more about what's going on. He's probably being kept in the dungeon beneath Lord Tin Hong's manor."

"We can't wait a week for Ngau Tau and Ma Min to leave!" I whispered frantically. "What if Tin Hong is torturing Leon for information right now?"

"He's immortal. He'll live."

My jaw dropped. "Oh, wow. I just remembered that you're a bad guy."

"I'm not a bad guy!" he protested.

"Really? Because you're sure acting like one." I shot to my feet. "I need a break. From you."

His eyes narrowed suspiciously as I stormed over to a window. Good. He could be as suspicious of me as he wanted. I'd been starting to think Henry Lam was a decent ghost, but I definitely couldn't trust him.

Glumly, I pushed aside the rattan blinds and peered down at the village below—and for just a moment, I let myself take in everything I'd tried so hard to ignore on my way to the restaurant.

This was a real village, with ghosts going about their business and living lives I knew nothing about. A cart stood in the centre of the road, filled with lanterns in dull shades of red, blue, and white. People limped up to the cart, plucking out lanterns and setting them back down.

The building across from us had several workers out front. They were lifting pieces of wood, passing them over their heads to one another. It wasn't the world I was used to, but things here were still real. Life went on, and ghosts in the Underworld needed enough offerings to tide them over until their next life.

Unless they became immortal, like Leon.

I tapped my fingers on the windowsill. Carefully, I checked over my shoulder.

Henry was still sitting at the table. His bowl of rice and plate of steamed chicken had arrived, and he was shovelling it all into his mouth like he'd skipped lunch period and was now making up for it after a long day at school. When he caught me looking, he swallowed, then chewed his next bite more slowly. Gross.

Henry was a jerk. Unfortunately, he was a jerk of many talents. Running wouldn't work when he could disappear and reappear at will. His syu fat mo outclassed mine by a painful amount. And I had no idea why his weaponry hadn't yet melded to him—he was packing more heat than a chili pepper with all its seeds.

I couldn't stop him from coming after me, but I could make it very, very hard for him to do so—because if there was one thing he couldn't do, it was create barriers so bad they kept the person in instead of keeping everyone else out.

I'd done it once before. It had been the very first barrier I'd created around myself—the one I'd made after trying to summon a ghost by whistling had gone horribly wrong. All

I had to do was re-create the barrier and hope that it held long enough for me to slip away. If I was lucky, maybe he wouldn't try anything with the restaurant as full as it was.

Experimentally, I shifted away from the window—just an inch.

Henry kept chewing.

I took another inch.

Nothing.

I started walking towards the staircase.

"I can see you, you know," Henry called around a mouthful of food.

I bolted. My feet flew down the stairs faster than I'd ever thought possible. Henry stormed down the steps behind me—and then all was silent.

I reached the bottom of the staircase and dared a look over my shoulder. Henry was nowhere in sight. Cautiously, I backed up until I hit a wall. The faded cloth lantern in the middle of the ceiling swayed gently, as if a quiet wind was passing through. Or maybe it was a noisy wind, but I couldn't hear it because of how loud my pulse was in my ears.

I pushed off the wall and sprinted towards the restaurant door. It was so close. All I had to do was push it open—

As soon as my fingers grazed the door, Henry popped out of nowhere and slammed the door shut. He had a couple of grains of rice on his cheek, and he laughed hollowly. "You wouldn't."

"You're right. I wouldn't." And as fast as I could, I jabbed out the nine strokes needed to call forth a barrier.

The familiar golden light flared out—but not around me. It shone out around Henry, enveloping him in a warm shimmer that did little to chase the shadows from his face.

His eyes narrowed sharply. "I'm not the one who needs protecting." To prove his point, he took a step forward, and then another—and he stopped. The toe of his boot rested against the thin golden wall of the barrier.

"What the Deiyuk is this?" he said, very quietly.

"A barrier," I said primly. "Never did learn to make them correctly all the time. Also, you've got rice on your cheek."

"You're an even bigger fool than I thought," he spat, flushing as he swatted the rice off his face. He reached into the pouch hanging at his waist and spun out his gwandou. It lengthened into its full form, scraping against the top of the barrier and sending little sparks of light flying.

"Well," I said. "I'm glad I surpassed your expectations."

"You're going to get caught, and then this whole journey will have been for nothing. Why can't you just wait? I told you I'd find Li Gwan."

All the hairs on the back of my neck bristled, but I shoved the restaurant door open.

"You're an embarrassment to the Wong Clan of Ghost Hunters!" he shouted.

That was it. I stomped back over to Henry and stood at the edge of the barrier, close enough that I could see the rise and fall of his chest. I wondered—not for the first time—why he pretended to breathe at all, or why he bothered to make himself seem warm.

234

His jaw squared. "Let me out of here and I won't hunt you down for the rest of your mortal life."

"I wonder what your ancestors would say if they knew you were helping a rule-breaking Ghost Lord," I said.

His mouth dropped—just slightly, just enough that I knew I'd discovered how to get under his skin—and then it clamped shut. The look he shot me could've scorched all the flowers in my grandmother's garden. But I wasn't in that garden. Not anymore.

I slammed open the door and ran out—right into Ngau Tau.

CHAPTER 22

"Oops," I said as I stared up into Ngau Tau's enormous nostrils.

"What did I tell you?" Henry yelled from behind me.

"Mortal," Ngau Tau boomed down at me. "You never told me the full spelling of your ancestor's name. Can you write it in Chinese?"

I couldn't, but that was beside the point. From around Ngau Tau's broad torso, I caught sight of Ma Min, one hand on his hip in severe disappointment. In his other hand he held his bladed polearm. Even if I tried to be quick, the two guardians would likely catch me before I got far.

"State your true business, mortal," Ma Min neighed gruffly. "Or we will return you to your realm immediately."

I glanced back at Henry. He was still stuck inside the golden glow of the barrier. And then it hit me. Henry wasn't the only one who could take me to the Ghost Lord.

"I'm here to speak with Tin Hong," I said, trying to keep my voice steady.

"Lord Tin Hong?" Ma Min made a loud rumble in his chest. "For what purpose?"

"Is this about your ancestor, Wong Wa Mui?" Ngau Tau hollered.

Ma Min stuck a finger in his ear. "Bro, please. Your inside voice."

"Oh, sorry." Ngau Tau cleared his throat, then continued almost as loudly. "I can take another look in my book—"

"I need to speak to Tin Hong directly," I said more firmly. "Can you take me to him?"

Behind me, Henry made a strangled sound, like he was choking on rice.

"Wong," he said. "That's not a good idea—"

I pointed at him. "He was taking me to Tin Hong, but we got sidetracked. You're a little intimidating with your . . ." I gestured to all of Ngau Tau, from the tips of his curved boots to the vicious horns on his head.

"Oh, thank you," Ngau Tau bellowed. Pleased, he adjusted the red kerchief tied around his neck. "I try. It's hard, you know. I'm not a morning demon."

Ma Min crossed his arms. "Is this true, Lam Kai Ming? Were you escorting her to Lord Tin Hong?"

I tensed, waiting for Henry to deny it, but before he could speak, another voice called out.

"It's true."

My skin prickled at the sound of that voice. Ngau Tau and Ma Min parted to look at the newcomer behind them.

Michelle gave them a deep bow. She was dressed in an embroidered white top and a long lilac skirt that fell to her ankles. The clothes weren't her usual hoodie and jeans, but the way she wore the frown on her face, the way she flicked her braid over her shoulder—that was all still the same. I wanted to cry and scream and hug her all at once, but I only balled my fists tight as she came up to us.

"Greetings, Ngau Tau and Ma Min," she said with a respectful bow. "I'm here to escort Tin Hong's esteemed guest to the manor of the First Court."

"Why has Lord Tin Hong summoned her to the Underworld?" Ma Min asked. "Mortals are not to step foot in this realm until their death has passed."

She gave him what was meant to be an apologetic smile, but I could see the teeth behind it. "It's a confidential matter, so I'm afraid all I can say is that Emma will be helping appease the ngo gwai who lost loved ones during the Year of Loss. If you must, you can ask the King of the Underworld, but he's entrusted this task to Lord Tin Hong. Isn't that right, Emma?"

She cranked her smile up a notch, and my heart fell. She was even worse than I thought. I'd trusted her all these years. She'd betrayed me. Sent my grandma to the hospital. How could someone be so cruel?

"That's right," I gritted out. "I'm here to help Tin Hong."

Ngau Tau let out a heavy snort of relief. "Finally! This court has been in chaos ever since the Year of Loss. I'll be happy to see all the ngo gwai here go back to their regular lives."

"We will let the King of the Underworld know you have brought the mortal to Lord Tin Hong," Ma Min said with a careful nod.

"Thank you," Michelle said sweetly. But as soon as she turned back towards me, her smile dropped. "Come on, esteemed guest. Lord Tin Hong doesn't like to be kept waiting."

"Great," I said, "because there's a *lot* I need to talk to you about."

• • •

Night fell like a splash of ink into water. One moment the town was coated in the hazy red of a setting sun and the next it was dark. It was almost as if the sky and the mountains in the distance were all part of a backdrop that was lifted and then dropped by a forgetful stagehand. The flatness of everything was unsettling—but what was worse was that Michelle wouldn't even look at me.

She hurried along as we crossed the Seoi Dang River and passed through a grove of bamboo. The woody stalks were thicker and taller than any I'd seen in the mortal world, but the leaves were dry and brown.

"You lied to me," I said once the bamboo had swallowed us.

"You don't understand anything," she said without turning around. Crumbling leaves brushed against her shoulders.

My voice grew louder. "You lied about who you *were*. You've been lying this whole time."

She tucked a lock of sleek black hair behind her ear. "No. Unlike your family, I've been trying to *help* people all this time."

"My parents and grandma haven't done anything!"

"But your ancestor did."

I halted. "I never even met my great-aunt. I don't know what she looks like. My grandma only remembers a sister that she lost." My voice cracked, but I kept going. "She never even wanted me to get involved with ghosts. She tried to keep me away from all this."

Michelle broke off a brittle bamboo branch and snapped it in half. "In the Underworld, we don't run from our responsibilities. Kai Ming's paying his debt by working for Lord Tin Hong, but your family is happily living out their lives in the Mortal Realm."

"Yeah, because they have no idea that Lin Wai ascended a ghost to immortality, and—" Realization hit me hard. "That's why Henry's working for Tin Hong? He's paying for helping my great-aunt?"

"Like your family should be." She tossed the branch to the ground and crunched it down to pieces. "The rest of us don't get to just forget what happened. You don't know what it feels like to watch your whole family waste away, Emma."

"I think I might have an idea," I said bitterly.

"You really don't." She lifted her chin, but I could see it

quivering. "You always know when a ghost starts to give up. They stop leaving their paper homes to get fake food." Her voice rose higher. "They wear their day clothes to bed, and when they wake up the next morning, they don't bother changing."

All the words I wanted to say died on my tongue.

"They forget your name, and don't sit with the rest of the family for dinner anymore, so you have to bring the offerings to their room, but it doesn't matter because Baba and Mama won't eat it anyway."

I looked at her teeth and wondered how much sorrow she'd had to feast on over the years. "You've been carrying that with you all this time?"

She angrily wiped at her eyes. "Not like you would've understood."

"You could've tried me," I said quietly. "I would've listened."

She went still. Her breaths came shallow. Abruptly, she turned around, continuing up the path again. "It's too late. If Lord Tin Hong's plan works, no ghost will ever have to waste away ever again."

Ice cascaded over me. "What does that mean?"

"Ghost hunters have significantly more spiritual energy than the average mortal. That's how Wong Lin Wai helped Cheung Li Gwan ascend to immortality. We've been waiting for another Wong descendant to have as much spiritual energy as Wong Lin Wai—and guess what?" Her face settled into coolness, and she jabbed a finger at me. "That's you."

"I don't know how to make someone immortal!" I shouted in frustration.

"I'm sure you'll figure it out." Her mouth stretched into a twisted grin. "Look how fast you learned syu fat mo."

But her voice was thick and wavered at the end, and we fell into an awkward silence. I rubbed at my eyes, but no matter how many times I wiped away the wetness there, they still stung. Talking to Michelle felt hopeless.

If I couldn't convince Michelle, I'd have to try harder at convincing Tin Hong. I held that thought in my heart as we continued walking. Eventually, the bamboo around us changed from dry and dead to verdant and vibrant. At the end of the bamboo path loomed an enormous gate, covered in a luxurious coat of black lacquer and gold accents that shone even in the hazy light.

"Calligraphy brush," she demanded, holding her hand out. "I know you have one."

My gut twisted, but I drew it out and handed it to her. As soon as it left my hands, an odd relief spread through me. If I didn't have a calligraphy brush, no one would expect me to write any syu fat mo, which knocked off one more worry from my list of things to worry about. At least I still had my great-aunt's dagger.

The spiritual energy here was thick like sap. It hummed through my body, low and insistent. Beyond the gate lay the largest manor I had ever seen. The double doors at its entrance were enormous and intimidating, with iron studs embedded into the polished wood. Elaborately carved wooden lanterns dripped from the tiled eaves, and the manor's gleaming red walls were adorned with gold-capped columns. It was beautiful in the way that white oleander flowers were, with poison that lurked beneath their pretty surface.

The two guards at the doors bowed mechanically when we approached. They were clad in matching sets of armour, with bladed polearms that flashed silver as they straightened with a strange rustling sound.

"Greetings, Chan Hei Nga," one of the guards said.

"Inform Lord Tin Hong I've arrived with Emma Wong," Not-Michelle commanded in a tone that sent chills up my back. She carried herself like this was her home.

"Certainly." He stepped aside to draw open the door, and there was that rustling again, as if his armour was stuffed with crumpled paper.

As we passed through hallways with large open windows that looked into the courtyard, I tried to plan what I'd say to Tin Hong. What the heck did you say to a Ghost Lord who was determined that your family make up for something they didn't do? *So sorry my deceased great-aunt messed up the balance of the Three Realms, but I bet you could find it in your heart to forgive her and leave my family alone.*

"Wait here while I fetch Lord Tin Hong," Michelle said.

Startled, I realized we were standing right outside a room with open latticed doors. No one was inside. I was so nervous I felt like running.

"Thanks," I said automatically.

Michelle's face went funny.

Right. We weren't friends anymore.

She hovered outside the doors like she wanted me to say something, but I kept my mouth closed. Finally, she drew the doors closed and I heard the sound of a lock click into place.

A tapestry stretched across the entire length of the wall, lustrous with an intricate scene of long-tailed peacocks amongst flourishes of peonies. Two high-backed chairs were placed in the middle of the room. They were covered in gilded carvings from arm to leg. There was more gold in the room than any other place I'd seen in my life. It was stunning. A speck of history, captured in a single glimmering room.

It didn't look like Tin Hong was suffering with the rest of the ngo gwai. In fact, he looked pretty well off.

I clamped my jaw tight as the doors swung open and a man stepped into the room. He looked old and young at the same time. His face was oddly smooth. His black hair was neatly parted on the side, and his eyes were calculating as they swept around the room before landing on me. Sweat beaded along my temple. The folds of his black brocade creased around him as he nestled into one of the chairs with lithe movements. I was terrified—his spiritual energy engulfed me in crashing waves.

Tin Hong, Ghost Lord of the Underworld.

"Welcome," he said, his voice like deep water, heavy and hollow all at once. It sank into me, weighing me down until I couldn't breathe. He rested his pale hands on the ends of the armrests. His tight-lipped smile didn't reach his eyes. "You have come a long way to see me."

My breath flooded back into my lungs. I drew myself up as best I could. He was right—I'd come all this way. I'd had a plan to talk to him reasonably. Negotiate something. But now that he was in front of me, all those plans flew away.

"Let Leon go," I said, my voice wavering. "And whatever you've done to my grandma—undo it."

He quirked an elegant eyebrow. "You're quite demanding for a mortal."

My fear gave way to anger. He was mocking me, treating me like I was no more than a weed he'd discovered in his garden. But I was more than that. I reached out for his spiritual energy. It was thicker than a tree trunk and more tightly wound than a ship's rope. As soon as I tried to dig into it, he was on the other side of the room. I felt his energy vanish from my grasp.

"I knew I hadn't made the wrong choice," he said, pleased. His smile was a hungry, greedy twist of the mouth. "You have just as much spiritual energy as Wong Lin Wai."

"I don't know how to make someone immortal," I ground out as I reached for his spiritual energy again. But this time, he whipped a calligraphy brush from inside his billowing sleeves and slashed out a character. A wave of fire encircled me, so tall I could only see his head. I stumbled back, only to be met with fire behind me as well.

"Alas," he lamented, "you do not have Lin Wai's training. But that's acceptable. I have been conducting my own research into what separates ghosts from those selfish immortals in the Upper Realm. I believe I can imitate what your ancestor did." He adjusted his black sleeves so they hung down. He was a narrow man and the thick brocade made him look like a skeleton wrapped in a shroud. "Besides, if you won't help me, there is always your grandmother."

My blood froze even as the heat from the fire around me licked at my face. "Don't you dare touch her."

He narrowed his eyes as he looked down at me from above the flames. "What will you give me in return for her safety?"

I swallowed. "I'll help you make someone immortal."

He nodded in satisfaction, but before he could say anything else, I continued. "But you have to leave the rest of my family alone. Forever. No more ngo gwai. No more curses."

He fell silent. Unlike Henry, he had an excellent poker face. My stomach turned when he scrawled out another character. The fire around me vanished.

"Then we have an agreement," he said smoothly. "You will stay here in the Underworld until I understand how to make a ghost immortal. The Ghost Festival will soon be upon us."

I shivered. The Ghost Festival was still three days away. There was no way I'd stay in the Underworld for that long. "I'll help you now."

"You will assist me when I tell you to," he said. He wrote out a silver character to the side, and the doors to the room opened. Much to my dismay, Michelle stepped in.

"Take Miss Wong to the dungeons," Tin Hong ordered her. "And find Kai Ming." My stomach dropped as his mouth sharpened cruelly. "I want a word with him."

CHAPTER 23

The dungeons were several dizzying flights of stairs beneath the surface. The deeper we went, the more musty the air became, until it felt like I was breathing in the dry earth itself. Michelle moved down the stairs quickly, as if she was eager to be rid of me—which was good, because if I had to look at her face again, I was going to liberally prune *something*. Like her hair. Or Tin Hong's robes. Or both of them, preferably together.

"You know, if you and Tin Hong just wanted me to help you make someone immortal, you could've asked," I said bitingly.

"We did," Michelle scoffed. "Remember Henry?"

I made a face at her. "All he said was that he needed me to go to the Underworld. He didn't explain why."

"Henry is more awkward than the recently dead. Also, don't pretend like that would've made a difference." She narrowed her eyes at me in judgment. "All you ghost hunters are the same. You don't trust ghosts, so we don't trust you. All you want to do is get rid of us. You forget we were once people."

"Just like you have?"

She whirled around. "Your family started this!"

"At least I didn't lie and pretend to be someone I wasn't for years!"

"I'm trying to help the ghosts here from losing more than they already have," she shouted. "You're one small, insignificant mortal. What you want doesn't matter!"

My face burned, but I forced my voice to remain steady. "You know what? I wish you'd stayed dead. Everyone would have been better off without you."

Her mouth dropped open. Immediately, horror washed over me, but I couldn't take back what I'd said. She whipped out a calligraphy brush from her sleeve—my calligraphy brush, the one Leon had leant me. The ink-stained tip wavered as she pointed it at me. We stood there, chests heaving. I felt sick. Of her. Myself.

"Michelle—"

"Shut up."

She scrawled something in the air before her. Each stroke glimmered silver before the character vanished altogether. A coldness slipped down my throat. I opened my mouth to say something, but nothing came out.

Michelle sighed. "That's better."

She'd *muted* me. Flustered, I sniffed. The quiet sound was almost immediately swallowed up by the compacted dirt walls, and Michelle turned away. Fine. I didn't need to talk to someone who'd betrayed me. That's what I told myself, anyway, as we descended a final flight of stairs. But deep down, I

MISADVENTURES IN GHOSTHUNTING

wished I could have taken back what I'd said. Despite every-thing she'd done, the hurt that had flashed across her eyes made me feel even worse.

Except she wasn't my friend. Friends didn't stop each other from saying what they wanted to say.

A mess of emotions swirled inside me. I couldn't afford to be sad. I didn't have any time to cry. Instead, I felt angry. It simmered inside me and I latched on to it. Being angry meant I was right. A dark corridor stretched out in front of us, lit by a wooden lantern at the end. Two guards stood on either side of a plain wooden door. They bowed as we approached.

"Open the door," Michelle said while I stared daggers at the back of her head.

One of the guards unhooked a large key from his belt and opened the door. Every time he moved, he made the same strange rustling sound as the guard at the manor entrance. He stared straight ahead, his gaze fixed on nothing, as we went inside.

My anger quickly gave way to dread as I faced the row of cells. A single lantern hung above the door, casting a weak yellow glow that reached only half the cells. Most of the cells were empty, except for one at the very end. For a moment, I thought about tackling Michelle and grabbing my callig-raphy brush. Lin Wai's dagger was heavy in my pocket. I could threaten her with it. Make my escape.

But as we approached the last cell, my stomach fell. An elderly woman with permed grey hair and a floral blouse lay curled in the corner of the cell. I tried to cry out, but my voice wouldn't work. Michelle unlocked the cell beside her and I stumbled in, desperate to get a closer look at the woman through the bars that separated us. She rolled over, and my head spun.

Mah Mah.

"She's fine," Michelle said, not meeting my eyes. She flicked her calligraphy brush, and I let out a gasp as warmth spread through my throat.

"Tin Hong promised to leave my grandmother alone," I said, voice shaking.

She shrugged. "She was already here. Lord Tin Hong will keep his end of the bargain as long as you keep yours."

"You're all liars—"

Abruptly, she left, closing the dungeon door behind her with a loud thud. As soon as she was gone, Mah Mah sat up wearily.

"I never expected your friend to be a ghost," she said sadly in Cantonese. "I should have been more careful."

"Why are you here?" I cried, clutching the cold iron bars. "How did you get here from the hospital?"

"Aiya, is that where my body is?" She threaded a hand through the bars and brushed away a spot of wetness beneath my eye. "Something is preventing me from returning to it."

"Your body?" I echoed. In a panic, I reached out to feel for her spiritual energy—only to pull back in surprise. Her energy was more a rope than a string, and unlike a ghost's, it was bright red. Relief flooded me when I felt the strength of it, binding her to her mortal life. It was thick and alive and ran deeper than I could reach.

"Mom and Dad are looking after you," I said, my voice thick.

"Good," she sighed. "I hope they remember to massage my feet."

Her arms wrapped around my back and she gave me an awkward half-pat. I buried my face into her shoulder as best I could with those stupid bars between us, breathing in the scent of laundry warmed by the sun and medicinal herbs. Her curls were so soft against my forehead.

"The ngo gwai got you," I said miserably, unwrapping my arms from around her.

Mah Mah chuckled softly and sat back. "Ai, my sister always made the best enemies."

I tucked my hands under my legs and glumly observed the four walls around us. "Have you tried to leave?"

"Yes." She spread open her hands, palms up. "These hands aren't as strong as they used to be, and I don't have a calligraphy brush to help channel my spiritual energy. Do you?"

"No," I said, then hesitated. "But I do have this."

I reached into my coat pocket and withdrew the dagger. The iron sheath looked even darker beneath the dim light. It had felt comforting to hold before, but now I wanted to get rid of it.

"My sister's dagger," Mah Mah said with a gasp.

"Take it," I said, holding it out. If I didn't have it, I couldn't use it on a ngo gwai.

She shook her head, and pushed it gently back towards me. "Keep it. It will help you more than me."

"I can't use it," I whispered.

Mah Mah's face softened in understanding. "A ghost hunter must do their part to maintain the balance between the Three Realms. If a ghost tries to harm mortal life, it's our duty to vanquish them."

I ran my thumb along the ridges of the hilt. "I'm not a ghost hunter." When Mah Mah fixed me with a level gaze, I slipped the dagger back into my pocket. "I didn't even know my best friend was a ngo gwai. I let her hurt you."

She studied me for a long moment. "You don't want to be a ghost hunter."

"No," I said honestly. As soon as the word left my mouth, I felt lighter. "You said you wanted to leave that life behind. I don't want to bring it back. I just want to keep our family safe, but I can't even write syu fat mo properly. What am I going to do with a ghost hunter weapon?"

She placed one hand on her knee and straightened to standing with a grunt. "When you young, I always try teach you how to write," she said, switching to English. "Number. Your name."

"I remember," I said with a wince. "I wasn't a very good student."

"It's too bad you can't write." She tried writing a character in the space before her, even though she didn't have a calligraphy brush. "My English not good, too."

"Your English is great, Mah Mah." With a sinking heart,

I watched as she tried yet another character. "Besides, you're good at other things. You taught me everything I know about plants. You don't need to be good at everything."

"Yes. No need to."

She tried writing one more character. Nothing happened. When I looked up again, Mah Mah's lower lip was quivering.

"I'm sorry," she said.

Guilt cut through me. "You don't need to be sorry, Mah Mah."

"No." She reached out through the bars. I thought she was going to pat my hand like always, but this time she didn't. Her hand wrapped around mine, encircling it, warm and comforting. "It was better to teach you. At the beginning."

My vision blurred.

I'd never heard Mah Mah apologize, and hearing it now . . . her words felt like spring seedlings. Maybe there was something to regret, just enough of it, that it pushed people forward. Encouraged them to do the right thing. Regret was making mistakes—and surviving them.

"I would've liked that." I sniffled. It was gross, and maybe I shouldn't have been crying so hard in the dank cell of a Ghost Lord's extravagant manor when I could've been plotting an escape plan instead, but I was done with behaving in ways everyone expected me to.

"It's not too late," she said with a toothy grin. "After we leave, I'll spend more time teaching you how to write Chinese."

I stifled a groan. "Thanks, Mah Mah."

She held out her hand. "I couldn't protect you before, but I can now. Give me the dagger, and I'll show you what a ghost hunter can do with a proper weapon."

Gratefully, I passed her the sheathed dagger—just as the dungeon door swung open. With a quick hand, she slipped the dagger beneath the waistband of her pants right before the guards marched in. I scrambled to the front of my cell when I saw the boy hanging limp between them.

"Leon!" I cried.

The guards didn't acknowledge me as they unlocked the cell closest to the door and threw him in. As soon as they locked the dungeon door again, I called out desperately, "Are you okay?"

Leon sat cross-legged and hunched over. His peacoat was ragged and torn, and his shoes were unlaced. For a long moment, I thought he hadn't heard me, but then he raised his head. Darkness lined his eyes. He looked defeated.

"Emma," he said tiredly, his gaze trained on the ground. "I tried. I really did. I just want you to know that."

My stomach dropped. "What happened?"

"I failed to keep you safe," he muttered. "That is what happened. Tin Hong cannot be negotiated with."

I hated how dead he looked. "None of this is your fault."

"I promised Lin Wai I'd keep her family safe. They took away my calligraphy brush, and I cannot do syu fat mo without it. We are stuck—"

"Leon."

"—now Tin Hong will sacrifice you to gain immortal life the same way Lin Wai gave me immortal life—"

"*Leon.*"

"—it will be soon," he continued muttering feverishly, "but when? How can I find out and stop him? First, I need to return you to the Mortal Realm—"

"Gwang Sam?" Mah Mah called out behind me.

At the sound of her voice, he looked up—and he froze.

"Lin Mui?" he asked hoarsely.

Mah Mah stood up. Her eyes were wide. She clutched the bars of her cell and spoke in Cantonese. "It is you. But you . . ."

"Died," he returned in Cantonese. His voice was softer and more melodious than when he spoke English. He tried to summon up a smile, but it only made him look more upset. "Your sister came to the Underworld and gave me immortal life."

Her knuckles went white as her grip tightened. Tentatively, she asked, "Is she immortal too?"

The silence stretched out as we waited for Leon's answer. It hurt to see the cautious hope in Mah Mah's expression, but I knew she needed to hear what Leon had to say.

"I'm sorry," he said, so quietly I almost didn't hear him. He dropped his head into his hands, and Mah Mah let go of the bars. She took a shuddering breath, but it wasn't sad, like I'd been expecting. There was a finality to it. Her grief faded into the rouge of her cheeks, the white in her hair. A part of her, but not a scar.

"There's nothing to be sorry about," she said. "It's good to see you again, Go Go."

His face crumpled. "I do not deserve you calling me older brother. You are both here in the Underworld. We must find a way to return you to the Mortal Realm as soon as possible."

"I can't," I said. "I promised Tin Hong I'd help him ascend a ghost to immortality."

Leon removed his hands from his face, revealing his ashen expression. "No."

I tried not to look at Mah Mah. "He threatened to use other people instead."

He lurched to his feet. "Lin Wai gave her spiritual energy to help ascend me to immortality."

"I know."

"*All* of her spiritual energy."

His eyes met mine, and I flinched when I realized what he meant. Lin Wai had died to give Leon immortal life. Mah Mah stared at us in worry, but she couldn't understand everything we were saying. If I didn't help Tin Hong, then he was going to go after her. He would use her in my place. If we could at least return her soul to the Mortal Realm, then I could figure out how to get around the promise I'd made to Tin Hong.

"Is Bo Liang able to help us?" I asked hopefully, remembering how fondly she'd spoken of my grandmother's family. "She held some sort of important position on the immortal council, right?"

Leon shook his head. "She has her own business to take care of, and she will not enter the Underworld unless she is forced to. She has . . . a history here."

An idea hit me. "When the guards return, we can promise them immortal life if they let us out."

Even from across the dungeon, I could feel the scandalized indignation radiating from Leon. "We cannot give everyone immortal life. It is impossible, and even if it was not, it would—"

"—destroy the balance of the Three Realms," I finished for him. "But they won't know it's impossible."

He shook his head. "It does not matter. The guards are paper guards. They only obey the commands of whoever crafted them. And who would defy a Ghost Lord?"

Well, no one. No one in their right mind, anyway. I was starting to understand just how much power a Ghost Lord wielded, how pointless it was to try to negotiate with one. I'd been trying to make the ngo gwai live in my world when they'd never left theirs. I couldn't force them to listen to a mortal.

"Then we don't bribe the ngo gwai," I said. "We make them more scared of us than they are of Tin Hong."

CHAPTER 24

Hours passed before the dungeon door finally opened again. A ngo gwai stepped inside, clothed in the turquoise garb of the manor servants. He was carrying a lacquered tray. On it were three steaming cups, small enough to fit in the palm of my hand. Mah Mah's gaze met mine, and she gave a tiny nod. Carefully, I shifted over to the cell wall I shared with Mah Mah.

"Tea," the servant said, passing a cup through the bars to Leon. When he approached my cell, Mah Mah clicked her tongue in disapproval.

"What kind of tea is this?" she asked in Cantonese.

The servant reared back, startled. "I . . . I don't know. Bou lei?"

She gave him a disappointed look. "Aiya, how can you not know what tea you're serving your guests?"

"Guests?" the servant said nervously.

"Yes, *guests*," Leon said from inside his cell, and I had to do a double take because he didn't sound like the Leon I knew. He sat imperiously straight, as if this dingy little dungeon was his palace. "Perhaps Lord Tin Hong did not inform you, but I have been sent from the Upper Realm to inspect the treatment of the ngo gwai here. Why do you not know what tea you are serving? How are your guests to know it is not poisoned?"

The servant cleared his throat. "Ah, yes. You see, I'm new here, and—"

"Give me the tea," I instructed, my voice more steady than the rapid pulse in my ears. "I'll check what it is before you give it to my grandmother."

"Of course," he said with a formal nod. Just like he had with Leon, he reached between the bars of my cell to hold the cup of tea out to me—and as soon as he did, I latched on to his arm with all my strength and tugged him forward.

"Now!" I cried out as he slammed into the bars.

Mah Mah unsheathed the dagger. In a flash, she had it placed against the servant's neck. The silver of the blade shone even in the dim light of the lantern above the dungeon door. The light flickered when the door shot open and the two guards outside stormed in. One of them aimed their polearm at us. I gulped nervously.

"Release him!" one of them shouted.

"Open our cells," Leon said calmly. "Please."

The guards rustled as they marched forward—and my pulse sped up when I realized their weapons weren't pointed at Mah Mah but at the servant.

"Um, we're the bad guys," I said, pulling on the servant's arm as a reminder. "Remember?"

"They're the bad guys!" the servant squealed in terror from beneath my hold. "Get this dagger away from me! There's a fresh offering of loquats and chicken I need to unload into the kitchens!"

"We are under strict orders to not allow any of the prisoners out of the cells," the guard stated. "No matter what happens." He advanced, his blade still pointed towards the servant. "You can give the servant the final death."

Oh, shoot. My grip tightened as Mah Mah warily watched the guards crowd in front of our cells, her dagger still pressed against the servant's throat. A choked sob escaped from the servant. I could feel him shaking beneath my grip—and I let him go right as Mah Mah lowered her dagger.

"Never mind," I said peevishly. "I forgot that dying apparently means nothing in the Underworld."

"Dying means everything here," the guard said—and he moved forward and sank the blade of his weapon into the servant's chest. The servant groaned and keeled over, his hand to his chest.

I scrambled to my feet. "Why did you do that? I released him!"

"We were also instructed to not listen to any bargains or threats," the other guard said. "You have nothing to use against us."

Beside him, his partner jolted—and folded forward. A dagger jutted out of his side. Mah Mah had her hands wrapped around the hilt.

"Did you just shank a ghost? Again?" I asked her.

She yanked out the dagger she'd plunged into him. She wore a fiery anger on her face. Any hope of quietly escaping the dungeon disappeared as the guard's body faded away into a swirl of dust. "Nooo," I moaned in despair.

"Watch out!" Leon shouted.

The remaining guard drew his polearm back, but I grabbed on to the string of his spiritual energy. It was a narrow, colourless string, and the energy in it felt stale and lifeless. I drew it towards me. But the guard didn't stop, his blade shooting forward towards Mah Mah. I had no choice. I squeezed my eyes shut and dragged his spiritual energy into myself.

I opened my eyes in time to catch his body vanishing into dust. Sickness rolled through me.

Mah Mah stared at me in horror. "What did you do?"

"I . . . I took the ghost's spiritual energy."

"Inside yourself?" Leon asked from his cell.

"Yeah." I willed my stomach to settle, but it only churned more vigorously. "I've done it before. It's okay. Really."

Leon paled. "You cannot take another's spiritual energy. It is exhibited."

"I know about the risks," I said, still ill. "And I think you mean prohibited."

"Ghost hunters do not take spiritual energy that is not their own!" Mah Mah said.

"I'm not a ghost hunter," I protested. "And the ngo gwai was going to attack you!"

"Mou so wai," Mah Mah retorted. "Our family are ghost hunters. Stealing energy is what ngo gwai do."

"It does matter! Why does no one seem to care about all the good things I try to do?"

Her face fell, and she spoke rapidly in Cantonese. I could pick out bits of what she was saying, but I couldn't understand most of it, and my frustration grew.

Leon cleared his throat. "She is saying that you need to be more careful."

"Great," I said, fuming. "I'll be sure to be more careful once we get out of the Underworld." *If* we could even leave Tin Hong's manor. The heat drained from me. "The guards had the keys."

Mah Mah pressed her lips together. She drew out a ring of keys from behind her and passed it to me silently.

"Thanks," I said stiffly.

I ran through the keys until I found the one that unlocked my cell. I stepped over the servant, still slumped against the bars, and unlocked Mah Mah's cell, then Leon's. We crept over to the doorway and peered out. The dark corridor leading up to the staircase was empty.

"We need to move fast," Leon said. "The servant has been missing for a while. Someone will eventually look for him."

I followed Leon and Mah Mah through the dungeon door, but then I looked back. The servant was still slumped against the cell bars, his forehead pinched in pain. I couldn't trust ngo gwai, but . . .

You forget we were once people.

I darted back over to him. "Can you sit up?"

"No," he moaned. "My spiritual energy . . . disappearing . . ."

I crouched down. He was going to become dust unless I did something. "We need to help him."

Mah Mah bent down beside me. "We need to leave, Ah Ling. They find us soon."

I looked back at the doorway. "We have time. Can you help me carry him?"

Leon ran an anxious hand through his hair. "If we take him to someone, they will capture us again."

"We could leave him somewhere upstairs where he'll be found," I said.

Mah Mah shook her head. "He not live so long."

"Still . . . here . . ." the servant moaned on the ground. "Listening to you . . . talk about me like . . . I'm not here . . . while the loquats and chicken go *stale* . . ."

"Sorry," I said miserably. "We shouldn't have gotten you involved."

I dropped to my knees and felt for the servant's string of spiritual energy. It was thin enough to break, as pale as a wisp of steam. Inside me, the spiritual energy I'd taken from the guard swirled.

"If I can take spiritual energy, can I give it?" I asked.

Leon shook his head, his dark eyes wide. "You can't."

"I can't—or I shouldn't?"

Mah Mah laid her hand firmly on my arm. "No."

I met her concerned gaze and realization hit me: she was worried about me. She always had been. "I have to, Mah Mah," I said. "Someone innocent is going to die because of us. It doesn't matter that he's a ngo gwai. He's still living."

I closed my eyes. Darkness settled in around me. All I could see was the ngo gwai's string of spiritual energy. Instead of pulling it towards me the way I usually did, I latched on and tried to push. Nothing happened. I squeezed my eyes shut tighter and tried again. What if it didn't work? The spiritual energy I'd taken from the guard roiled unpleasantly through me. What if we *were* the bad guys?

I was about to give up and open my eyes again when I felt someone else join me. The string of their spiritual energy was strong and thick and red with mortal life, and I realized it was Mah Mah.

"This way," she murmured. Her spiritual energy twined along mine and pushed into the ngo gwai. He gasped and my eyes shot open. The ngo gwai was already on his feet.

With his mouth agape, he patted his body like it was brand new. "What's in that stuff? I haven't felt this alive in decades!"

"Uh, good ol' mortal energy?" I ventured.

Leon cleared his throat. "You two may have given him too much. He will be . . . extra lively for the next while."

I took Mah Mah's hand in mine. "Thank you. For trusting me."

"It was the right choice to make," she said softly in Cantonese.

She was looking at me as if noticing something she'd never seen before. Self-consciously, I smoothed down my hair, but all she did was give me a gentle pat on the shoulder.

"Zau lo," she said, nodding towards the door.

"Wait!" the servant cried. "If you head straight up the stairs to the ground floor, the guards posted at the entry will catch you."

"So where do we go?" Leon asked hesitantly.

"Take the second door to the west once you go up the first flight of stairs. There will be a hallway through it that only the servants use. It'll take you to a door that leads out to the side courtyard."

"There are no guards there?" Leon asked.

"Oh, certainly not," he said with a wave of his hand. "That's where all the servants here go to relax during their breaks *because* there aren't any guards. I never did like those paper guards. Just because they don't eat offerings, they don't care about preserving the freshest flavours from the offerings. It's not every day that we get loquats."

Mah Mah clicked her tongue. I tensed, waiting for her to say we couldn't trust a ngo gwai. But to my surprise, a small smile crossed her face.

"Do ze," she said gratefully.

"Thank *you*," the servant said. "Although I wouldn't have almost died if it wasn't for you—"

Mah Mah glowered at him, and Leon let out a nervous chuckle.

"Let us go forth, Mui Mui." Leon grabbed her by the

shoulders and steered her out of the dungeon before she could do anything. "Or do I call you Po Po?"

"You're still older," she said, looking rather pleased with the question. "Mui Mui is fine."

We climbed the stairs. When we reached the first landing, I looked up. The stairs continued upwards, but just as the servant had said, there were several doors to both the east and west of the landing. We crept to the west side towards the servants' hallway, passing a display of leafy paper vegetables clustered around a realistic piece of pork belly folded from hundreds of tiny pieces of paper that slotted into each other. Leon carefully pressed his ear against the second door before pulling it open.

We moved into a long, narrow hallway. It was eerily quiet. Just when I was beginning to think we were really going to make it out of Tin Hong's manor without bumping into anyone else, we rounded the corner—and ran straight into Henry Lam.

CHAPTER 25

For a moment, I almost mistook him for a guard. He'd replaced his hooded jacket with a cross-collared black robe that fell just below his knees. Below his medallion-studded belt, the bottom of his robes flared out in wide, pressed pleats. The hem was decorated in embroidered dragons that snaked through swirls of red-and-blue clouds. Suddenly, his boots with the pointed toes and thick white soles made a lot more aesthetic sense.

He crossed his arms. The leather bracers around his wrists gleamed in the light of the wooden lantern hanging above him. It almost seemed like he was weirdly happy to see me—and without thinking, I started smiling back. A shadow fell across his face, and he snarled, "*You*."

"What are you doing here?" I complained, taken aback by the malice in his voice. He hadn't sounded nearly as murdery back at the restaurant in the village of ngo gwai.

He scowled, but it lacked the punch it usually had. "You mean why am I here when you trapped me in that reversed barrier of yours? Real funny. Ngau Tau and Ma Min didn't stop laughing for an hour before releasing me."

I glared at him. "Don't be melodramatic."

"I'm not," he gritted out. "When you've got literally all the time in the world, laughing for an hour at someone's misfortune could be the highlight of your day."

"Let us pass, Henry," Leon said in a low tone. He was standing in front of my grandma, his stance protective.

Henry's expression turned flinty. "I can't." He drew out his gwandou, and as its tasselled blade stretched to the ceiling, my stomach flipped.

"You promised to help me in exchange for a year of offerings," I said. "You're not going to get any siu yuk or pomelos if you stop us from leaving."

"Things have changed," he said frostily.

I backed up until I was beside Leon. I caught sight of Mah Mah drawing her dagger. Unfortunately, Henry noticed too. His gaze flicked to it for a moment before he passed his gwandou to his other hand. "Lord Tin Hong has given me another chance to complete my contract. If I break it, he'll come after me."

"What about the other Ghost Lords?" I tried, not liking the resignation in his voice. "There are nine others, right? Tell them what Tin Hong is doing."

He thumped his gwandou on the wooden floor with an angry thud. "You think that sei lou gwai will let me skip around to all the Ghost Lords in the Underworld? He has

268

ngo gwai watching me. If I stick a toe out of the manor grounds, he'll know."

Mah Mah nudged me. "Move, Ah Ling."

I didn't budge. She wanted to fight Henry, but she didn't know what she was getting into. Leon had no calligraphy brush. I still felt sick from the transfer of spiritual energy I had done earlier. But more than everything else, I didn't *want* to fight Henry. The truth of it hit me hard. He was a snarky jerk, but he'd helped me several times.

Henry glared in Mah Mah's direction. "You're Lin Wai's sister? Shouldn't you be taller or something?"

I took everything nice I'd ever thought about him back. "Watch your mouth, Ghost Boy," I warned. "That's my grandma you're talking to, and she could whup your butt in a second."

He snorted. "As if Po Po's creaky joints will even work—"

The dagger whizzed by Henry's face. It landed with a *thunk* in the door behind him. A few shorn strands of his hair drifted to the ground.

"Aiya, your hair too long," Mah Mah said pleasantly. "I help you cut, okay ah?"

Henry looked flabbergasted. He raised his gwandou and Leon tackled him. They both fell to the ground, and I took my chance. I sprinted to the wall and yanked the dagger out. When I spun around again, I froze.

A dozen guards marched down the hall towards us. Some of them held the same bladed polearms as the guards in the dungeon, while others drew back bows with notched arrows.

"Run!" Leon shouted, shoving Henry back.

Mah Mah grabbed on to me. We pulled open the door—and an arrow flew into it, slamming it shut again.

"Mah Mah, behind you!" I shrieked, but it was too late. A guard grabbed hold of her, yanking her up by the arm. He started to drag her back down the hall. Quickly, I closed my eyes, searching for the guard's string of spiritual energy, but there were too many—I didn't know which one belonged to the guard that had my grandmother. I tried tugging on one and opened my eyes again. The guard that Leon had been fighting was sprawled out on the ground, but Mah Mah was still getting dragged away.

"They've got my grandma!" I cried.

Right on cue, Henry spun out his gwandou and swept it clean through the three guards around her, including the one dragging her away. His eyes widened when they all faded to dust, and he cursed. "Why did you have to yell that? Tin Hong is going to think I've betrayed him."

"It's not like I forced you to help her!" I dashed over and wrapped my arm around Mah Mah's back, supporting her with my shoulder. "Are you okay?"

"Mm sai geng," she said as she shakily got to her feet.

Leon rushed over to us and hoisted her up onto his back, piggyback style. "We must leave before more guards come."

He ran out the door with Mah Mah on his back. I followed him, only to be cut off when Henry appeared in front of me. He slammed the door shut.

"Where do you think you're going?" he said coldly.

"You don't really want to do this," I said. I could hear Leon pounding on the door and shouting on the other side.

Henry slashed out a character with his calligraphy brush and all the guards stopped behind us. His jaw tensed. "Don't pretend like you know what I want."

I forced myself to meet his glare. I had every reason not to trust Henry Lam. In fact, he was probably the worst person I could trust. He wasn't a good person—but he wasn't exactly a bad person either. He just made bad decisions. I'd made plenty of them. I knew what it was like to want to run until there was nothing left to run from.

"What do you want, Henry?" I asked. "Do you want to keep working for Tin Hong?"

"I'm a ghost hunter. It's my duty to help maintain the balance between the Three Realms by eliminating ngo gwai that cause trouble."

I was quiet for a moment before I said, "That sounds like something you have to do. Not what you want."

He let out an exasperated groan. "It's the same thing."

"No, it's not."

"Yes, it *is*."

"It's not," I said. "If you feel like you have to do something, but you don't like what you're doing, then that's not something you want. Like me doing math tests—I hate doing them, but I have to do them in order to pass the class. I think you don't want to help Tin Hong. I bet you hate hunting ngo gwai on his behalf, doing his dirty work. It makes you feel like you're not really a ghost hunter anymore." I lifted my chin. "Or maybe I'm just pretending to know what you want, and all of this is wrong."

His eyes flickered with an emotion I couldn't read. His throat bobbed. He raised his gwandou and I suddenly remembered that I hadn't watered the monstera in my room for two weeks. I was going to die, and so were my plants. My parents would never remember to water them.

He vanished.

Guttural cries echoed out behind me. I turned around to see Henry cutting through the guards like they were made of the custard inside sweet egg tarts. Fascinated, I watched as he took out the last four guards with a single swipe of his weapon. He always wore a serious expression when he was fighting, like he was focused on nothing else. I shuddered.

"What's wrong?" Henry asked as he appeared beside me again. "Are you hurt somewhere?"

"I must be. For a second there, you almost looked cool." I cleared my throat to calm the weird fluttering in my stomach. "You're really extra. You know that, right?"

"I hate you," he said, but his tone was one of admiration. My face flushed with warmth. Bodies did weird things when you thought you were about to die.

"Help us and I'll give you enough offerings to last a lifetime," I bargained.

He stood his gwandou up. "Make it two lifetimes and it's a deal."

I squinted at him. "I can tell my family to make it a tradition, but I don't know if they'll pass it down."

"Tin ah, did you forget where you are?" he groused. "What do you think all the ghosts are doing down here in the Underworld? Lying around like corpses? Haunt your descendants and get them to offer you double offerings to share with me."

"Yeah, I'm still not promising you that. Then I'd have to share my offerings with you forever."

"It's not forever!" he complained, like I'd personally offended him somehow. "It's only until one of us gets reincarnated. I'm pretty sure I only have about 214 more years to work off until I get to drink from Mang Po's soup of forgetfulness so I can reincarnate without the annoyances of my previous life, like memories of you."

I gritted my teeth and wrenched open the door. Leon had set Mah Mah back on the ground. Both of them perked up as soon as I stepped out into the side courtyard. They were surrounded by trees with jade-green leaves and ivory flowers, and a sudden pang of homesickness struck me.

"Are they all gone?" Leon asked in a rush.

I jerked my thumb back at Henry. "There's one more."

"Wait!" he said. "I'll help you."

I crossed my arms. "I don't trust you."

"I think you can," Mah Mah said, walking up to us. "He comes from a good ghost hunter family. I can tell."

Henry flushed pink, looking exactly how I imagined I did whenever my parents gave me an unexpected compliment. "You're just saying that."

She waved Lin Wai's sheathed dagger—the dagger that I was supposed to be carrying. "He didn't take this when he easily could have. It was right behind him in the door."

"When did you take that off me?" I asked in disbelief.

She clicked her tongue. "When we go home, I am training you. Not to be a ghost hunter—just to be more aware of your surroundings." She faced Henry. "Like this boy. Your parents taught you well."

"You're right." He looked off to the side. His gwandou shrank back into its short form. "They did."

Leon extended his hand to Henry. "Armistice?"

Henry made a face, but accepted his handshake. "What?"

"I think he means truce," I volunteered.

Leon raised his pointer finger. "Actually, I did mean armistice. An armistice is a synonym for truce, and is a temporary cessation of fighting in order to come to a collective agreement. I read all about it in an English mortal dictionary."

Henry yanked his hand away. "Why did Lin Wai save you again?"

Leon's smile dropped. "That is a good question, but one better saved for another time. We need to return Emma and her grandmother back to the Mortal Realm."

"How do we get back?" I asked.

"There will be boats docked at a town near the Seoi Dang River."

"Samlin Town?" Henry asked.

Leon inclined his head in agreement. "It is the closest."

Henry's face shuttered. "You're right. Let's get going, then."

I gave Henry a questioning look, but he marched past me and followed the path that ran to the outside of the courtyard. Leon bent down, and my grandmother hopped onto his back again. I gave the manor one last look before I followed them. I had to remember how to return to this place, because once Mah Mah was back in the Mortal Realm, I needed to return to keep my deal with Tin Hong. He wouldn't hurt any of my family ever again.

CHAPTER 26

We left Tin Hong's manor and crept along the edge of a pine forest that led us west. The cold light of the moon gave the trees a spectral glow. The rich green of the trees faded the farther we travelled from the manor as if the colour was getting leached away. I kept sneaking glances over my shoulder, expecting to see more manor guards following us. But none appeared, and after an hour of walking, we finally snuck into the back of Samlin Town.

"Stick to the less crowded areas, and duck your head if any ghosts approach you," Leon whispered. He poked his head out around the side of a building. "We should try not to attract attention so close to Tin Hong's manor. The guards will be searching this place soon."

"Where are the boats?" I whispered back, looking out around the building as well. The street was empty, but it didn't lift the unease I was feeling. It felt like we were being watched. I didn't have a good sense of time in the Underworld, but the moon had been up in the sky since we'd left the manor. Once daylight came, there would be nowhere for us to easily hide.

Leon adjusted his hold on my grandmother, hoisting her higher onto his back. "We have to cross the town to get to the docks down at Seoi Dang River."

"Let me down," Mah Mah told him in Cantonese.

"I am not sure that is a good idea," he said hesitantly.

She slapped her thigh. "I don't look as young as you, but my legs still work fine."

Worried, I watched as he lowered her to the ground. But when she took a few steps towards me, her knees buckled and she nearly fell.

"Mah Mah!" I gasped, just barely catching her.

"Mm sai geng," she said. "Don't worry."

"Of course I'm going to be worried!" I cried. I mean, I was worried about a lot of things. Like dying. Or her dying. Or any of my other family members doing the big D-Y-I-N-G. "You nearly went splat on the ground."

She frowned. "Splat?"

"Never mind," I said. "Actually, no. Splat. Like an egg." I mimicked dropping an egg on the ground and having it explode on impact. D-Y-I-N-G. "You need to rest, Mah Mah."

Leon pressed his hand to her forehead, and his expression filled with concern. "You have been in the Underworld for a long time. It is draining on mortal energy."

"I rest when I alive again," she said, swatting his hand

away—and as she did, I caught sight of a red stain on the side of her shirt.

Blood.

"You're hurt," I said hollowly. "When did you get hurt?"

She sighed and reverted to Cantonese. "The guard cut me when he was dragging me away. It's only a small scratch—"

"That doesn't look like a small scratch!" I squeaked. The red splotch on her shirt seemed to be growing the longer I looked at it.

Henry glanced at her, then at me. "Come on. There's a place where we can check on Po Po. It's hidden with complex syu fat mo, so Tin Hong shouldn't be able to find it."

We followed Henry through the side streets of the town. Thankfully, Mah Mah didn't argue against Leon carrying her on his back again, and that worried me even more. She never gave up. I forced myself to look at my surroundings to keep my mind off her injury.

Samlin was painted in the colours of the earth, all clay-tiled roofs and wooden slats for fences. We walked past tiny houses with chickens that pecked to and fro in rigid lines. We tried to keep to the side of the road as much as possible, but when the shops began opening their shutters for the day, we let ourselves fall alongside carts pulled by oddly upright horses. A child ran by with a long-tailed kite, painted to look like a red carp. Her giggle was quickly lost in the low murmurs of the awakening residents.

"The ghosts here seem . . ." I didn't want to say *more alive*, but it was the most suitable description I could think of.

Leon veered gracefully around a shopkeeper dragging a table out onto the road, his hands looped around Mah Mah. She had her head rested against his shoulders. "They receive more offerings," he said.

Leon and Mah Mah were attracting some stares, but at this point I didn't care. I just wanted to get her back home. "I guess the offerings don't include paper airplanes back to the Mortal Realm."

Henry snorted. "Oh, they do. Huge jets. Helicopters. I think I've even seen a few commercial airplanes. There's a whole collection of them out in the seventh region Seventh Court of the Underworld."

"Nobody flies them?"

He shrugged. "Fuel doesn't come in paper form, and most ghosts don't have enough spiritual energy to move them with syu fat mo."

We wound through a series of side streets until we came to a simple arch, built from three logs of wood balanced precariously against each other. The houses here were squat, with tiny courtyards filled with yellowed grass. There were even a few plants in mottled greens. They were the first living plants I'd seen outside Tin Hong's manor. I felt another pang of homesickness. The sooner I dealt with Tin Hong, the quicker I could get back to gardening with Mah Mah.

We stopped outside a house at the end of the street. Like the others, it had a plain wooden door and two square windows on its front.

"Welcome home," Henry announced as he sauntered up to the front door.

"You managed to hide something so large from a Ghost Lord?" Leon asked skeptically.

"Better study up more, Roasted Squab."

". . . I am offended," Leon said, more perplexed than anything.

"Don't be," Henry said cheerily. "It's a compliment. Roasted squab tastes great. Maybe I'll get Wong here to include that in my year of offerings she promised me."

I gave him the evil eye. "I won't. I get twenty bucks in allowance every week."

"Time to get a job." He beamed, and my heart beat faster. "You could go ghost hunting with me."

A job was a good idea, but not with him. If I had to hunt down ghosts with Henry, I'd be distracted the entire time—in a bad way, of course. Definitely a bad way. "Yeah, no thanks."

"Too bad. We'd make a good team." Henry walked up to the front door. He paused as if he didn't want to go inside, his grip tight on his calligraphy brush. After a moment, he wrote something on the door and pulled it open.

Calm sank into me as soon as I stepped inside. The dust sat undisturbed. Two chairs were tucked neatly into a small table. The house was a single room. Along the back wall I spotted a couple of empty bowls beside a wok set into a stone counter. A fat log sat inside a hole beneath the wok, ready to be set alight.

"Who lives here?" I asked.

He dropped his gaze. "No one does. Not anymore." He shut the door and wrote a glowing silver character on it. "Not for a long time."

I let out a relieved breath. Mah Mah would be safe here. Leon walked over to the side of the house where a reed mat lay on the ground. He bent down and gently, like he was holding a porcelain flower, lowered Mah Mah onto the mat. He muttered something to her. She raised the hem of her shirt and my stomach turned queasily. A gash cut from her ribs downwards.

"Mui Mui, you are terribly injured," Leon said in a tight voice.

"It's not bad," Henry said.

"No bad," Mah Mah agreed. She patted her hip. "See? Still work."

"*That's* not bad?" I said faintly. Her entire side was coated in blood.

Henry examined her injury carefully. "A cut through the neck is bad. A lost arm is bad."

Mah Mah chuckled, even though she didn't have any right to. "Haiya, no head also bad."

Henry smirked. "Po Po mou gong cho."

I stood up, my hands clammy. My grandma did *not* just make a joke with the ghost who had once tried to deliver us to certain death. I would've dragged her away from him, but Henry poised his calligraphy brush over her, a look of consternation on his face as if he was deliberating what to write.

"May I?" Leon asked quietly.

Henry passed him the brush. "Give it a shot, squab. Healing isn't my strong suit."

I held my breath as Leon wrote something over her wound with careful movements, as if every stroke was precious. The character hovered there, glowing gold, but unlike all the other syu fat mo I'd seen, it didn't vanish.

"What did you write?" I asked.

"*Yu*," Mah Mah replied.

"*Heal.*" Leon placed a hand over the character. Sweat beaded along the bridge of his nose. "This spell requires a lot of spiritual energy."

Without thinking, I rested my hand on his shoulder. Spiritual energy coursed up through my chest and down my arm, where it spread out through my fingers. The warmth of it seeped into him, and he jolted.

"Did your grandmother teach you to do that?" he asked.

"No," Mah Mah interjected proudly. "She learned that all by herself."

Warmth rushed to my face and settled happily into me. "You helped."

She gave my hand a pat. "It is okay for me to not teach you everything. You are smart, Ah Ling."

I swallowed down the ball of emotion in my throat and concentrated my thoughts on giving more spiritual energy to Leon. I closed my eyes. The room faded away. The calling of the roosters outside dulled to silence.

"Stop!" Leon jerked away from my grip. "You are giving too much of your energy."

Dizzy, I snapped my hand back. An emptiness lay low inside me. It chilled my insides. "Is she going to be okay?"

Henry unlaced his leather bracer and tossed it to the ground. "Mm hou yuk. Don't move."

Mah Mah sat still as he shook out his sleeve then tore off a strip of fabric. I waited, stomach roiling, as he wiped away at the blood until there was nothing left but skin, unmarred and unbroken.

The wound was gone.

Leon rubbed at his neck tiredly. "I only closed the surface. There might be some internal damage, but it does not seem dangerous."

"Hou ah," Mah Mah grunted. She swatted off the dust on the back of her pants, then swiped at my shoulder after. "Wash clothes later," she said, and my throat closed. Later meant home.

"How far is the harbour from here?" I asked.

"Look through the back door," Henry said, wiping his bloodied hands on his face. The movement left a smudge of red on his cheek.

Reluctantly, I stood. Leon was still bent over Mah Mah, sweeping the grey curls out of her face. She was in good hands. Tears pricked at my eyes. I rubbed them away and walked to the back door. It was beside the stone counter with the inset wok. I was about to push the door open when something red beneath the log under the wok caught my eye.

Gingerly, I pulled it out. It looked like a red lai see envelope, but there was no money inside. Instead, there was a folded letter. It was hastily written in black ink. I couldn't read any of the Chinese characters except for one—*Wong*. My last name.

"Put that back."

Henry stood behind me with a stricken expression.

"I didn't mean to snoop," I said carefully. "But why is my family name written on this?"

"It's nothing," he said. "I meant to burn it a long time ago."

I looked down the length of the letter again. "Is this about Lin Wai?"

"What?" Leon called from across the room. "There is a letter about Lin Wai?"

Henry grimaced like hearing the name physically pained him. "No. Lin Wai is the one who wrote it." He turned his gaze to the ground, kicking at nothing. "You read it, squab."

The colour drained from Leon's face. In a moment, he was beside Henry. He took the letter with trembling fingers. He scanned the letter, then read it again. His eyes watered.

"What does it say, Go Go?" came Mah Mah's tired voice.

With a heavy heart, I went over and sat on the reed mat beside her. Leon looked over at Henry, who nodded and crossed his arms.

Leon lifted the paper again and read—once in Cantonese, then a second time in English.

CHAPTER 27

Dear Lam Kai Ming,

I thought for a long time about how to write this letter. I thought about starting with "sorry" for all the trouble I've given you since coming here to the Underworld. Then I thought about beginning with "thank you" for how you've helped me in my journey to bring back Li Gwan. Yet neither felt right, and I am terrible at letters, so instead I'll tell you what it was like to have you as my friend.

When we first met, you didn't trust me. I lied to you about why I'd come to the Underworld. You thought I was simply trying to find my dead fiancé. But you gave me time to think. And space to breathe. You understand what it feels like to lose people you love. We've had so many conversations about the people we miss. It never gets easier, even in the afterlife. But you said it well: time passes, and we learn how to live again.

But now I've finally discovered a way to bring Li Gwan back to life, and I need to try. You would do the same, right? If you could give someone you love immortal life, no matter the cost, wouldn't you?

If things don't work out, and I leave this world for the final time, please don't worry about me. I've only returned to the dust, and dust is all around us.

Thank you for being a good friend. I hope you find what you're looking for.

Wishing you a thousand years of health and happiness,
Wong Lin Wai

CHAPTER 28

I wrapped my arms around Mah Mah as she buried her face into her hands. My body felt heavy, like I couldn't get up. But I didn't want to. Not yet. I let Lin Wai's words sink in. Accepting them felt like a part of me had come home.

Henry looked towards the back door. "I lost a good friend that day."

"You helped her," Leon croaked, his fingers tight around the letter. "That's why you knew who I was that day when I stopped you from taking Emma to the Underworld."

"I didn't help make you immortal," Henry said gruffly. "That was all Lin Wai."

Leon crossed over to Henry and engulfed him in a hug. Henry went absolutely still, like a ngo gwai had attacked him.

"You're supposed to hug back," I said. "You know—with your arms."

"This doesn't make us friends." Henry gave him an awkward pat on the back. "But you're welcome, squab."

Leon smoothed out the creases of Lin Wai's letter. He

glanced at it one more time before holding it out to Henry. Henry shook his head.

"You should have it," he told my grandma.

"Let Go Go keep it," she insisted. "He and my sister were meant to be together."

Leon smiled sadly. "What I remember of her is already enough. I don't need anything more."

He brought the letter closer to her, and Mah Mah took it with quivering hands. She pressed it to her chest and closed her eyes. I looked around the small house—at Henry lingering by the two chairs at the little table in the corner, at Leon's faraway gaze trained on the lonely wok on its stove. We were separate, but together. We'd all come together because of Lin Wai. I leaned my head on Mah Mah's shoulder, and she let out a shuddering breath.

"I wish I could have met her," I said.

"She wasn't afraid." She wiped at her eyes and examined the letter. "Like you."

"I'm scared of a lot of things," I whispered.

She set the letter down in her lap. "Being afraid is okay as long as you don't let it stop you."

She cupped my face between her hands. I closed my eyes. Being able to see ngo gwai wasn't as much of a curse as I thought if it meant giving me moments like these— moments with Mah Mah. With Leon and Henry. With our family, and all the stories that led me to this point. The ngo gwai were as much a part of my life as everything else, and I wouldn't have traded that for the world.

Suddenly, I knew what I needed to do.

"The boats will take me anywhere along the Seoi Dang River, right? Not just to the Mortal Realm?" I asked.

Leon gave me a worried look. "Yes, but—"

Quickly, I drew myself to my feet. "I need to see Michelle."

"Why?" Leon asked.

"She wants to make sure that none of the ngo gwai here starve from lack of offerings." I met Mah Mah's eyes. "I'm going to make her a deal better than what Tin Hong is promising."

Henry's brow crinkled in confusion. "You can't one-up a Ghost Lord on what they're able to provide to a ngo gwai."

"Even if I got a whole city involved in making offerings?"

"That would be very difficult. No one believes in making offerings to the dead to sustain them in the afterlife anymore," Leon said, but he had a faraway look on his face, as though he was mulling the idea over in his head.

"I just need to talk to Michelle," I said. "She's always been better at figuring out the details. I'm sure she'd be able to think of something."

"Wong, wait—" Henry started after me, but Mah Mah grabbed him by the sleeve.

"Go, Ah Ling," she said, her voice wavering.

I gave her a grateful smile and pushed open the back door. The house backed onto a ridge. Below it lurked a sliver of the hazy green-blue currents of the Seoi Dang River.

Four docks branched out into the water, but they were all empty. Another chorus of rooster calls rang out in the quiet of the morning. I wondered if Michelle could hear them too—only I didn't have long to think because the door behind me slammed open as Leon and Henry joined me at the ridge.

"Why is Po Po so strong? She almost took my whole arm off!" Henry grumbled, rotating his shoulder.

"Please tell me the boats are invisible," I said, looking down the ridge.

Leon sighed. "The boats are invisible. Emma, if this is about wanting to see Michelle—"

"No, seriously. Are the boats there? Because I don't see any."

Leon frowned as he peered over the edge of the ridge. "This is very odd. The harbour should be filled with—" His last word was drowned out by a rooster call, so loud that it could've been right behind us.

"What?" I asked.

"With—" Leon was cut off as the rooster called again, and Henry's mouth twisted into a snarl. He vanished, only to reappear a short moment later with a skinny rooster in his hands.

"Quiet," he seethed, giving it a little shake. "Unless you want to become chicken stew. Who even thinks of burning paper roosters for the dead?"

He dropped it on the ground and it gave a spiteful squawk before Leon scooped it up.

"As I was saying," Leon said, shooting Henry an offended look while petting the rooster, "the harbour should be filled with vessels, but it is not."

Panic gripped me. I wouldn't be able to send Mah Mah back home *or* find Michelle if the boats were missing. "Where are they?"

Henry cursed. "I'll check the harbour."

He popped out of existence. As soon as he was gone, I turned to Leon. "If we can't get a boat, promise me you'll take care of my grandmother."

Leon nodded sympathetically. "Do not worry, Emma. We will find a boat."

"Leon, *please*. I need to find Michelle, but I can't risk my grandma being here—"

Henry poofed back beside me, his mouth twisted in irritation. "Sei la, they're getting all the boats ready for catching the offerings during the Ghost Festival tomorrow. They're doing everything from making repairs to attaching decorations. I swear, no one prepares ahead of time in this accursed place. They've had all year to get ready, but do they? No—"

"Is there any other way to return to the Mortal Realm?" I interrupted.

Leon cupped his chin in contemplation. "We need a vessel that will carry us along the Seoi Dang River. It is the only way for mortals to enter and leave the Underworld."

"We could ask someone to borrow their boat once it's fixed," I said desperately.

Henry paced back and forth across the ridge. "No one's going to lend us their boat and risk missing out on the biggest day of offerings for the year."

My stomach dropped. If we couldn't get a boat from the town, then we had to try somewhere else. I gave the harbour one last, disheartened look before heading back to the house. "You two take care of my grandma. I need to head back to Tin Hong's manor and find Michelle."

Henry popped up in front of me just as I was reaching for the door. His face was red with anger. "Are you crazy? Tin Hong wants you here for the festival to take your spiritual energy!"

"Henry is right," Leon said. "We need to return you and your grandmother to the Mortal Realm before the start of the festival."

"Tin Hong isn't going to stop coming after my family just because we return home." I glanced at the closed door, then lowered my voice to a whisper. "He threatened to use Mah Mah instead."

Leon froze, his eyes wide. "You never told us that."

"I thought we could return her to the Mortal Realm before then."

Henry squinted at me suspiciously. "You mean both of you."

I shook my head and went inside the house. "I already made Tin Hong a promise."

"But he will take all your spiritual energy." Leon followed me, running his hand through his hair and trying to flip it out of his face. It only resulted in a messier flop. "You will die and become a ghost."

"Henry's a ghost and he's alive-ish," I said, trying to be brave. "I'd never have to do math tests ever again."

Leon looked really upset. "There is more to being a ghost than not doing math tests. What if you do not receive enough offerings and are forced to wander the world as a ngo gwai?"

"Anyway, that's a terrible idea," Henry spat. "Only I would want your paltry offerings. Any other ngo gwai would demand that you burn a new paper house every year and offer crab, lobster, and duck during holidays."

"What's your genius plan, then?" I asked.

Henry went around the small house, drawing the window shutters closed. "We'll hide you both during the festival. Once it passes, Tin Hong won't get another chance for a whole year."

"So, we're just going to hope he doesn't find us?" I asked, frustrated.

"Yep." He circled around and kicked the back door shut. Darkness fell over us. "This house is veiled with syu fat mo. Tin Hong doesn't know about it. We're going to stay right here and make a plan to stop him before next year's festival."

Next year's Ghost Festival. Another whole year of looking over my shoulder for Tin Hong and his ngo gwai. One more year of wondering which family member would land in the hospital next—or maybe Tin Hong would just start

293

sending us to an early grave one by one until I fulfilled my promise to him.

"If you don't want to help, then at least take care of my grandma."

I stomped over to the side of the house where my grandma lay resting, only for Leon to call out, "Emma, wait." He'd been quiet while Henry and I had argued, but now I could see how his bottom lip quivered. "I will go with you to Tin Hong. He can use my spiritual energy instead."

"He specifically said he needed someone from my family."

"But you can draw out spiritual energy," he said. "You can funnel it through yourself. I have more than enough spiritual energy to ensure that Tin Hong can conduct his ritual, and prevent you from becoming a ghost."

He hovered there, hands clasped behind his back, waiting for my answer. He looked hopeful—but it was hungry and desperate, like he needed to do this more for himself than for me.

"You can come with me," I said, and I only felt a little guilty when his face broke open in relief. Silently, I apologized to him. He could come along, but I wouldn't use his spiritual energy.

I walked over to the reed mat where my grandma lay beneath a blanket. She must have been sleeping deeply because she hadn't woken up from all the noise we were making. I didn't want to wake her, but I needed to say goodbye, just in case.

I bent down—then squinted.

"Mah Mah?" I asked.

"What is wrong?" Leon asked, alarmed. "Did the wound open up?"

"No, but something's weird." I threw back the blanket. Beneath it was . . . nothing. The blanket had been hovering over an empty space made to look like the shape of a person. My heart thudded as I scoured the dark corners of the house, but it was a tiny room with no hiding places.

"Where's my grandma?" I asked, terrified.

Leon flapped out the blanket like she'd tumble out if he shook hard enough. "She is not here?"

"Not unless she's shrunk!" I cried.

"Hold on. I'll use syu fat mo to see if anyone else has been in here while we were outside." Henry patted his belt, then wrenched open the black pouch hanging off it. He dug around inside. With every passing second, his eyes bulged larger.

"That conniving Po Po!" he howled. "She took my calligraphy brush! No wonder she was holding on to me for so long."

"What was she doing when you two came outside?" I asked in a panic.

"Resting," Leon said, but even as he spoke the word, his eyes widened in realization. "But she was not sleeping."

Henry drew out the short form of his gwandou and cinched the strings on his pouch closed with a scowl. "She's a ghost hunter. She wouldn't go to sleep while danger's around."

My pulse was going so fast it was making me dizzy. I threw open the front door and checked the small courtyard and the empty street in front, but no one was around. "She heard us talking. She knows that Tin Hong will use her if I don't show up."

Henry bent down, examining the dusty dirt path that led from the house to the street. "We'll find her. How far can one injured granny go?"

"This isn't a regular grandma we're dealing with." I rushed out onto the road, scanning the houses and barren trees. "This is Mah Mah!"

Leon gulped. "I will fly above the town. It will be easier to spy her."

He transformed into a pigeon and soared off into the skies, while Henry and I tackled the streets on foot. I tried to keep myself calm as we split up, but I was massively freaking out. What if Mah Mah ran into Tin Hong or his guards before we did? There was no point in trying to hide anymore. If Tin Hong's guards were already here, we had bigger problems to worry about than them spotting us. Mah Mah would probably willingly hop onto their backs and order them to carry her to Tin Hong.

We had to find her. Fast.

CHAPTER 29

Henry and I raced between throngs of people. The main roads of the town had filled with ghosts—crowds of them, chattering away in their plain robes and swinging around lanterns on sticks. Some of them were stringing up paper lanterns along the eaves of shops, while others carried their boats in pairs, holding the narrow, flat vessels above their heads. Small lanterns rimmed the sides, dripping down like heavy red peonies.

I was skimming their faces, trying to find my grandma, when a girl bumped into me. She was holding a paper lantern on the end of a stick. Before she could walk away, I quickly asked her, "Have you seen an older lady around? Grey, permed hair? Wearing a floral shirt? Looks like she could take on a bear with her bare hands?"

"No, but— Hey, hold on." She leaned closer with her lantern, peering up at me with a sudden intensity that made my stomach flip. "Aren't you a mortal?"

"No," I said, because the last thing I needed was to stand

out in this village of hungry ghosts. I tried to casually back up, but she swung her lantern out close to my face.

"Really? Because you feel awfully mortal—"

"Nope!" Henry interjected loudly, jumping in between us. He was holding the short form of his gwandou like he was ready to swing it out, but he tapped it on his shoulder instead. "She just ate a huge amount of fresh offerings. Oranges, peaches, steamed fish. If you head to the river, you might catch some of the earliest offerings."

She perked up. "The offerings have already started coming in? All right, good luck finding who you're searching for!"

When she slipped into the crowd of ghosts, I turned to Henry. "We should check the river. Mah Mah would definitely be able to badger someone into letting her catch a ride with them."

His face darkened as he considered the possibility. "She would, knowing her. Come on. We can check."

We made our way to the west of town, down to the river. Henry wound his way around the crowds, his eyes flicking to each side—and suddenly, as if a candle had been blown out, the sky went dark as the sun was replaced by the moon.

I skidded to a stop behind a line of ghosts walking the path down to the river. The pathway was lined with wooden stalls of ghosts selling everything from paper lanterns to clothes to mounds of stacked fruit that all looked eerily similar. "What's going on? It was only morning not too long ago."

Henry squeezed through several ghosts clustered around a stall that smelled faintly of something sweet and soft. "The

Ghost Festival lasts for a full day and night in the Underworld so none of the offerings are missed. It's harder to spot the lantern offerings during the day."

The moon was full and bright. Its light illuminated the town in ethereal shades of silver. A golden glow spread through the streets as people lit the lanterns that hung from their houses and shops. Wafts of fried fish and steamed rice kept drifting across my path, but when I tried to see where the food was, the smells vanished. When we reached the river, I sucked in a breath.

In the dark of night, the Seoi Dang River was an empty vastness that stretched along the length of the land. Several ghosts pushed their boats out onto the water before hopping in, and the bottoms bobbed along the dark surface like petals floating on ink. The shop stalls continued up the riverbank, lit by hanging lanterns.

"It doesn't look like she's here," I whispered as we walked across the riverbank. The pebbles crunched beneath our feet, but the sound was swallowed up by the loud scraping of boat hulls as ghosts pushed them into the slow-moving waters. I peeked inside the boats, but they were shallow enough that I would've easily been able to see her if she was in any of them.

"We should try to find Leon and see if he's seen anything," Henry said.

Something bright caught my eye upstream. It was a golden orb of light, floating down the water towards us. When more lights joined it, the hair on the back of my neck stood on end. "Are those what I think they are?"

"Lanterns." He grimaced. "The Ghost Festival has started."

Desperately, I searched the riverbank one last time. The ghosts on the sampans pushed their long oars into the river and drifted off upstream towards the lanterns. I trudged up the riverbank, where the forest lay behind the shop stalls— and I spotted a bobbing light in amongst the trees.

I pulled back. "The guards are here."

"Blend into the crowds," Henry said. "We can head back to town before they notice us—"

"I see Mah Mah!" I only caught the top of a head and the bright flash of a shirt amongst the guards, but it was impossible to mistake that head of curls for anyone else. I ran to the closest stall, hiding behind a display of embroidered robes. She was walking in between the guards, chin held high as though she was an empress and they were her escorts.

I hurried out from the stall once Mah Mah and the guards were far enough ahead, then stopped before I entered the forest. If the guards turned around, there'd be nowhere for us to hide.

"It doesn't look like they're headed to Tin Hong's manor." Henry looked behind us, then started pulling robes off the displays. "Try this on."

"Mah Mah is being taken somewhere by a bunch of Tin Hong's guards and you want to go shopping?" I hissed loudly.

"We're going to follow them."

Even more confused, I held up the clothing Henry had

passed me. "Yeah, I don't think Tin Hong is going to change his mind about the whole 'using my family to become immortal' thing no matter how nicely we're dressed."

He went to the other side of the stall and flipped through the outer robes, shoving one into my hands. "It's a disguise, ban dan. If the guards see who we are, there's no way we're going to be able to get close to Po Po."

While he paid the shopkeeper with the same spirit money he'd used back at the restaurant, I put on the first two robe layers. There was an inner white layer and a midnight-blue robe that went overtop. It came with a simple tie that I knotted around my waist. Embroidered gold ginkgo leaves ran along the crossed collar. "Huh. Our embroidery kind of matches."

Henry peered down at his chest, where golden dragons flew between red-and-blue swirls of clouds. "Oh. Yeah."

"Did you do that on purpose?"

He rubbed the back of his neck. "No. Just thought you liked plants."

My cheeks went warm. "Thanks. I do."

"You're welcome." He glanced away, but not before I caught how his eyes softened. "You look nice."

I squinted at him. He was acting weird, and that was making *me* feel weird. "Thanks?"

The tips of his ears reddened. "Come on, we should hurry if we want to catch up."

We rushed along the riverbank in the direction that Mah Mah and the guards had gone. Unlike before, no one's stares lingered on me. When the strip of riverbank narrowed, we slipped into the forest.

It didn't take long to find the bobbing lantern again. Mah Mah and the guards were walking along a cleared pathway, just far enough ahead that we could see there were about four guards with her. As we followed them deeper into the forest, the shouts and bustle from the town faded into the hush of the pine trees. The trees became denser the farther we went. I couldn't hear anything anymore—not even the gentle lapping of the Seoi Dang River. All the noises from the town had disappeared.

"Something doesn't feel right," I whispered.

Henry looked behind us. Worry clouded his expression. "We should keep moving."

I nodded and stepped forward, only to step down on something hard. It looked like a black stick. "What the—"

"My calligraphy brush!" Henry snatched it up and furiously dusted off the dirt on its white brush head. "That's the last time I trust your grandma around my possessions."

"Shhh," I said, turning my head to peer into the darkness around us. My feeling of unease was growing with every passing moment.

"It's true," Henry insisted. "Your grandma has lighter fingers than a ngo gwai without hands—"

I backed up into him. His brow pinched in concentration. A strange shushing sound was rippling through the space around us. It sounded like the wind blowing through a stack of papers.

"The trees are tightening together," Henry yelled. "Move!"

The gaps between the trees were narrowing so quickly we had to squeeze through the trunks. Trees pressed against me. Branches scraped at my face. It was hard to breathe. Just when I thought I couldn't force myself through another tiny opening, I stumbled out from the forest and into the most beautiful garden I'd ever seen.

Around us were persimmon trees, standing in two weeping rows of dripping fruit amongst clusters of vibrant jade and gold, their bounty red and plump. A cover of white and lilac wisteria hung overhead. Beyond them lay the Seoi Dang River, a gentle current of dark water. The offering lanterns bobbed along it. In the lifeless dark, they were unnaturally beautiful. They glowed like a million strands of spiritual energy, all woven together to create a semblance of a wish.

"Guess we followed the right path," I said nervously.

Beside me, Henry stumbled out into the garden with a gasp. "Whoever made that pathway really doesn't want us here."

I rubbed my arms. "Yeah, I'm going to guess that's Tin Hong."

"Of course," he snorted, plucking off a lilac-coloured strand of wisteria above his head and tossing it to the ground. "Only he would have enough spiritual energy to spare to create a place like this. So wasteful."

Cautiously, I walked between the two rows of persimmon trees. Their cloying nectar permeated the air in a long-ago memory of sweetness, sun-faded until there was only one note remaining. I didn't want to go near them. Jewelled tendrils of gold and green from the wisteria overhead brushed against the top of my head. Ahead, the passageway opened, and the persimmon trees split into a circular clearing. It felt . . . wrong. The feeling crawled up my spine and settled at the base of my neck like a poisonous spore.

Henry swatted a branch out of the way. "Where did they go?"

"They must be here somewhere. They can't have just disappeared into thin air—" Abruptly, I stopped. What if that's what really had happened? I closed my eyes and felt for my grandma's string of spiritual energy, only to discover something else instead.

The whole garden was covered in thousands and thousands of tiny strings of spiritual energy. They formed a net over the area, so thick I couldn't feel past it.

My mouth dropped open. I spun around to tell Henry, only to see him already standing in the middle of the clearing.

"You feel it too?" he muttered. He elongated his gwandou, accidentally cutting off several strands of wisteria in the process. He thudded the end of it into the ground. "Right here. There's something hidden here."

"There's spiritual energy woven all over this place." I stood in the middle of the clearing and closed my eyes. I tried tugging on the net of spiritual energy, but I only managed to pull it slightly towards me before it bounced back like a rubber band. "Can you try removing it with syu fat mo?"

"I can't move around spiritual energy." He crossed his arms, looking at the spot beneath his feet. "They've taken her somewhere we can't go."

I came up beside him, feeling the low hum of energy rising from the centre of the garden. If I concentrated hard enough, I could feel a hint of Mah Mah's spiritual energy behind the net surrounding us. It was faint, but reachable.

"Then we need to find a way in," I insisted.

CHAPTER 30

I walked around the garden, testing for any spots where the spiritual energy wasn't knitted together as tightly. Whoever had made the veil had done an excellent job, and probably should have been doing something better with their time than hiding my grandma from me. I bent down to look at the roots of the trees, but shot up again when a crack sounded behind me.

Henry was twirling his gwandou around with a practised ease, slicing off branches from the surrounding persimmon trees. Before any leaves or persimmons could touch the ground, they vanished into dust.

My mouth dropped. "Who looks that happy destroying plants?"

He paused in mid-swing. "Me?"

"Not letting *you* near my house again," I muttered.

"I'm trying to clear the garden so I can see what's around us." He ran his gwandou through another tree, shearing off half its leaves. "This place is strange, even for the Underworld. I keep trying to cut down an entire tree, but every time I do, the tree rights itself like nothing happened. And then there's the Seoi Dang River."

"What about it?"

"Every time I try to move towards it, I don't get any closer."

"Maybe it only looks like you've been moving towards it." I walked to the edge of the clearing. The river was only several steps away, but no amount of walking seemed to bring me nearer. "Weird. What happens if you try throwing something towards the water?"

He looked around. "There's nothing to throw. Anything I pluck off the trees will turn to dust before I can lob it."

I pointed at his weapon. "Try throwing that."

He reared back with a horrified expression. "My gwandou? Not for all the offerings in the world. You know how long it took me to enchant it so that it can shrink down and fit inside my magical pouch without cutting up my hand every time I withdraw it?"

"Yeah, well, you're not going to get any offerings if we can't get through and find my grandma." I sighed and scuffed at the dirt with my shoe. "Anyway, the river doesn't matter right now. I can't figure out how to get past the spiritual energy veil. This is the worst garden I've ever been in."

"It's not really a garden. It only looks like one." He spun his gwandou up and resumed hacking through the trees like he had a personal vendetta against them. "Like everything else in the Underworld, it's only a replica of something that exists in the Mortal Realm."

I plucked a ripe persimmon from the closest tree, only for it to turn to dust before I could examine it more carefully. Experimentally, I reached out to the spiritual energy of the trees. They stood free of the veil cloaking the garden.

Eagerly, I turned to Henry. "Maybe I can't touch the veil of spiritual energy, but I can pull in the energy from these trees."

"Don't," he said warningly. "You keep consuming all this spiritual energy without thinking about the consequences. Remember how sick you felt last time? If you take in all the spiritual energy from these trees, you're going to feel at least ten times as bad. You might die."

"Then *I* could be the one haunting *you*."

"Ha ha," Henry said unconvincingly.

"I'll just try a tree or two and see what happens."

He lowered his gwandou, watching as I sat down in the middle of the garden. I took a deep breath and closed my eyes. I gingerly pulled on the spiritual energy of the closest trees. The energy flowed into me. It felt just as awful as when I'd taken the spiritual energy of the ngo gwai. Eventually, after what felt like ages, the last of it ebbed into me. I opened my eyes again, only to see Henry was right beside me.

"Are you okay?" he asked, bending down.

"Yeah. I only feel like I'm one-tenth of the way to dying," I wheezed. My head spun like I'd just been on a roller coaster, but I managed to point to the moon above us, no longer cloaked by tree foliage. "I think we cleared a large enough space. How much spirit money do you have?"

"Enough," he said suspiciously. "Why does it sound like you have a questionable plan in mind?"

"Because I do. We're going to build a lantern large enough to attract Tin Hong's attention and send it through the clearing I made. And we're going to use your spirit money to do it."

Henry's scowl deepened exponentially. He looked pained, and slightly fearful, as if half-baked plans were his idea of torture. "If we build a lantern large enough to be noticed by Tin Hong, any ghost might show up. It might not be him."

"It might not be," I agreed, "but it will. He asked me to assist him, not my grandma. She's his backup."

He sighed and uncinched the black pouch hanging off his belt. "How much do you need?"

"As much as you can spare."

"All right," he grumbled, "but you owe me big time."

And he reached into his black pouch and started pulling out dagger after dagger after dagger. Then a sword. A wicked-looking crossbow. I think I even spotted a throwing axe or two.

"How much can that thing carry?" I asked in disbelief.

"I fit a whole horde of ngo gwai into it once," he said proudly.

When he was done pulling out all the weapons in his arsenal, he finally withdrew a bundle of spirit money. It was a stack of square papers, all with the same silver stamp in the middle, and bound together with a piece of pink twine. He tossed it to me.

"Is this all you have?" I asked, already untying the twine.

Henry grumbled as he dug around in his black pouch. He flung another wad of papers onto the lush grass beside me. "You still need more?"

"As much as you have." I picked up the wad. It was lighter than it looked. Like the other bundle, it was tied together with a piece of long pink twine. I started untying the knot in the middle. "The lantern needs to be large enough to stand out from all the other lanterns in town, otherwise it'll just blend in."

"You know what will be easier than using all my spirit money?" Henry said sourly. "If I just pop in to Tin Hong's manor and tell him to come over here."

I fanned out a stack of spirit money on the ground. "Not with how weak you are now. Tin Hong's cut off your offerings."

He stopped in the middle of taking out more money, startled. "You can tell?"

"Yeah. Your spiritual energy feels . . . dimmer." I closed my eyes and felt for his spiritual energy. The edges of it were even more frayed than before.

Henry grinned. "There's hope for you yet, Wong."

I didn't smile back. "Tin Hong knew."

"Knew what?"

"That you were helping us."

He threw down another bundled wad of spirit money. "Of course. That sei lou gwai was watching me just as much as I was watching him. He never fully trusted me." He sat down beside me, cross-legged, and I realized, with a start, that his chest wasn't rising and falling the way it usually did. He rubbed at the back of his neck, hesitating.

"I never wanted to work for Tin Hong," he finally said, "but I saw the power that he wielded as the Ghost Lord of the First Court of the Underworld. When my ancestral offerings started to run low, he came to me with a job offer: get rid of the beng gwai harassing the folks in the nearby town and I'd get a year's worth of offerings."

I bent down and picked up some of the spirit money. "Why would Tin Hong ask you to get rid of a sick ghost?"

"Not a sick ghost, a beng gwai. A ghost that spreads illness. It was blackmailing the more fortunate families in town for offerings."

My fingers tightened around the papers in my hands. "Everything comes back to family, huh?"

He scratched at his cheek. "It always does. And when you don't have any family left, you start looking for anyone who sticks with you long enough to remember your name."

"Tin Hong remembered your name," I stated. It was kind of a hard name to forget, or maybe that was just me.

He nodded. "A few weeks later, he asked me to take care of another troublemaker. Then he came with another job, and another." He used his sleeve to wipe a speck of nothing off his gwandou blade. "I figured that even if I was dead, I could at least continue hunting ghosts and help maintain as much balance as I could between the Three Realms."

"I didn't know hunting ghosts included handing my family over to a Ghost Lord," I said bitterly.

His jaw worked back and forth, like he was chewing on something. "I don't have any excuses. I know I'm not . . . a good person. I've done many things I'm not proud of for the sake of survival. I've tarnished the clan name. My ancestors would have disowned me, but there's no one to give them offerings anymore, and they've faded from the Cycle of Death and Rebirth."

I looked him right in the eye. "I don't owe you any forgiveness."

"No, you don't." He clasped his hands together and ran his thumb over the calluses and scars across his knuckles. "I'll spend as long as I need to make it up to you."

Heat flushed across my face. "This doesn't make you any less of a jerk."

He finished drawing out one last bundle of spirit money and solemnly said, "I know. But it does make me broke. That's the last of my spirit money."

I rose to my feet and inhaled to brace myself. "Hey."

"What?"

I pointed over to the Seoi Dang River. "Look that way."

He stiffened. "What? Is Tin Hong here already—"

I leaned over and pecked him on the cheek. Immediately, he went as red as a lai see envelope.

"W-wh-what—" he stuttered. "What?"

"Thanks for giving me all your spirit money," I said. "Maybe I'll include some roasted squab in your offerings every now and then."

"I was joking. About the offerings. But not really," he stammered. "I do need them to survive."

"I know," I said, spreading out the spirit money at my feet as much as I could. "All right, Ghost Boy. Time to work some magic."

He drew out his calligraphy brush from his pouch and offered me the handle. "You want to start?"

"You're better at it—" I started, then stopped.

I sucked at syu fat mo. A lot. It reminded me of all the times when I came home from Chinese school with poor quiz marks because the teacher couldn't read my writing, and Mom and Dad and Mah Mah's brief glances at my scores. I wasn't good at it, but just because I wasn't good at it didn't mean that I had to avoid it. I had to start somewhere. Using syu fat mo to attract the attention of a Ghost Lord seemed like a pretty good place to begin anew. Gingerly, I took the sleek black handle of Henry's calligraphy brush with its soft head. "You know what? I will."

He grinned. "Let's make the ugliest lantern in existence."

"The largest," I corrected, and I wrote out the character for *move*.

The spirit money drifted up from the ground, surrounding us in clouds of paper. When I wrote the character for *move* again, they slowly started flattening against each other, forming the skeleton of a paper lantern. The shape of it came together the more syu fat mo I scrawled out, and I fell into a rhythm before I knew it.

"Trade me," Henry said. "You're starting to look sick."

I passed him the brush and wiped away the sweat forming on my forehead. Henry started writing. He was a lot quicker, and the rest of the lantern was almost complete when I caught sight of something swirling in the midst of the last spirit money.

"Wait, something's mixed in with the papers," I said.

"You mean mixed in with my money," Henry said in a strained voice, but he paused in the middle of writing and the remaining papers fell to the ground—except one. It soared slowly through the clearing. Something about its folded beak and wings looked hauntingly familiar.

"Don't touch it," he said out of the corner of his mouth. "That's a scouting bird."

We backed up slowly. I pressed my back against the trunk of the nearest persimmon tree, and my heart beat furiously in my ears as the bird floated closer. Once it came within arm's reach, I took a deep breath and grabbed it out of the air.

"Why did you do that?" Henry groaned. "Release it! It's scouting for its creator—"

"I know," I said grimly—and I did. I knew exactly who the bird belonged to.

The paper bird was folded with crisp lines. I turned it over and felt a tiny thread of spiritual energy connecting it to something larger. I squeezed my eyes shut. There was no going back after this.

I tore the bird in half, snapping the string of energy. Henry readied his gwandou beside me as the spiritual energy that had been connected to the paper bird suddenly swelled.

Michelle appeared in the middle of the clearing. I tightened my fists at my sides.

She lifted her chin, her gaze darting between me and Henry. "Here for grandma?"

"Yes," I said—and to my surprise, I didn't feel angry. "And you."

CHAPTER 31

Michelle sauntered up to me. Henry raised his gwandou, pointing its sharp blade towards her.

"Don't worry," she told him. "I'm not doing anything to Emma. Yet."

I didn't budge as she picked up the two halves of her paper bird off the ground. She had her lips pursed as she always did when she was thinking about something difficult. That's when I realized that maybe she'd never really changed at all. She'd always been this person, and no amount of wishing otherwise would make her different.

"I have an offer to make," I said.

She brushed one of her twin braids over her shoulder and tucked the remains of her paper bird into her sleeve. "Lord Tin Hong has been planning for the immortality ritual since last year's Ghost Festival. I doubt he'll agree to anything you have to offer."

"Not to Tin Hong—to you."

She raised an eyebrow. "Right. I think you've forgotten how I expect you and your family to fix all the problems your great-aunt caused here in the Underworld. To do that, you need to work with Tin Hong."

"I want to make sure the ghosts here have enough offerings too." I nudged the paper lantern built from spirit money. It rustled with the movement. "If Tin Hong succeeds with his immortality ritual, he's going to use up another year of offerings. More ghosts will suffer."

"What are you talking about? He can't use the offerings. They would need to be gathered up from the Seoi Dang River before they can be of use to anyone."

I frowned. "Then why is he conducting the ritual during the Ghost Festival?"

Henry glared at Michelle. "What Hei Nga's saying doesn't make sense. Tin Hong needs more spiritual energy than what one mortal can provide, even if that mortal has enough spiritual energy for the Sight and syu fat mo."

She shrugged, but her brow was creased in a hint of doubt. "Tin Hong told me that he wouldn't need to use any of the offerings. It would take the whole day to collect all the offerings, anyway, so your point is moot. Nice try, ghost hunters."

"I'm not a ghost hunter," I said.

"I am," Henry said proudly, standing his gwandou up beside him. "And you'd do well to remember that."

I shook my head. "I don't hunt ghosts. I don't want to do anything to you, Michelle. I'm not even asking you to be my friend. I'm asking you to work with me. We can make sure the ghosts here in the Underworld have enough offerings without Tin Hong trying to make ghosts immortal when they shouldn't be."

She lifted her chin. "That was a lot of words to say you don't actually have anything solid in mind."

Henry coughed. It sounded suspiciously like a snort. I ignored him and continued, "The offerings in the Underworld are dwindling because not enough people actually make offerings to the dead anymore, right? What if we brought the Ghost Festival to Victoria?"

"That would require a lot of planning, and hoping that people in the Mortal Realm would actually want to participate. We'd have to get the city council on board, for starters. Besides, no one's going to want to buy a bunch of food and leave it out for some ghosts they don't believe in."

"That's why I need your help," I said, taking a tentative step towards her. "You've always been able to figure out how to make a plan work."

"Maybe I'm tired of planning," she said, but even as she said it, I could see the reluctance twisting her face into the person I thought I knew—and maybe I still did.

"That's okay," I said. "We can still figure it out together."

"Someone's here," Henry hissed.

My stomach dropped as the verdant branches of the persimmon trees parted. Leon stumbled into the clearing, his face sickly pale, and behind him was Tin Hong, clad in robes of royal-blue brocade. A gilded scabbard was at his side. He pushed Leon forward and fixed me with an unimpressed look.

"You have a loyal dog, Miss Wong."

My heart leapt into my throat. The energy was frantic inside me. I looked at Michelle, but it was too late—she'd already drawn her calligraphy brush and was marching towards Leon. Any chance I'd had of convincing her vanished. "Let Leon go."

"You and your grandmother are rather adept at escaping, so I don't believe I will." Tin Hong gestured at Michelle. "Unveil the pagoda. It's time for us to ascend."

"I should have killed you long ago," Henry sneered at Tin Hong. He readied his gwandou, but before he could do anything, I darted over and gave his hand a squeeze.

"You don't have to do anything," I told him, trying to get him to back down.

He shot an offended look my way, but it lacked the sharpness it usually had. "I'm not going to let him use you and your grandma for his creepy ritual—"

My heart sank as I took in how tired he looked. His sallow cheeks. The darkness under his eyes. He was no longer pretending to breathe, either. His spiritual energy dwindled with every passing moment. If he tried to take on Tin Hong, he'd be dead before he could even touch the Ghost Lord. I couldn't let that happen.

"I'm sorry, Henry," I whispered. I reached out for his spiritual energy.

He froze.

I yanked on it until he bent forward onto his hands and knees, gasping, fingers clutching at his chest. Finally, he collapsed at my feet. His eyes closed. I released my hold on his energy and looked up, only to see Leon's shocked face staring back at me.

"Impressive," Tin Hong said, hungrily taking in Henry's prone form. "There is a reason why I prefer you over your grandmother."

Michelle wrote out a character in the space before her. The lines shimmered gold and silver, and Henry's body sat up, only to flop back down again a moment later. Satisfied, she lowered her calligraphy brush. "You've changed."

"Yeah," I said. "I have."

She pursed her lips together and turned towards the empty space in the middle of the garden. Tin Hong stood at her side as she scrawled out a series of complex characters. As soon as the last shimmering stroke faded away, I felt the spiritual energy cloaking the area lift. A shudder went through me when I realized that the middle of the garden was no longer empty.

A pagoda loomed over us. It was a slender tower with eight sides that seemed to stretch up forever. The five tiers of eaves had corners that curved towards the sky. Michelle aimed her calligraphy brush at Leon, and he fell into step beside me. As we approached the pagoda, the cold light of the moon slunk across the shadowed reliefs carved into the walls. Flying deities wound around the sides. Their faces were smooth and blank, and they sent chills up my spine.

"Do not worry," Leon whispered beside me. "We will find a way to rescue you and your grandmother."

I shook my head. "You've fulfilled your promise to Lin Wai. You're free, Leon."

He went perfectly still. "Pardon?"

"I know you've been helping my family because of the promise you made to Lin Wai. But you don't have to help us anymore. You've already done more than enough. You need to live for yourself now."

"That—" he said, his voice strangled. "That is not—"

For a brief moment, his face crumpled, and I could see everything that had been written in him from the start. His pain in losing the person he'd loved the most. His fear and anger. And spread across it all was a sheen of guilt, the kind that had had years to grow and fester into something more—something that dogs a person and nips at the heels of all their happiness.

The four of us entered the pagoda through an arched doorway. A winding staircase circled the sides, stretching all the way up to the ceiling until it led outside. Each of its eight walls had large openings to the garden, and they continued up each tier in perfect symmetry. The starless night sky peeked through the very top openings.

I followed Tin Hong up the stairs of the pagoda until we reached the doorway at the top. When I stepped outside onto the roof, I drew in a sharp breath.

An enormous lotus lantern sat on top of the pagoda, balanced on the tip of the decorative spire in the centre of the roof. Its many petals were softly aglow with a warm yellow light that seemed to radiate from within—and in the middle of the lotus was my grandma. She lay on her back like she was sleeping.

"Mah Mah!" I cried. I tried to rush over to her, but Tin Hong caught my arm.

"Nothing has happened to her," he said. "And nothing will, as long as you're the one who assists me."

"Fine." I yanked my arm out of his grip.

"Good," he said, pleased. "Take her place in the centre of the lantern."

Slowly, I walked up to the lantern. With every step I took, the finality of the situation sank in deeper. I hadn't been able to rescue Mah Mah and return her to the Mortal Realm. Tin Hong and Michelle had entrapped us. All along, I'd thought I had a chance at escaping and saving my family.

I'd failed.

I forced myself to move forward. Everything about the situation made me uneasy—from the strange garden below, to the towering pagoda I was standing on, to the lotus lantern in front of me with my unconscious grandmother.

Then she cracked an eye open, and I nearly jumped back.

"Aiya," she gasped in dismay. "You come here too quick."

Tears welled in my eyes. "You shouldn't have run off. We could have returned you to your body in the Mortal Realm by now."

Mah Mah shakily sat up on the bed of paper petals as Michelle came up beside us. "Ah Ling, I think we both know that's not true."

"Come on," Michelle said. She wrapped her arm around Mah Mah's back and tried to escort her away from the lotus, but Mah Mah refused to budge.

"I stay here," she announced, thumping the bed of the lantern beneath her. "Use me. Send Emma home."

Michelle bit her bottom lip. Then her face firmed in resolution, and she pointed her calligraphy brush at Mah Mah. "I didn't want to do this, but . . ." She wrote out a character, and a swirl of papers lifted from the top of the pagoda and engulfed Mah Mah from the head down. I resisted the urge to run after her as the papers carried her away and dropped her beside Leon. Quickly, the papers rearranged themselves into a cage around them.

I stood in the middle of the lantern and tried to block out everything around me. I could hear Mah Mah arguing with Michelle and Tin Hong, but I didn't want to look over at them. I kept my focus on the moon above and tried to block out everything else.

Tin Hong lifted his calligraphy brush. The jewels on his fingers glimmered like shards of glass. "Shall we proceed?"

Michelle looked over the edge of the pagoda, then back at Tin Hong. She seemed hesitant. "You aren't going to use the lantern offerings on the river, right?"

"Of course not," Tin Hong said coolly. "We have an immortal gracing our presence as well." He pointed his brush at Leon.

Fear crashed through me. He was going to use Leon too? "Wait a second, this isn't what I agreed to—"

"Let's begin, Emma. Draw out the immortal's spiritual energy and pass it to me."

He flicked out fast strokes with his brush and Leon keeled over with a groan.

I reached out for Tin Hong's spiritual energy—just as the gold light of a protective barrier flared up around me. My heart shot into my throat as Mah Mah struggled to her feet, also enclosed in a barrier. She had a calligraphy brush in her hand, and she was frantically writing out characters faster than I could follow. Another barrier appeared around Leon.

"She's got my calligraphy brush!" Michelle yelled.

Mah Mah slashed out the last stroke of a character, and one of the petals of the lantern vanished into a thousand tiny pieces of paper.

"Stop her!" Tin Hong roared, tossing Michelle his calligraphy brush. "Do not let her interfere! Once the immortality ritual begins, I must see it through to completion."

Michelle snatched the calligraphy brush out of mid-air and sliced out the character for *move*. The cage papers shot upwards before diving down towards Mah Mah, who rolled away to avoid the swarm.

"Aiii," she moaned, rubbing her hip. "My back."

"Get up!" I shrieked as I raced over to her. I fell over her just as the paper swarm came back. My hands and face erupted in pain as a hundred tiny papers sliced through my skin. They darted away and I jolted up with a gasp.

"Please, Mah Mah. We have to move!"

"Mm sai geng," she groaned, waving me away. My heart twisted when I noticed she had cuts on one of her hands as well.

Michelle wore a look of concentration as she guided the papers back up, but before she could finish the character she was writing, I launched myself up and felt for her spiritual energy. I gave it a hard tug. She stumbled forward, her eyes wide—then I tackled her, and we both fell off the pagoda.

CHAPTER 32

There are few things worse than falling off the top of a five-tier pagoda with your ex–best friend.

As we fell, she shouted something. It sounded an awful lot like "sorry," but it was hard to tell. I squeezed my eyes shut and braced for impact—only to land on something that crinkled. My eyes shot open. I was on an enormous paper dragon made of spirit money. Henry was sitting at its helm, slashing out characters to make the dragon rustle and glide.

"I knew I shouldn't have trusted you," Henry grumbled when he glanced back at me. "How could you just knock me out like that?"

I gave him the evil eye. "Would you have left Tin Hong alone?"

"No, but—"

"Then sorry, not sorry. I prefer you alive, or whatever it is you are," I said non-apologetically as Henry's ears went red. I hunched down, flattening myself against the paper dragon. I tried not to be impressed with the quality of the dragon—it even had scales. *Scales.*

"Is this made out of spirit money?" I asked.

"Do you mean *my* spirit money? The money you wanted to make the lantern we never ended up using? Then yeah, it is made out of spirit money."

The wind blew the hair out of my face as I peered over the side of the dragon. "Do you see Michelle?"

"No," he said, guiding the dragon up the side of the pagoda with a final flick of his calligraphy brush. "But I can still feel her spiritual energy—"

The back of the dragon dipped. Startled, I looked back, only to find that Michelle had clambered atop. She panted, grasping at the dragon's scales to pull herself up. I scrambled for purchase and tried to locate her spiritual energy. If I could stop her—

"Give me that brush!" she shouted as she dove towards Henry. He rolled over—too far. My heart stopped as he tumbled over the edge, only to grasp the side of the dragon at the last second.

"Hold on," I shrieked as he tried to pull himself up. I reached for him, but the dragon swerved away from the pagoda. Michelle held Henry's calligraphy brush up triumphantly. She scrawled out a glowing word. In desperation, I jerked on Michelle's spiritual energy. She let out a gasp. The paper dragon tipped to the side. We both nearly fell off before she managed to rebalance its long, winding body with another hurried character.

"Can you not?" she snapped, brandishing the calligraphy brush. "We're both going to fall if you keep doing that."

"I'm trying to help Henry up!"

"And I don't want you to!"

"Will you just grab my hand?" Henry roared. "You're literally right in front of me—"

I grabbed on to his hand and hoisted him up. He spun out his gwandou and swiped the blade down at Michelle. She screamed as it sliced into her shoulder.

"No!" I cried out. "What are you doing?"

"She's fine," Henry said, prying the calligraphy brush from her hand.

She moaned, clutching her shoulder. "Give it back—"

She tumbled backwards as Henry directed the dragon back up to the top of the pagoda, and I caught her by the hand as she fell past me. She had a stunned expression on her face, as if she couldn't believe I'd caught her. My shoulder ached from the strain. We flew up to the top of the pagoda and the dragon righted itself again. As soon as it did, she fell fully back onto the dragon.

On top of the pagoda, Leon and Mah Mah were fighting off Tin Hong. He'd drawn his sword from his gilded scabbard, and it flashed every time he slashed at them with it.

"Hop on!" Henry shouted at them.

"We are a tad preoccupied," Leon panted out as he dodged Tin Hong's sword.

I jumped off the dragon and back onto the pagoda. "Mah Mah, get onto the dragon!"

"No, no," she crowed, stabbing out a shimmering gold

character. A flurry of papers clouded Tin Hong. "Most fun I have in long time!"

Carefully, I crept closer to her. She seemed to be winning against him—until Tin Hong leapt through the cloud of papers and swung his sword towards my grandmother. A scream rose inside me. He stopped it just before her neck.

"On second thought," he said, his chest heaving, "perhaps I don't need your grandmother after all. Or the immortal. All the offerings on the Seoi Dang River will suffice."

"You said you wouldn't use them," Michelle gasped as she stumbled up beside us, holding her arm. Wildly, I looked around for a way out. There was nothing I could use.

Nothing except the spiritual energy all around us.

"I keep no promises to mere ngo gwai," Tin Hong sneered, his hold steady as he aimed his sword at my grandmother. "Once I become immortal, I'll ensure that all ghosts have enough offerings to sustain them until their next life. Think of how much more access to spiritual energy I'll have once I can leave this wretched realm. Now help me restrain the ghost hunter descendant."

Michelle turned towards me, her hand still clasped to her shoulder. Her eyes were hollow, and they met mine for only a split second before they darted away, as if she was ashamed. Something inside me lifted.

"The deal's off, Tin Hong." I kept my glare focused on him even as I felt for the spiritual energy around us. It lingered in the remnants of the lotus lantern and the persimmon trees in the garden below. Every petal breathed it out. All the leaves quivered with it.

I called the energy to me—and the last layer of papers forming the lantern burst into a flurry of movement.

"Don't you dare," Tin Hong warned. He pressed his sword into my grandmother's throat. Blood welled along its edge, yet she stood tall and unwavering. Her gaze was fierce. In it, I read everything she wanted me to know.

But I was done with sacrifices. Tin Hong only knew how to take. He didn't know how to give, but I did. If I had enough energy to give someone immortal life, then I had enough energy to share.

I gathered up the energy inside me—as much as I could manage—and I redirected it into Michelle. She shuddered as the energy seeped into her. She let go of her injured shoulder and hunched forward, her hands on her knees, her face contorted in pain.

"No!" Tin Hong howled, lurching forward towards her. "That spiritual energy is meant to be mine—"

I grabbed hold of his spiritual energy and wrenched it towards me.

He jerked forward then gathered himself back, teetering like he'd been shoved off balance. He lifted his sword, but it was too late—I already had his string of energy. It was strong as rope and bright as the moon.

"Emma." Henry's face was pale. He stood frozen to his spot. "Stop. You're going to—"

"Don't be selfish," Tin Hong said, backing up, stretching

that string farther between us. "You could grant ghosts a longer life, if not an immortal one. They could reach their next lives without needless hardship." An accusation lay in his eyes—disapproval tinged with disbelief. He was telling me I was making the wrong choice.

And maybe I was.

All these ghosts down here, they'd suffered because of what my great-aunt had done. Maybe I owed it to them to help them.

But I didn't need to be perfect, or even good. Not anymore. And maybe I'd never really had to, but it took shutting out everyone's voice to hear my own.

I tightened my grip.

"Stop," Tin Hong commanded. His voice sounded of exhaustion and mistakes. "If you kill me—"

"Let me guess," I said. "I'll be just as terrible as my great-aunt."

And I grabbed on to his spiritual energy and yanked it into me.

He sank to his knees, his blue brocade robes pooling around him.

His feet faded.

His hands.

His nose and mouth.

His cold, accusing eyes—until the last of his spiritual energy slipped into me like a swallow returning to its nest, and everything he had been faded into dust.

I let my legs go weak. The dust was all over me. All

over the ground. It hung in the air and snuck into my every gasping breath. And inside me, something was growing. Climbing. Clawing. It wanted *out*.

Out out out out out—

I sank back. The world seemed too bright. My ears rang. My head spun until the spinning became a blur and the blur became pain and the pain became darkness.

CHAPTER 33

"My foolish granddaughter," someone murmured above me. "Nei ah zeoi ma fan ah—"

I opened my eyes, wincing against the brightness. Pain shot through my head again. It felt like it was slicing me in half.

Mah Mah's face hovered above mine, in that space between emptiness and light. Her eyes were scrunched up as if she'd been crying. But she wasn't. My strong grandmother, too proud for her own good. I opened my mouth to tell her how proud I was of her, to wait a little longer and I'd take her back home, to ask her to teach me more about our family history, to tell me about her sister, Lin Wai, who only did what she had for someone she loved.

"Love you, Mah Mah," I whispered, but the words sounded far away.

She took my hand, entwining her warm fingers with mine. Her lips moved, but my head was abuzz. Inside me, the spiritual energy writhed, like roots with nothing to burrow into. It tried to worm itself deeper into my body, into space that didn't exist.

Her voice fluttered across me. "This time, I'll protect you."

And she grasped that writhing bundle inside me, dragged it out—and planted it inside herself.

CHAPTER 34

I bolted up, gasping. The last dregs of Tin Hong's spiritual energy left me in a nauseating swirl. Mah Mah swayed on her feet. Her face was grey. She tipped over.

"Why did you do that?" I asked frantically, fumbling to grab on to her before she sank down onto the ground. "I was okay. I didn't need your help. You didn't need to—"

She tried to wave me away as she wheezed out, "Mm sai geng."

I rested her heavy body down on the ground and knelt beside her. I closed my eyes and felt for her spiritual energy, and as soon as I found it, I flinched back. Her energy was a mess. It twisted inside her uncontrollably, slithering around like a tangle without end.

"We need to do something," I babbled frantically.

Henry knelt down beside me. "Emma, there's nothing we can do."

"I'll take it back." I squeezed my eyes shut again and tried to grab on to her writhing spiritual energy. "I can give the energy to someone else."

But as hard as I tried, I couldn't hold on to her spiritual energy. It slipped away from my grasp whenever I thought I had it. The harder I tried, the more panicked I felt. A hand on my shoulder startled me into opening my eyes again.

Leon's mouth was thinned in determination. "Take my spiritual energy."

"What? No!" I protested, shooting to my feet.

"With Tin Hong's spiritual energy, it should be enough to ascend your grandmother to immortality. She's still mortal. She doesn't need as much as a ghost." He took off his peacoat and placed it over my grandmother, whose chest was rapidly rising and falling. "Quickly. We do not have much time."

Flabbergasted, I stared at him. "I'm not going to take your spiritual energy. You'll die."

He nodded solemnly. "I am well aware."

"I just need to try harder," I said desperately. "I can drag out the excess spiritual energy. I just need time—"

"You told me to live for myself." Gently, he rested his hands on my shoulders. "I am already living for myself, Emma. This is what I want to do. You and your grandmother are as much my family as Lin Wai was." A small, tentative smile crossed his face. "We do not share the same blood, but we do not have to. A family is built from shared memories."

"Being family doesn't mean you sacrifice yourself," Henry shot back.

"Quickly, Emma," Leon said, and he sat down beside my grandma.

My mouth was dry. My heart beat loudly in my ears. *Thump, thump, thump.* It was all I could hear. My hands shook. I didn't want Leon to sacrifice himself, but if I didn't do something, Mah Mah would die. The energy in her roiled wildly. I could feel it now without even closing my eyes. It would swallow me whole if I reached back inside her.

How could I take away someone's life to save another?

"Go Go," Mah Mah murmured. She cupped Leon's cheek with a warm smile. "Enough. My sister gave you a second life. What a gift, ah?"

He laid his hand over hers where it lay against his cheek. "Yes. It has truly been a gift."

"Then treat it as such." She turned her eyes to me, and my stomach sank. "I think I have grown to like the Underworld. We've only seen a small part of this realm. I wonder what else there is to explore."

Leon's fingers tightened around hers. He was determined to see his death through, but he'd already died once. That's how everything had started.

Maybe we were just going back to the beginning—and maybe it wasn't the right beginning, but it was what had brought us here. I didn't want to go back anymore. Lin Wai had loved someone so much that she gave up everything to bring him back, but love wasn't about sacrifice. Love was about knowing how to treasure someone when they're gone just as much as when they're alive. How to keep living with what they've given you.

Knowing when to let go.

"I'm not going to take your spiritual energy, Leon," I said thickly.

His head shot up in alarm. "You must. Your grandmother is too weak to do it now."

Michelle cleared her throat. She was standing apart from us, in the middle of all the fallen pieces of paper from the lotus lantern. She wasn't holding her shoulder anymore, but her eyes were rimmed in red. "No one knows yet that Tin Hong is dead."

I swallowed. "What are you saying?"

She tugged on one of her braids, not meeting my eyes. "The Underworld is missing a Ghost Lord, and we have someone here who's really good at disguises."

Henry's face contorted into a mix of disgust and fear. "I am *not* becoming the next Ghost Lord of the First Court."

Michelle huffed. "I'm not talking about you becoming a Ghost Lord, egghead. I'm talking about you helping Po Po to become the next Ghost Lord of the First Court."

Everyone's eyes swivelled to Mah Mah.

"Are you joking?" I asked nervously. "Because I can't tell if you're joking—"

"Aiya, me?" Mah Mah said, flattered. "No, no. Very bad idea. I just regular ghost here, no need to worry about problem. Afterlife very relaxing. Maybe I garden."

"You need spiritual energy from offerings to grow anything worth gardening," Michelle pointed out.

"That is an . . . idea," Leon said carefully.

"A bad idea," Henry spluttered. "Are you all listening

to yourselves? Sooner or later, someone's going to find out she's not really Tin Hong, and we're going to have even bigger problems on our hands."

My head spun. Mah Mah, the new Ghost Lord of the First Court of the Underworld? It was worse than a bad idea—it was terrible. A disaster waiting to happen. Yet I could see the possibility taking root in Mah Mah's head. She wasn't outright refusing. In fact, her eyes sparkled with the same look she got when she spotted a wilted orchid on discount at the grocery store.

Maybe Mah Mah replacing Tin Hong meant I could still see her as much as I wanted. The Underworld was only a short trip away if you had the right passage.

"What kinds of problems?" I asked.

"Like . . . like . . . Look, I don't know, okay?" Henry said, flustered. "But the King of the Underworld isn't going to be happy when some random Po Po is wandering around, pretending to be Tin Hong. There's going to be some kind of crazy punishment involved, like getting cursed to live the next thousand years as a rock in the Mortal Realm."

"One thousand years of peace and quiet," Mah Mah said with a pleased sigh.

I found her hand beneath the peacoat laid over her and gave it a squeeze. "You don't have to do this. You can just be a regular ghost, like you said." My vision blurred. "I'll make sure you get lots of offerings with all of your favourite foods. I'll . . . uh . . ."

"Or maybe," Mah Mah said, preening and leaning close

339

to me with a mischievous twinkle in her eye, and continued in Cantonese, "I pretend to be a Ghost Lord. I fix the problems that my sister caused. I do a better job than Tin Hong did with managing the First Court of the Underworld."

She waited there, like this was my choice. It wasn't my choice. She didn't need my permission. I loved her for asking anyway. I took her hands in mine. Squeezed them. Rested my forehead against hers. I needed to be brave, just like she'd been for me.

"Okay," I whispered.

CHAPTER 35

After I spoke to her, Mah Mah let out a slow exhale. Her eyes closed. My breath hitched in my throat. I squeezed her hand more tightly. What if we were making a terrible mistake? What if things didn't work out the way we'd planned?

"Mah Mah," I choked out. "Wait—"

Her eyes flew back open, and she sat up with a groan. She whacked her back with a fist. Then her eyes widened, and she stood up. She touched her toes like she was doing pilates. She spun on one foot, then the other. My jaw dropped, and I felt for her spiritual energy, only to release it right away as if I'd been zapped. Gone was the vibrant red that had coloured her energy. Now it was pure white, the colour of death.

"Aiyo, dying isn't so bad after all," she chortled with another little hop. "Imagine that! I was worried for nothing."

"That's it? You're . . . dead?" I asked, too astonished to even cry.

Leon studied her in puzzlement. "I see. Her spirit was already in the Underworld, so when she died, it only broke the connection between her spirit and her mortal body. It did not need to travel anywhere."

"So Ngau Tau and Ma Min won't know a new ghost's entered the Underworld?" Henry asked, slightly green.

"Nope," Michelle said cheerfully.

"Hold on," Henry said, terror dawning on his face. "That means there might be other ghosts roaming around that no one knows about—"

Mah Mah rested a hand on his shoulder and squeezed down with a sweet smile. "No time to worry about that. You need to help me become Tin Hong."

"Emma," Henry spat, whirling around to face me. "Tell your grandmother she can't be a Ghost Lord!"

I met her eyes. They were warm and brown, and full of the same fiery strength I'd always known. My lips tugged into a smile.

"My grandma can be anything she wants," I announced.

Henry groaned. "I want everyone here to remember that I thought this was the worst plan ever. Got it?"

"Please hurry before the King of the Underworld finds out," Leon said quietly. "I do not want to be a rock for a thousand years."

Henry flipped his calligraphy brush between his fingers in agitation. "All right, Po Po. Tin Hong isn't here for me to steal his voice, so I'll try to imitate it as closely as possible. This might itch."

He raised his brush to the empty space before him—and paused. His gaze flicked back to me. I gave him a tiny nod.

He puffed up his chest and started writing. Silver, glowing brush strokes filled the air. They hung there for a moment, and then they vanished into shimmering wisps.

When I looked at Mah Mah again, she was gone. In her place stood Tin Hong, with his royal-blue robes and sneering mouth. Involuntarily, I shivered. But then she clicked her tongue as she adjusted her waist belt, and my heart lifted.

"How do you feel?" I asked hesitantly.

"Heavy. And large. Too tall," she complained, trying to loosen her belt. "I think your nice friend made this too tight."

Henry glowered, but his cheeks flushed pink. "Pretty sure that's how he always wears his belt."

She lifted her new, heavy brocade sleeves. "How do I look?"

"Strange," Leon admitted.

"Like an overcooked piece of roast goose," Henry said.

"I'll talk to you later," she scolded, wagging a finger at him. Then she turned to me, with her face that wasn't my grandma's face, but with a warmth that could only belong to her. "What do you think, Ah Ling?"

"Creepy," I said, trying to summon up a grin. My throat swelled with sadness. She was trying to make me feel better, but I was still trying to summon up the courage to leave her here in the Underworld. Even if I was eventually able to see her again, it wouldn't be the same.

"Good," she said with a satisfied nod. "Now change me back."

"What?" Henry howled. "After all that work I did to transform you into Tin Hong?"

"And you'll change me back again after," she tutted. "Right as soon as I'm done seeing my granddaughter back to the Mortal Realm. It'll attract more notice if I say goodbye as a Ghost Lord."

My heart dropped. I took in the garden with its dried, shrivelled trees beneath us. The full moon above with its eerie light. And farther away, through the treetops of the forest around the pagoda, the inky waters of the Seoi Dang River, rolling along with the lantern offerings floating upon it, softly aglow with unspoken promises.

And in the middle of it all was Michelle, standing in the scattered papers of Tin Hong's failed attempt to ascend to immortality. She gave me a quick glance. Before I could say anything to her, she vanished.

CHAPTER 36

We descended the pagoda on Henry's spirit money dragon, all of us crowded onto its writhing back of paper scales. Everyone was quiet as we wound down towards the Seoi Dang River. The waters were alight with hundreds of lantern offerings. Up the river, ghosts plucked the lanterns out of the water with long poles. A strange emptiness pulsed inside me, and it had nothing to do with how the dragon twisted through the air.

"I think I'm going to be sick," I whispered once the dragon landed on the pebbled riverbank. I stumbled off and bent over, fingernails digging into my knees. My stomach felt hollow.

Henry scrambled off behind the dragon's head. "What's going on?"

"I think your dragon gave me motion sickness," I moaned.

Leon's brow furrowed. "We should hurry and return you to the Mortal Realm. You look like you have been macked around by a ngo gwai."

Henry pretended to retch. "You mean smacked? It's smacked. *Smacked*."

"Just—" I swallowed. "Wait here. I'll be back."

Mah Mah gave my hand a pat. Worry dragged her mouth down. "Don't take too long, okay ah?"

"I won't," I said, gulping down my nausea.

I left the three of them standing there, and I followed the river along its pebbled bank until it narrowed. Lanterns bobbed gently along the slow-moving, shallow current. On the water, the lanterns had no shadows. There was only the light of their reflection, glowing softly in ripples. They drifted along in clusters as I walked.

My head pounded, and the hollowness inside me swelled. I stooped against a tree. Sank down. I couldn't feel my fingers.

"If you need to throw up, don't do it in the river," called out a familiar voice from across the water, and the tension in my chest unravelled. "You'll get it all over the offerings. You'd basically be puking in someone else's food."

On the other side of the river, Michelle sat beneath the thatched straw eaves of a dilapidated hut. Cracks arched down along its hardened mud walls.

"I thought you left," I said, trying to keep my voice level.

"I did. But I figured I should see you off. You know, just in case." She drew up her legs and wrapped her arms around them. "I don't expect you to understand why I did what I did."

"I don't." I forced myself to focus past the throbbing in my head. "I don't think I ever will."

She played with the end of her braid and said matter-of-factly, "And I'll never forgive your great-aunt for being so selfish."

For some reason, her words didn't sting as much as they could've. There was no malice behind them, or even bitterness. I exhaled. It felt like a weight had been lifted from my shoulders.

"Come on." She nodded upstream, where I'd left everyone else behind. "I'll help you back."

"You don't need to." I braced myself on the tree trunk and pulled myself up. Dark spots dotted my vision, and before I knew it, Michelle was right there beside me, hoisting me up—her arm around me, mine around her.

"How much spiritual energy did your grandma take from you?" she asked, scrunching up her nose.

"Uh . . . a Ghost Lord amount?"

"You feel sort of empty." She heaved me up around her shoulder again. "You want some of my spiritual energy?"

I looked at her, incredulous.

"No strings attached," she promised.

"You're a ngo gwai," I pointed out. "You need offerings to replenish your spiritual energy. I don't. I'll just go home and sleep for twelve hours."

She shrugged. "I'm not a full ngo gwai. I've been living in this mortal body for years. My spiritual energy can recover from sleep too. Besides, with all the energy you gave me from the garden . . . I'll be more than okay."

I thought about it, but the more I thought, the less I

wanted to take anyone's spiritual energy anymore. I'd taken so much from different ghosts. I wanted my energy to just be my own for a while, even if some of it was missing. I especially didn't want to take Michelle's. Even though she wasn't who I thought she'd been, she also wasn't a stranger. Maybe I could get to know the real her.

"Maybe in the future, when I'm dying or something," I said.

"Deal," she said, brightening.

We walked back along the river. As soon as my grandma and Leon came into view, Michelle froze in place. Henry was standing beside Michelle, the blade of his gwandou bright at her throat. He looked furious.

"Let go of her," he snapped.

"Leave her alone, Henry," I said.

He lowered his blade, glaring at Michelle. She passed him with a smug smile and stuck her tongue out as soon as he looked away. My chest lightened. She wasn't so different from the Michelle I knew after all.

Mah Mah and Leon were still chatting at the water's edge when we approached them. Someone had conjured up a stool for her, and she was sitting on it, chattering away happily. Leon's smile dropped as I came up with Michelle.

"I'm not trying to pull anything," she said, raising her hands defensively.

Leon's frown deepened. "That is even more suspect."

"I'm being serious." She removed her shoulder from under mine and took a step back. "I'm just here to say goodbye."

An alarm bell rang in my head. "Goodbye?"

"I'm staying here." She shifted from one foot to the other. "I'll help your grandmother. It sounded like she had an idea for making sure offerings were better distributed for the ghosts here. It won't make up for all the ghosts that died during the Year of Loss, but it's a start."

"But . . ." I started, then closed my mouth.

She wanted to help Mah Mah. It wasn't sorry, but apologies wouldn't fix anything. I couldn't go back in time and make things right with them. For now, this was enough.

I swallowed down the lump in my throat. "You can always come home, Michelle."

She kicked one of the stones on the riverbank. "It was never my home to take."

"No," I said, "but it became yours."

She bit her lip. Despite all the travelling and fighting she'd done, her robes were immaculate. It was like she didn't exist.

"Yeah," she said in a small voice. "It did, didn't it?"

"Your family will miss you," I said, and my eyes stung.

She blinked. "I know. I'll miss them, too."

Mah Mah took her hand gently. "You should visit them when you have a chance."

She shook her head. "It's better if I stay away."

"Come and visit," I said firmly. "That includes me. And school starts again in another couple months. Robotics Club needs you, and I need you to tell me what my grandma's up to."

349

"Okay," she said, her voice wavering, and her face split into a toothy grin.

I ran my sleeve under my eyes. Mah Mah gave my arm a comforting squeeze. She held up a piece of paper with inked characters scrawled down the length of it. My heart thudded when I realized what it was.

Lin Wai's letter.

"Ready?" she asked.

I wasn't. I didn't think I'd ever be.

"Yeah," I croaked out.

She nodded, and pulled out the calligraphy brush she'd stolen from Michelle. She wrote in the air. Silver shimmers followed her brush tip. The letter rose up. Folded over itself. Creased.

When the paper boat was finished, she plucked it out of the air and set it down at the water's edge. She swept out another character, and the paper boat was aflame. As we watched the flames engulf the boat, she found my hand and gave it a pat.

"I'm proud of you, Ah Ling," she murmured.

Fresh tears blurred my vision, and I held on to her hand tightly. "I'm proud of you, too."

She wrapped me in a hug that felt warmer than the sun. I buried my face into her shoulder and clung to her. I didn't want to leave her in the Underworld. I needed her to come back with me—back home, to our family, to the garden in the backyard that needed pruning. We were supposed to do so many more things together.

"Mom and Dad will miss you," I sobbed. "*I'll* miss you. I already do."

She gently grasped me by the shoulders and pushed me back. "It's okay to miss me. But I'll always be here. Just follow the ghosts and you'll find me."

"I'm going to visit you," I replied, weeping. "All the time. And you can haunt me."

"Okay, okay."

"Maybe don't haunt Dad too much, though. He's scared of ghosts." I snivelled. "And don't haunt Mom at all. She'll call in an exorcist and get rid of you for real."

She patted my shoulder. "Hai, hai."

The ground beneath me felt like it was rocking back and forth. From up the river, lanterns parted as if someone had taken a pair of shears and cut right through the water. The bow of the boat appeared amidst the hazy glow travelling the current. It lit up all our faces with an otherworldly radiance.

"When you see your Baba and Mah Mee, tell them . . ." She hesitated as the boat slowed to a stop in front of us. Behind her, the mountains rose as tall as gods. "Tell them I . . ."

"I'll tell them you're with good friends," I said.

"Gwai ah," she said, and she smiled.

I took a deep breath. The boat swayed gently in the water. Beckoning. Leon gave me a gentle nod of encouragement. Henry crossed his arms and looked away. Michelle raised her hand hesitantly in farewell. Mah Mah stood there on the bank, her smile saying everything else she wanted to tell me.

I jumped onto the boat without saying goodbye. A goodbye was an ending, and this wasn't an ending.

This was a beginning, and this time, my family was going to do it right.

EPILOGUE

Lunar New Year festivities were coming to an end.

Mom handed Dad another bowl of tong yun. The sweet, nutty dumplings floated on the surface, sending wisps of steam into the night air. Behind us, the light from the house cast a warm glow over the garden in the backyard. It was late January, so nothing was in bloom, but I could feel growth starting. Spiritual energy slipped along the barren bushes and coiled itself in roots deep underground.

Was it me who put that spiritual energy there? Yeah, maybe. Was it cheating to make sure we had the best garden in the entire city? Definitely not. I was only making sure Mah Mah's garden was taken care of. When she visited a few weeks ago, she'd scolded me for not starting the seedlings inside the house yet. It was weird seeing her complain with Tin Hong's face, but I'd got used to it. Mostly.

We held Mah Mah's funeral a week after the doctors officially declared she'd passed away. They said it was heart failure, but I overheard them talking to Mom and Dad about not having an exact diagnosis. I wanted Mah Mah to come, but she declined, insisting it was unlucky to attend her own funeral. Sometimes I still caught Mom dabbing at her eyes with tissues when she looked out into the garden, and Dad lingering in front of her black-and-white portrait on the family altar.

But they were still here, and so was I.

On this cold start to the new year, the sky was so thick with clouds that none of the stars shone through. Every time one of us opened our mouth, a breath of air puffed out like a soul escaping for one brief moment. I shivered, my hands frozen around the tin box of incense Mom had handed to me.

"That's the last bowl," Mom scolded Dad. She shook out a match from the tiny box in her hands. "Too much tong yun isn't healthy for you."

"Last bowl," he promised around a spoonful of chewy tong yun. When I looked over, he winked at me, and I grinned back.

Mom stood over the incense pot on the lawn. The pot was an old, oversized clay planter, chipped along the rim and scratched along the sides. Instead of soil, it was filled with years of incense ash atop a layer of nga fui—white stone powder.

I flipped open the lid of the incense box. Inside the tin, joss sticks were neatly piled into flat rows. I offered the box to my parents first, and then I picked out two sticks—one for Henry and one for Mah Mah.

The incense sticks were fragile and skinny, and I could already smell the camphor on them. I rolled them gently between my thumb and my finger, then stuck them in the pot. Mom handed me a match.

"Hey," Michelle panted, running into the backyard, a plastic bag swinging from her hand. She came to a stop beside me and my parents. "Sorry I'm late. I got caught up with some last-minute details for Project Paper Airplane."

Project Paper Airplane was the plan Mah Mah and Michelle were working on to better distribute offerings to ngo gwai in the First Court of the Underworld. Mah Mah couldn't spend too much time in the Mortal Realm because it looked suspicious, but Michelle could spend as much time as she wanted. She was pulling double duty on finishing her classes *and* trying to solve the issues in the Underworld. When Henry visited me the other day, even he'd grudgingly admitted that she was working impressively hard. They still didn't get along, but knowing they were around left a warmth in me, like a bulb I'd secretly planted was sprouting shoots.

"Did you figure out how to make the planes run yet?" I asked.

"Not yet," she groaned. "The spirit—u-uh ... the energy needed is still missing something."

"You're working so hard," Mom said. She took out a few incense sticks from the tin box, then paused. "Just like Emma."

I almost dropped the match I was holding. Mom *never* gave compliments unless she was obligated to. She stuck her incense sticks into the pot as if to signal the end of what she'd said. It wasn't a very long compliment, but it was a start.

"Do you want some tong yun?" she asked Michelle, to change the topic.

"No, thank you, Mrs. Wong," Michelle said, chipper. "I just ate a billion dumplings before I came here." She held up the plastic bag. It was heavy with a Tupperware container at the bottom of it. "Here, we made you some, too. My parents say happy new year."

"Oh, how kind of them!" Mom said, taking the bag from her. "I'll pack up some tong yun for you after we give our offerings to the ancestors. You don't have to, you know. You can go back inside."

"Oh, no, Mrs. Wong, I'll stay and help." She pointed at the box of incense in my hand and gave me a hesitant look. It was taking time, but we were slowly figuring out how to rebuild our friendship on truths instead of lies. "Can I take some?"

"Sure," I said with a smile. I passed the box to her, and a warbling coo rang out in the night. I looked up into the leafless branches of the maple tree above the shed. A pigeon was perched on one of the upper branches, illuminated by the moon. My heart beat faster. Leon hadn't shown himself since I'd left the Underworld, but every now and then I spotted a pigeon lingering in places it shouldn't be.

"A pigeon?" Dad said. "At this time of night? Hold on, Emma's scared of them. I'll grab a rake and shoo it away—"

"No!" I shouted.

Dad gave me a quizzical look. "But you always want me to chase them off."

"I've . . . uh . . . had a change of heart." Nervously, I caught the pigeon's beady orange eye—and then smiled. If it really was Leon, I hoped this was his way of saying that he was also trying to find a way to move past everything that had happened. Maybe he was also building a new beginning. "It's not bothering anyone. Maybe it's a spirit, making sure we light enough incense for all those hungry ghosts out there."

"That is . . . very creative, Emma," Dad said.

Mom shuddered. "Don't say such unlucky things. What would Mah Mah think?"

The pigeon cooed softly, as if thanking me, and I grinned when I met Michelle's eyes. "I think Mah Mah would say to light more incense."

I struck my match against the worn pot rim. The flame was small in the night, but so bright. It flickered as I brought it down to the tops of the incense. A heady scent filled the air and sank into my chest. Somewhere in the Underworld, Mah Mah and Henry were eating the offerings that were floating down the Seoi Dang River. Maybe they were also thinking of ghosts, of people they once knew, of sisters and friends and family.

I extended my hand to Michelle. "Can I have another stick of incense?"

"Sure," she said with a shy smile, and she shook out the stick into my hand.

I leaned against her shoulder. With a new match, I lit the stick and stuck it in the pot with the other ones. The wisps of smoke rose to the night sky as one steady trail, paper-thin and blooming full all at once.

It was good to be with family.

ACKNOWLEDGEMENTS

A huge thank you to my editor at HarperCollins Canada, Yashaswi Kesanakurthy, and my incredible agent at Transatlantic Literary Agency, Amanda Orozco, for believing in my ability to build this book to its full potential. I'd also like to extend my gratitude to everyone else on the HarperCollins Canada team who contributed to making this project a reality.

Many thanks to all the beta readers and critique partners I've had over the years, with an extra special thank you to Dana Lau, who encouraged me to dig deep into my writing abilities to find the heart of this story. For everyone who had to suffer through earlier manuscript drafts, I'm sorry. I hope I gave you decent nightmares at least.

I'd like to acknowledge all the friends I met through working at the Canadian International Institute of Art Therapy for encouraging me to follow my dreams. Thanks for helping me see that creativity is a process.

Much love and appreciation for the BOBAPOP writing group for keeping me sane through this wild journey.

Melody Thio (President of Leon's Fan Club), Nessa Assara (Squab Connoisseur), J.A. Moy, Andrea Parijs, T.L. Coughlin, and Jessica A. Kassin, you've stuck with me through all the screaming and yelling and terrible fanart I've done. I can't wait to throw more publishing parties, especially once your books find a home on my shelves.

Thank you to my favourite person in the whole world, Dan. I couldn't have done this without you and Ollie supporting me through every cup of tea gone cold and late-night ramble session.

And finally, thank you to my grandma, Mah Mah. You've inspired me in so many ways. There are so many things I wish I could say to you. I might've even written a whole book to get me started.